ADVANCE PRAISE FOR *DAYS OF MOONLIGHT*

"Loren Edizel's fiction speaks through the passage of time itself—the poignancy of what history erases and what only the written word can save. Lovingly written, *Days of Moonlight* reveals the passionate love and friendship of two women who embody the history and culture of a passing age, and the tender bonds of family and place.
—CAROLE GIANGRANDE, author of *All That Is Solid Melts Into Air*

"This is a little gem of a book, full of all the tales that make us and unmake us—real and imagined ones, past and present ones. I am infatuated with the voice of our protagonist Mehtap, at times poignant, at times funny—it is totally unique and, at the same time, all of us. It is a story about love, the choices we make, and the choices that life makes for us."
—CECILIA EKBÄCK, author of *Wolf Winter* and *In the Month of the Midnight Sun*

"From the first page, via two simple bracelets, Loren Edizel's *Days of Moonlight* brings the reader to heartbreakingly real crossroads where desire, family secrets, and the legacy of Greco-Turkish conflict all meet—and yet, thanks to the author's concise images and considered style, the novel also succeeds in reading with the dreamy timelessness we love in the greatest myths and fables. It's wonderful."
—DANIEL PERRY, author of *Nobody Looks That Young Here*

"Reading this novel was like sliding into a warm bath. It's a luminous work, a love story that spans several decades. There is also much wisdom and insight to be found along the way. Reader, you are in for a treat."
—**Morris Berman**, author of *The Reenchantment of the World*

"A beautiful, moving portrayal of the complexities and richness of life, and love gained, lost, and re-found—a poetic novel full of visceral imagery. You can hear the clinking of the tea glasses, taste the salt of the Aegean Sea, and see the red-tiled roofs of Izmir. You will be transported to Crete, Turkey, and Canada where past and present comingle in the sensual and often bittersweet power of memory, and become immersed in the stories of strong women, and the women and men they love."
—**Melinda Vandenbeld Giles**, author of *Clara Awake*

DAYS OF MOONLIGHT

For my dear friend Donna

With all my love,

Loren
July 21, 2018

Copyright © 2018 Loren Edizel

Except for the use of short passages for review purposes, no part of this book may be reproduced, in part or in whole, or transmitted in any form or by any means, electronically or mechanically, including photocopying, recording, or any information or storage retrieval system, without prior permission in writing from the publisher or a licence from the Canadian Copyright Collective Agency (Access Copyright).

We gratefully acknowledge the support of the Canada Council for the Arts and the Ontario Arts Council for our publishing program. We also acknowledge the financial support of the Government of Canada through the Canada Book Fund.

Cover artwork: Gerar Edizel, "Steps in Izmir," 2017, watercolour on paper, 21 x 20.5 centimetres.
Cover design: Val Fullard

Days of Moonlight is a work of fiction. All the characters and situations portrayed in this book are fictitious and any resemblance to persons living or dead is purely coincidental.

Library and Archives Canada Cataloguing in Publication

Edizel, Loren, author
        Days of moonlight / Loren Edizel.

(Inanna poetry & fiction series)
Issued in print and electronic formats.
ISBN 978-1-77133-477-8 (softcover).— ISBN 978-1-77133-478-5 (epub).—
ISBN 978-1-77133-479-2 (Kindle).— ISBN 978-1-77133-480-8 (pdf)

        I. Title. II. Series: Inanna poetry and fiction series

PS8609.D59D39 2018   C813'.6   C2018-901517-9
                                            C2018-901518-7

Printed and bound in Canada

Inanna Publications and Education Inc.
210 Founders College, York University
4700 Keele Street, Toronto, Ontario, Canada M3J 1P3
Telephone: (416) 736-5356 Fax: (416) 736-5765
Email: inanna.publications@inanna.ca   Website: www.inanna.ca

MIX
Paper from
responsible sources
FSC® C004071

DAYS OF MOONLIGHT

a novel

Loren Edizel

inanna poetry & fiction series

**INANNA PUBLICATIONS AND EDUCATION INC.
TORONTO, CANADA**

For Alfredo, Nikola, Maura, and Jacques

Silence is the language of God, all else is poor translation.
—Mevlâna Celâlleddin-i Rumî

Izmir, January 6, 2010

My dear Mehtap,

I will be brief. I have two golden bracelets, my inheritance from Crete, which I bequeath to you. If you have daughters, you may give one to each. I haven't heard from you in very many years. I hope you're happy and fulfilled.

These bracelets represent the story of the Labyrinth. For a long time, I thought they represented the Minotaur's tale. But the labyrinth will do you in long before the Minotaur. This is what I believe now. Hard to say why such savagery is embossed on women's jewellery. Those involved are long dead, so we shall never know.

You must come before they are stolen. I hardly ever wore them. No one has ever worn them. They've spent their lives in the darkness of tidy drawers, wrapped in cloth.

In this package are some of my old notebooks. Those I could find to take with me to this wretched place. The others are somewhere in the house ... I couldn't remember where. I've asked that they be sent to you when they're found.

I hope you'll remember me with kindness in spite of some things you'll read here and offer my soul refuge in your generous heart.

Your loving aunt,
Mehtap

Notebook I. The Journal

I DON'T LIKE THE MEN I DATE, in general. I don't like the coarseness of their features, the stubble on their faces which most don't seem to bother with. I want to smell perfume and aftershave. Is that too much to ask? For instance, today, on the ferry, the man the girls from work set me up with. He was taking me to Karşıyaka for tea. The breeze blowing through his white shirt kept bringing acrid odours to my nose. Nice enough man, otherwise. Not much hair on top, and a belly, mind you. The creases in his pants seemed a few weeks old. Works at the post office in Pasaport. The girls tell me I'm too picky, and I'll never find a husband. They use the expression "you're going to stay on the shelf," my expiry date having already passed at twenty-nine. I keep my thoughts to myself, but I feel like telling them, "Why do I need a husband? So he can sentence me to a life of disillusionment like the rest of you?" I mean, when they talk about marriage it never sounds like something you'd want to do. Not one of them talks about how she can't wait to get in the sack with her husband at night. Why is that? Out of modesty? I doubt it. As for the security of marriage, I think they are all fools to think their puny, bureaucrat husbands are actually offering them "security." They are working women, aren't they?

HE WAS TALKING TO ME about his wife today, how she gives him a hard time and is always nagging. He rolled his eyes and stretched the vowels in "always" when he said it. His mistress, for whom he has set up an apartment in a small cul-de-sac at the other end of the city, also complains. Do you love your wife, or your mistress? I asked. My wife has morphed into my mother. My mistress is delightful, but her whining is beginning to make things less so. If she morphs into my wife, I'm done. She is gorgeous though, in an addictive sort of way. She has cost me a furnished apartment already and if I give her jewellery, she whines a little less. I'm an idiot he said, laughing. I'm a damned idiot. I waited for him to stop and asked: What was it about your wife that made you want to marry her in the first place? She was handsome, and distinguished. My parents approved. She wouldn't give me the time of day when I was courting her. I found that intriguing. After I married her, she continued to give me a hard time. But I no longer find it intriguing. His wide-mouthed laughter made him snort. As for her distinguished airs, well, on closer observation, I would define them as bourgeois arrogance. Underneath it all, she has a coarse and petty heart, you know what I mean? You're not like the women I know, he said. I can tell you anything, and I feel free. So I told him he was bourgeois and arrogant himself. Underneath his lordly pretensions he was rather coarse, too. See? he exclaimed. I'm your boss and you're not one bit afraid of me. I cannot live without your truth! Shall we now write that letter to the pompous fool in Belgium, the one who is charging me a fortune for the equipment I need? You know the routine, anyway. I'll sign when you're done. And upon these words, he went back to his office and closed the door.

Today, on the streetcar, on my way home after work, I was watching the girls from a nearby high school who boarded in a noisy, giggly group; their skirts considerably shorter than the prescribed rules, their pigtails limp and their faces littered with pimples. They seemed so fresh and vivid compared to everyone else. Compared to me. We all sat there, working women, working men, with our grey faces, the dust of our boring lives muting even the most colourful purse or dress, staring in envy. What are these girls' ambitions? I imagine they must have so many, nowadays. What were mine?

WHERE IS THE ELECTRIC FAN when I need it? It must be in the attic and I don't want to go crouching in the dust and cobwebs to find it. The summer heat is making the asphalt on the street soft. Even the gevrek[1] boy with the large pan on his head is fanning himself with a newspaper going up the stairs. He isn't shouting "Gevrek!" with his usual gusto either. He must be twelve, thirteen. Out so early in the morning, carrying hundreds of gevreks on his head, on a Sunday. He looked up as he passed the house. He knows I'm sitting in the cumba[2] having my tea. I buy half a dozen every Sunday to help him finish his job faster. Problem is I eat all of them, too. Well, I'll go call him. He looks so desperate in this heat.

I'm back, having bought a dozen oven-warm gevreks. I shall not eat them, this time. I'll bring them to His summer house in Çeşme, along with the box of baklava. It's tradition. Every summer, the first Sunday of July, he invites me to his summer house so I can swim and enjoy the beach as his guest, with his family. He has three daughters. His wife, of course. Me. The servants. And the gardener. More like a summer palace, surrounded by palm trees, pines, and dozens of fragrant oleanders in bloom buzzing madly with concealed cicadas. This is what usually happens: he sends the chauffeur to pick me up at my house. The stout man is clad in a black suit with tie and comes out of the car to open my door, dabbing a damp white handkerchief on his ever-expanding forehead to stop the flow of sweat. I call him Fehmi Bey. He calls me Mehtap Hanım. As soon as we settle in the car, I say, "Fehmi

---

[1]gevrek: sesame-crusted bread ring, similar to a bagel
[2]cumba: bay window particular to Greco-Turkish houses in Izmir

Bey, aren't you going to take off that black jacket? It must be so uncomfortable in this sweltering heat. I cannot bear to see you like this." He chuckles and removes his jacket. The back of his short-sleeved white shirt is soaked.

"Thank you Mehtap Hanım," he says. "Patron (this is how we all call Him) would get mad if he knew. He wants me in the suit at all times. I'll stop the car and put it back on before we arrive."

I reply, "Patron should try to spend five minutes in a black suit, in this boiling car, himself."

Fehmi Bey chuckles, "Mehtap Hanım, we should not criticize Patron. Thanks to him I have raised my children. May the grace of God be with him."

"Yes, yes, of course, Fehmi Bey," I retort, "but somebody has to bring him to his senses."

On the way to Çeşme, with all four windows rolled down and hot air rushing through the vehicle to flatten itself on my damp face like an invisible iron, we continue chatting. He likes to talk politics. Rather, how the government is corrupt and fails us all. On this subject, he is voluble, and the conversation takes us to Kennedy Meydanı. He does honk irritably a few times on the way and digresses from politics to interject, "Who is giving these donkeys drivers' licences, I want to know!" He never curses in my presence, of course, but by the end of this ride, I'm assured we have donkeys in parliament, on the roads, in high and low places. Tragically, the list includes the sons of these various donkeys waiting patiently in their mothers' wombs to burst forth and unleash their ignorance onto the wondrous landscape of Turkey. We are passing Narlıdere with its endless citrus groves on both sides of the road now. Perhaps driving all day will turn the most cheerful person into a pessimist.

I ask him about his wife, to change the subject. "How is your Hanım doing?"

"Don't ask…" he starts. This is the overture for a long lament on Hanım's sciatic nerve which capriciously enough acts up whenever he is tied up with Patron on road trips. "I come home after a week of non-stop driving," he says, "to find piles of laundry to be ironed, dust bunnies everywhere, the children running amok instead of doing homework. Hanım, in her nightie and curlers, having tea. Mehtap Hanım, you tell me now, if your sciatic nerve were so raw that you couldn't do anything around the house and had to sit in your nightgown all day, why would you have curlers on? Forgive me. I don't mean any disrespect, and don't get me wrong, I have great respect for her; she is a good mother, a kindly soul, and all that, but some things I just don't get." He takes out his limp handkerchief and dabs the top of his bald head, then smiles as he looks at me through the rearview mirror.

I smile back, "She probably wanted to look pretty for you."

"Mehtap Hanım, may God forgive me for saying this. The first time she came to bed with those things on, in the dark, my heart stopped. She looked like an extraterrestrial in drag. If she wanted to look beautiful for me, she would remove them when I was around. But no! She wants to look nice for the neighbours and grocers."

I can't stop a guffaw. He grins at first, and soon enough we are laughing together, wiping our eyes. I see the road sign for Kilizman. "Fehmi Bey, would you stop here for a moment, please? I need to stretch my legs, a little," I say.

If I told him I wanted to buy ayran[3] for us, he would rush out and buy it himself. There is just no drink in the world that equals the delicious, fresh taste of the ayran made in Kilizman. And I'll tell you what I love, precisely: getting out of that stifling car and into the dusty road, bright yellow light squeezing into every crevice of that noon hour filled with the gentle noises of the small town going about its business. With baked muscular shoulders and kerchiefs on their heads, the young men walk

---

[3]ayran: buttermilk

here and there in hurried steps carrying things, whistling and talking to each other over a medley of noises coming from the blacksmith's and the garage farther away, the bakery, and the traffic. Old men in grey pants sit with caps on their heads in the shade of a luscious plane tree, next to rusty, wet, tin cans fragrant with basil, worry beads sliding between their fingers, gazing at everything with the detached curiosity of the elderly. Waves rolling and crashing behind the houses, and dusty bare feet moving on sidewalks, *zzzing-zing-zings* of an electric saw cutting slabs of marble for tombstones. Fresh ayran is handed to me in a tall cold glass. I tilt it into my mouth. The tart, salty liquid flows down my throat, making everything cool inside me, making everything in that moment, happy. Fehmi Bey realizes what I'm doing and waddles to my side in his sweat-stained pants, wanting to pay. I have already settled the bill, however, and he drinks the ayran handed to him in a few gulps. He goes, "Ahhhh!" after he's done and smiles with two wedges of white on each side of his mouth.

When we get back in the car, he turns on the radio. "Surfin' USA" is playing. He changes it to some jazz, momentarily, introduced as "Take Five" then settles on Zeki Müren singing "Yıldızların Altında."[4] We listen to his melodious tremolos all the way to Zeytinalanı. "*My heart is drunk under the stars, ah how sweet it is making love under the stars,*" he goes and we slightly move our heads from side to side with the melody—on one side the crashing frothy waves, on the other, fields dotted with small houses and olive groves. "Mehtap Hanım," he smiles, "this is your song." He means because of my name, moonlight. I nod with a smile and keep looking out the window at the world speeding by. In three quarters of an hour we will be in Çeşme. I don't want to arrive, really.

When we get there Patron's wife will come to the car, alone,

---

[4] "Yıldızların Altında": "Under the Stars"

and embrace me with mechanical air kisses, rattling on niceties all the way into the house, dispersing Chanel 5 into the atmosphere. He will be nowhere in sight, as usual. Taking a nap, I bet, in his shorts, in a chaise-lounge under the parasol in the garden. "Just in time for a swim!" she'll say with enough high-pitched drama to remind me she once studied to be a soprano (a second-rate one, no doubt), and then send me upstairs to the guest room to change into my swimsuit. I'm glad he is sleeping, so I don't have to worry about the whiteness of my thighs or the size of them since I have not really succeeded in sticking to the punishing grapefruit diet I found in a magazine last week in preparation for this day.

In any case, away we go, with our straw hats and towels to the white beach surrounded by blue skies and emerald water. She looks a bit crusty, the boss's wife, from staying in the sun too much, but I have to admit she is attractive, with those large Audrey Hepburn glasses and fake blondness with black roots showing. I feel white and shy and totally out of place until we get in the sea and the freshness hits my chest to bring out a breathless sigh. After the initial shock subsides, the Aegean Sea, turquoise and limpid, enveloping my limbs feels like a gigantic womb. I think, as we swim side by side moving our legs and arms in unison like synchronized frogs, of the sea as the mother of the first creatures who crawled out of it and somehow, eventually became me and Patron's operatic wife. She is still wearing her glasses and is careful to keep her teased puffy hair out of the water. We talk about this and that, mostly office news and her daughters. Despite swimming side by side, the formality of our conversation makes me feel subservient and tight inside; a sentiment I will not shake off until I leave their house.

Later, after a shower, I slip into a light summer dress and meet them on the marble veranda for lunch. The daughters are there, sitting at the table, impatient to eat and leave the house to meet their friends. They're not particularly sociable, and I'm already too exhausted from the mannered conversations with his wife to try and engage them in further nonsense. He is smiling in his white shirt, unbuttoned enough to show some chest hair and tanned skin. He's got some grey scattered among his dark brown hair. The blue eyes are exactly the colour of the sea behind him. Very trim and sinewy, his body. My knees weaken. I can see nothing else when he stands there smiling at me. Am I blushing? Can his wife see what I feel? It's profoundly embarrassing to become so overtaken by the beauty of a man. If I were to swoon looking at the hazy seascape stretching beyond the terrace, it would make me a curiously sensitive person, perhaps a poet, a nature-lover. I would not stammer or blush. Swooning over a man is foolishness. In my defence, he is not merely attractive or handsome. His nose is slightly crooked, and perhaps his eyes are a tad too close. His eyebrows could use a trim. Yet, these irregularities enhance his magnetism. Not that he would ever; but if he asked to sleep with me I would. Immediately. No matter the cost. There, I've said it.

"So, Fehmi has brought you safe and sound, Giritli! Welcome!" He calls me by my family name. My parents are from Crete, thus the name. Giritli. Apparently his father's ancestry is also Cretan. This, he told me when he hired me. Since then, I've been Giritli, to him. I like it, too. It makes me feel masculine in a sexy way, independent, special. As we embrace and chat standing around the table, I wonder if he would call me Giritli in bed, immediately blushing at the thought, hoping it could pass for sunburn. I look at my plate as the housekeeper heaps it with pilav and chicken and some okra cooked with tomatoes in olive oil. Farther away, on the veranda at the side of the house I see the driver, sitting and smoking at a small table set for two. He will be eating with the housekeeper. She's wearing a uniform. A short-sleeved dress with thin white and grey vertical lines, buttoned in front, a white collar, white shoes, and stockings. He bought this uniform in Germany for her, as a gift, as if getting a uniform would ever enchant a maid. "I want her to quit wearing that flowery shalvar[5] and look like a modern housekeeper," he had explained. When the sweaty housekeeper returns to pick up the empty plates in her squeaky white orthopaedic shoes, I thank her for the delicious meal and for toiling in this hot weather to prepare it. "Good health to your hands," I say. She wishes me a good digestion and pats me in the back with familiarity. The boss's wife has a generic, ready-made smile. "Sultan, we will have coffee in the living room." The housekeeper's name is Sultan.

"Giritli, what do you think of my garden?" the boss asks suddenly.

"It looks exactly the same as last year," I reply, uninterested.

"So you have not seen my new rosebush! The one I brought from Denmark." I cannot say I don't care about his rosebush and I don't want to pretend admiration for an anaemic little stick of a plant from a distance, but he's already dragging me towards it and away from his wife. "I have to get away from here and you must help me," he whispers as we walk toward the stub. We stand about two feet away from the plant. The gardener is a few feet to the left, planting some other things. "I know it doesn't look like much yet, but the roses will be the colour of peaches, and very fragrant when they bloom, and the size of grapefruits," he says loudly and cups his hands to show me. "I have asked Fehmi to drive you back in a couple of hours. Gönül will call me in an hour. I'll pretend I got a call from a client, the Belgian, and have to go to the office and take you with me to send an urgent telex. About a shipment. Big problems. Okay?" he whispers.

"Don't involve me in your lies, Patron!" I hiss. He begs like a boy, the sea in his eyes rolling here and there to invoke sympathy. I nod, "Well, you'll have to send me some of these fabulous roses, then, when they bloom," I speak louder hoping the gardener and

---

[5]shalvar: baggy trousers gathered in tightly at the ankle

the wife will hear it as we turn around and walk toward the house.

My visit to Çeşme will probably end before I get another chance to swim. On the long way back home, Fehmi will ooze into his soggy jacket with stoic professionalism, Patron will fidget with the radio button absentmindedly thinking of his romantic escapade with Gönül, and I will pout trying to suppress my inner torment. It will be an hour of silence, interrupted by the Beatles and Bach. But I will surely say, "For the love of God, Patron, please tell Fehmi Bey to remove his jacket. The mere look of him makes me sweat!"

And Fehmi Bey will raise his hand in dutiful objection, "Please, Mehtap Hanım, I'm used to it."

When Patron turns to look at me, I will glare back. "Go on, Fehmi, you heard the lady; take it off," he will say, looking sheepish.

I MISS MY GRANDMOTHER. I believe she is the only reason why my parents did not die of heartache and grief when they had to leave Crete and arrived in Izmir as teenagers. That is what they always told me. Even though she was not my real grandmother by blood, she was the best a child could hope to have. Her tenderness made me feel safe even from the other side of a room, even when I could not see her, even now. Some days, like today, I awaken and she is present within me. I feel her gaze, and her hardened palm caressing my cheek and momentarily a wave of grief-filled happiness washes over me. How does one describe this feeling? I'm not sure. When I say, "I miss her" can those miserably common words truly describe the moment when my love reaches for her and tumbles down the precipice of absence? Death is a formidable enemy and I cannot forgive God for it. I cannot forgive God for leaving us here, at the mercy of a universe we don't understand, without enough words, without enough solace, endlessly waiting for our turn to disappear and become nothing.

WHEN MY PARENTS DIED one after the other a few years ago, I thought I had lost all my anchors. Whom else did I have in this world? Some cousins I have not met, others I have met only once or twice in my life, all scattered along the Aegean coast after the population exchange. I took a bus soon after I buried my father and went to Bodrum where some of my relatives lived, running a small family bed-and-breakfast. Another bus took me to Marmaris, where one of my great-aunts lived. In Ayvalık another uncle and cousins in the olive oil business consoled me, greeting me with affection, as Mehmetaki's daughter. I was told stories of my father's childhood, my grandfather, our ancestry, and everything to do with Crete. The hope remains, in some of these elders that they will return to Crete someday to see it once more before they die, or to be buried there. We all speak Kritika when we get together. I and all my cousins born here are not fluent, so we incorporate many Turkish words into the conversations. I love the sound of it; there's a lot of "*tch-tch-tch*" and hearing it soothes me. Spending time with my extended family gave me a deep sense of comfort and belonging at last, and freedom from practicing the art of invisibility in public, my Cretan origin with its broken Turkish and its Greek customs, my Christian mother, safely unseen and unheard.

FROM MY GLASS-COVERED CUMBA I get a westerly view of the sea and the sunset, every evening. I've just realized I'm spending a lot of time sitting here, so much so that it wouldn't surprise me if the wooden floors caved in one day to drop me onto the sidewalk in my broken chair, glass of tea in hand. Especially if I keep buying—and eating—so many gevreks every morning! Every time he passes at six in the morning, I ask the boy if he'll go to school after work. Every time, he shrugs without responding. "Look," I said yesterday, "I can see you're a very hard-working boy. You would do very well in school if you put that effort into studying and advancing in life. You're still young. Why don't you do it?"

He gave me half a smile, a sad one, and nodded. Then asked "Is this going to be all, ham'fendi?"[6]

I nodded and gave him the money. "One day, you'll be an old man with crooked legs and a hunchback if you keep doing this, and how are you going to sell your gevreks then?" I shouted after him as he slinked away and up the street, placing his pan on his head.

My westerly view, I was saying. If you touch gold and make a wish as you gaze at the sunset, it will come true. I have been doing this since I met Him. I want to have him all for myself; I want him to need me and to be the whole world to him, as he is to me. I don't care about his money and his idiotic notions. I just dream of a moment, here in this cumba, when he will say, "Why have I not noticed you before? It is you I love. Not my wife, nor my mistress. What a fool I've been!" And kiss me, with a long and passionate kiss, like in the movies, where men are hopelessly blind where women are concerned, except momentarily, when the veil of obtuseness lifts from their minds and they see true love in all its splendour. Would he ever realize that this love would overflow from the confines of the reality to which he is so accustomed? Would he dare enter it and get lost in its vastness? Would he sense that love is to life what death is to nothingness? And I, insignificant, homely secretary to the king of zippers, can I live this entire life, day in and day out with such secret and painful yearning?

I CALL HIM THE KING OF ZIPPERS because we manufacture zippers at the factory and it makes the girls at work laugh to hear the epithet, especially when he is in a bad mood and gets tyrannical, which is often. I suppose it coincides with instances when Gönül has a headache or tortures him with some new caprice, or when his wife nags. I know immediately from the way he opens the

---

[6]ham'fendi: M'am

door to the office. He turns the knob and pushes it open with sudden force, as though he were coming to arrest someone, and then his face appears from behind the half-opened door, rigid, jaw clenched, ready to find fault with the dust on top of the file cabinet that he otherwise rarely notices. "Mehtap!" He barks. No "Giritli" when he is mad. "I want to see The Books, now! And have the girl bring me some coffee."

I do some very simple bookkeeping for him, but the accountant is responsible for The Books. They are under lock and key, in the glass cabinet right behind his large and ornate oak desk. If only he would turn from his desk, he could unlock the door and take out all the books he wanted. They are chronologically placed. But no, he is fuming, so I have to go around his desk, squeeze myself behind him and unlock the cabinet to take out the books he wants to examine, because he is in a terrible mood, because his mistress spent too much money or his son wants to go to summer school in England or something. It is a great emergency. The King of Zippers needs the girl to bring him coffee. Cancel all the meetings, stop people from entering his office. Send them back where they can make more zippers. Why do I get the feeling that my year-end bonus has just shrunk by a third?

So, I'm sitting at my desk outside his office, writing in my journal. Might as well ... nothing else to do. I watered the plants. The girl came with his coffee. Her name is Gülşen. He never remembers it. The other day he called her Gülbahar and reminded me of my elementary school teacher, that awful witch. I won't have him call her Gülbahar; and not just because it is the wrong name for the poor girl, but because it is a terrible memory for me. I said to him, "Patron, what is so difficult about the name Gülşen? Think of a laughing, happy rose. Picture it and you'll never forget her name. It is insulting to be called by all sorts of names. At least call her 'daughter,' if you can't remember, for heavens' sake!"

He started calling her Gülen. Then he said it was my fault, because now he thinks of a laughing woman. Why is laughing and rose the same blasted word, he exclaimed. "Why is everyone naming their daughters a variation of Rose or Laughter? Why can't her name be Star, or Fish or some other thing? Have we run out of names?" He jumps a little—more like a spasmodic little hop—when he gets excited or upset. I find it endearing to see that little boyish hop and the arms going up in the air and his thick dark eyebrows pushing his forehead up into a crease. If only I had met him when he was younger. Perhaps I would have had a chance. There are so many movies—Turkish movies—about rich men falling in love with poor girls. Well, it takes an entire movie and a large string section to make it happen, but still, in the end, the moral of the story is that these things do happen, and the rich spoiled boy gets a chance to redeem himself. Of course, the poor girl never looks truly poor in a Turkish movie, plus, she has to wear puffy wigs tied in pig-tails and braids to look young, and all that does is make her look like an older woman in denial. But it's all about the idea, naturally. The rich boy will abandon her and take up full-time drinking after he marries a girl of his class he ends up mistreating. He may throw furniture around in one of his drunken rages, spill his drink or slap his wife. She will pack her bags and leave, rubbing her cheek, never to be seen again. Life may deal him a terrible blow, after more decadence, making him lose his fortune, which now opens the way to accidentally running into his poor long-lost beloved on her way to the factory, because he too now lives in a working-class neighbourhood. Or very many years will pass before they meet again, and she will be wearing a puffy grey wig and really awful makeup. Sometimes the rich one is the girl. She is made to marry some other rich boy who cheats on her, throws furniture around, spills his drink, slaps her face etc. He may die in a car crash at the opportune time, after the poor boy has managed to educate himself and become an engineer, thus affording a convertible Chevrolet in which he is driving around with a platinum blonde woman of dubious morals on their way to a party where everyone is debauched and dancing the twist. He sees the rich girl crossing the street, and she sees him. Her face darkens with sorrow. He drinks some more, remembering the rejection he faced when he was a young man. This causes another car accident. His convertible Chevrolet days are over. He must now buy a Devrim.[7] The first Turkish automobile ever made, in 1961, which conked out after one hundred metres when our president Cemal Gürsel got in it with great fanfare to pay a visit to Anıtkabir, Atatürk's eternal resting place. But before he buys a Devrim, our sultry hero will lie covered in plaster in a hospital bed struggling between life and death. The heroine is coincidentally a nurse now, with a different kind of wig and a little white nurse cap, having lost her fortune when she was married to that abusive rich brute with a gambling habit. With money and good cars out of the way, they can finally reunite and be happy.

I'm mixing a few plots here, from different movies. I probably watch too many. What else is there to do?

THE ACCEPTED NOTION IN SOCIETY, at least here and now, is that the destiny of a girl is to get married and bear children. Past the age of twenty-five, which has been my case for more than a decade now, we are not desirable. Then, family and friends conspire, as I said before, to arrange meetings with mature men who may still be living with their mothers. They may be widowers or divorcés. There may be a damn good reason why they are still out there, unclaimed and should remain so. And so as a single woman, I can't help but remain suspicious of divorcés and men

---

[7]Devrim: first ever automobile designed and produced in Turkey; the word "devrim" also means "revolution" in Turkish

whose mothers have ironed their shirts for too long. Widowers are another category. They have children who will not accept a replacement to their beloved mother.

I'm picky. I admit it. I want love. I want passionate fumblings in dark alleys. I want a man who looks and smells exactly like my boss to ravish me, spend my body, and cast my soul to the open seas. I want to be treated like a lady. I want to make my own choices. I'm too strong-minded for my own good. Perhaps my independence is all I have to hold on to:

1) Despite the dusty silence that descends upon my evenings in this house.

2) Despite the fact that my girlfriends have disappeared one by one into the world of marriage, diapers, and laundry blue.

3) Despite the lonely trips to the movies where I'm the only unaccompanied young female, prey to creeps moving in the darkness of theatres.

Kerime who has lived in Germany for the last two years writes me she can go to the movies alone, to a restaurant or a café unaccompanied and will not be accosted by lewd men. Mild-mannered, they are, in tight jeans, reading Albert Camus in used pocketbook editions, pulling their beards and sipping espressos. They'll ask permission to sit at the same table with her. They will smile and dive straight into deep conversation without small talk. She is lucky. She really is. She says she has had lovers, and I'm the only friend she can tell about it; the others will not understand and will judge her as being immoral.

NURAY WAS TELLING ME ABOUT HER FRIEND today, at work. Apparently, this friend of hers had an arranged marriage, the modern way. They were made to meet at a family function or such, and then made to go out a few times chaperoned by her younger brother, and an engagement date was set when the couple decided that they liked each other enough. He was a catch, she thought. He had gone to university in America, a chemical engineer now, with a good job, apparently modern ideas, not bad looking, and from a well-to-do middle-class family. All was well until the wedding night, when the expected blood stain did not materialize on the sheet. The groom threw her out of the house in her nightie and told her never to return. The girl swore she was a virgin. Her parents took her to a doctor who confirmed that hymens could tear without causing bleeding, and that she'd most likely been a virgin until her wedding night. They made him write a note to the groom. The groom's family would not budge and a divorce ensued within a week. The bride tried to commit suicide in the bathtub, with the same Gillette razor that shaved her legs. She was hospitalized for some weeks. Then, she returned to her parents' house with her emaciated face and haggard eyes and was rarely seen in public. She tried to kill herself another time, apparently, and was saved, until she jumped off the balcony of a seven-storey building and died instantly.

The girl was Nuray's childhood friend. And so she wept, disconsolate. To be maltreated so horridly over some skin, to be considered nothing more than an intact membrane; is there truly greater insult to a human being? I hugged Nuray as she sobbed into my shirt at work. There was not much more I could do, except nod as she swore she would never ever let that happen to her. "So, we, the so-called daughters of the Republic, are still ruled by the hidden veil within us in this men's world. I'm so angry...." She sputtered and I held her in my arms, rocking side to side a little to calm her down, thinking, "Here we are, two spinsters forever." What else? You either die an old maid so that you never give any man the satisfaction of seeing you as a prized piece of membrane, or you get rid of it somehow so that if it doesn't belong to you, then it will belong to no one else either.

WEEKS HAVE PASSED, but I'm still thinking about the suicide and Nuray's anger, which is also mine. A plan is coming together in my mind. Nuray, like me, lives alone, at the other end of the city. I've asked her today how she feels about coming to live with me. She can rent out her own house, then she would have fewer expenses, and so would I. We would go to the movies together. We could even take trips with the money we saved. Go to Europe, for instance, visit Kerime in Germany and perhaps I'd meet a university professor with modern ideas, have a torrid affair, and return to an unsuspecting Izmir, disguised as a Shelved Virgin. Perhaps he would keep me there, in Cologne, beg me not to leave. We would smoke in bed after lovemaking, like they do in French movies. I would make him Turkish coffee to sip and kurabiye to nibble on while reading Deutsche Zeitung or some such thing. Or better, the Kamasutra, with pictures, like the one the boss keeps in his office. I may go to university and study philosophy, like Helmut or Werner. Not Helmut. It rhymes with Kel Mahmut[8] or Armut.[9] Helmut, Armut, Kel Mahmut! No. Werner, possibly. Or Dieter. My family name would change to something unpronounceable like Kreutsbergerschmidt. My daughters would not have to wax from head to toe like I do. They would be bald in all the right places, tall, and naturally athletic.

She seemed interested. Said she'd think about it and get back to me. It's exciting to have someone like a sister to do things with; perhaps a new and more exciting chapter in my life is about to begin.

IT'S DONE. SHE'S MOVING IN by November. I'm surprised at how fast she organized everything; I would have taken at least a year to think it over, then another one to decide how to move. But she accepted almost immediately as if she had already pondered it long before it occurred to me. She has asked me to go to her house to see about the furniture she should move to my house

---

[8]Kel Mahmut: bald Mahmut
[9]Armut: pear

other than her bedroom set. A renter has already been found; a distant cousin from the provinces, moving to Izmir with his wife and children.

She prepared a list of her potentially annoying habits, "so you have time to adjust yourself," she laughed. (A numbered list!)

1) Singing in the bath
2) Squeezing the toothpaste tube in the middle
3) Putting a tea-soaked spoon in the sugar bowl
4) Leaving wet towels on the bed, underwear on the floor
5) Smelling the food in the plate before eating
6) Washing sheets every two days
7) Sleeping naked.

I anticipate two, three, and four will be a problem; I like order. Number One is fine, unless her voice is atrocious. And it probably is. I should ask. Number Five I can live with. Number Six, I don't care as long as she does the wringing and hanging and ironing of those sheets herself. As for sleeping naked, it gave me a little jolt to hear this, like the time I unexpectedly fell upon dirty pictures in Patron's desk drawer. My heart raced. I felt like a spy, uncovering secrets that could start wars. It embarrassed and confused me with those nameless yearnings that rise from the depths of forgotten dreams.

I HAVE TO FIND THE FLAG TODAY and hang it out the window. Tomorrow is October 29, the anniversary of our Republic. The crescent moon and star reflected in a pool of red will be exhibited from every house or apartment balcony. You can tell where the foreigners live at a quick glance by the absence of flags on their balconies. My father had bought this flag thirty years ago. The cloth is of very high quality and still looks good as new. I can easily wrap it twice around me and it will go all the way to the floor; my parents made sure they bought the largest and most expensive flag they could find in those days. He used to hang it out ceremoniously, as if to show all the neighbours indubitable proof of his citizenship. Although he had learned Turkish relatively well, his accent gave him away as a non-native speaker. "Where are you from? Are you Greek?" he would invariably be questioned. "Turkish, from Crete," he would stress the word Turkish and soften the rest, so that Crete came out sounding like an afterthought. He had been called infidel sapling too often in his life and the large flag was his defiance. As he lay dying in the hospital, a few days before October 29, he opened his eyes wide and I knew he had something important to tell me, his parting advice. "Don't forget to hang the flag. Top shelf, my closet." He fell into a coma soon after that, so these were in fact his last words to me. *Don't forget the flag. Top shelf, my closet.* In Cretan Greek. Every time I unwrap the flag, the smell of his hospital room returns to my nostrils; iodine, alcohol, and various medicated smells emanating from an emaciated frame topped by his shrunk head with terrifyingly large protruding eyes, their whites yellow. I hear the traffic sounds coming in from the open window, one particularly abrupt nurse letting a door slam somewhere down the corridor, and the moans of patients rising from the ward like a tone-deaf aria, an a cappella ode to pain, reaching my dying father to remind him of his finite number of minutes and days which will stretch longer and longer at the very end; Mother Nature's sadistic indifference meant to extinguish all hope in another fleeting moment of well-being. *Don't forget the flag.* One could say my father died a patriot. Until his last minute, his thoughts were with the Republic. I should have had such words carved on his tombstone. But I did not. Now he is with me every time I unfurl the flag and hang it from the window. I wished for different last words, such as: You were everything to me. I did my very best for you. I have loved you so much. But, "*top shelf, my closet*" it has to be.

NURAY'S VOICE IS DECIDEDLY ATROCIOUS. She sings loud and off-key as she monopolizes the bathroom for hours on end. She did warn me, didn't she? If she takes her bath as soon as she returns from work, her repertoire consists of songs learned in elementary school, joyful marches sung to the beat of a drum. She splashes water around too. Who does that at our age? Late at night, if she takes her bath before going to bed, she sings à la turca, all the vowels rising and falling through the entire gamut of possible and impossible notes, the tremolos and falsetto mockingbird sounds. She extends those vowels, and replaces *do* with *fa, sol* with *re*. In fact she replaces entire keys, to make the songs unrecognizable. I can't stand it! But she is such a sweet soul, and how can I forbid her from singing? I'd rather hear chalk screeching on a blackboard, though. And that is the honest to God truth. I know I won't last if she continues singing. On top of all this, she wets the entire bathroom floor with her splashing, leaves her wet towel crumpled on the floor and walks around in the nude while I run frantically to pull curtains shut. Any neighbour passing in front of the house could crane his neck and see her pubic hair.

The gevrek boy is infatuated with her. She waits for him, sitting on the steps, her voluptuous pale flesh escaping from armpits, v-necks, and false pleats around her hips, like sausage meat stuffed into a sheath too small to contain it. She is bursting at the seams. And she intends to remain single all her life. How? Even the stray dogs and tomcats must get erections when she sits on those steps. She has taken my gevrek boy away too. He pays no attention to me whatsoever. She pats his head and offers him a gevrek that she just bought, invites him to sit beside her on the steps and eat it. He does, too. He puts his platter down and munches away next to her with a beatific smile. I watch them from the cumba above, envious, and the rancour remains within me like tapeworm, discarding innocuous bits here and there; distant proof of the jealousy eating me from within. Yesterday, as she was reaching for yet another slice of bread during supper, I said, "Are you sure about this? Your dress may rip in the bum when you least expect it." Her hand stopped before touching the basket and retreated. I felt ashamed as soon as I saw that. She avoided my eyes until we finished eating. It's not as if I'm thinner. We are probably the same weight. Bread makes me look boxy, whereas on her it settles on the hips and bosoms; making her look even more opulent and voluptuous.

WE WERE ON THE TRAM HOME TODAY. She asked the driver if he could leave us close to our street, and not at the designated stop so we wouldn't have to walk on account of her new shoes which are KILLING her. "Look, look at the back of my ankle! I'll DIE if I have to walk home from the bus stop," she told him theatrically. The man could lose his job if a controller would see it, or if the small and sweaty ticket guy in the grey uniform rushing to and fro to sell tickets on the streetcar reports him. But no, he had a large grin and stopped the streetcar right in the middle of the street for the Countess to descend. He added, "Only for you, Missy! I'd do it for no one else." She neighed a sort of "*hneehneehnee*" with her head tossing around as if she wanted to unscrew it and winked before going down swaying her hips.

I followed feeling like her ugly cousin, head down, sulking, and burst out once we had crossed the street, "What was that all about?"

She shrugged and lit a cigarette, removing bits of tobacco from the tip of her pink tongue. "Cheer up, I just saved you two blocks of walking!" Smoke came out of her nostrils.

"When did you take up smoking?" I demanded to know, breathing all that noxious cloud in.

She raised her eyebrows and closed her eyes, "Sometimes, I smoke. Is that a problem? What are we cooking for supper today?"

"I don't know; are YOU preparing?" I made sure to add all the sarcasm I could.

She didn't flinch. "Yes. We're eating fried eggs. Soft yolks, lots of butter. I'll make tea and toast too. When I was a little girl, this was supper when mom was too exhausted to cook. It was my absolute favourite and I'm starving."

We walked up the stairs leading to our narrow street. She flicked her cigarette and took another deep breath pushing the smoke out of her nose, like a bull about to take on a torero. Stone buildings were covered by a bluish hue in the dusk, their windows shimmering with the last reflection of the sun's glow. We walked through the tentative scent of jasmine that blew our way from someone's backyard mixed with the paper and candy smell of the grocer's shop. Abdullah Efendi was sitting with his son on the sidewalk, playing tavla.[10] We greeted each other and as we approached my house, Nuray took out the key from her purse and skipped up the steps to open the door, entering quickly in what struck me as a proprietary move. She seems at home and happy; and instead of simply rejoicing in that fact, my mind seems to perpetually make lists of grievances and slights. I envy her carelessness. I only know how to be careful and proper. I blend in; she stands out. If she wants to laugh out loud, she does. If she wants to shake her popo when she walks, she does. Next to her, I look like I have a severe case of haemorrhoids impeding my stride.

I ASKED HER TO HELP ME LOOK MORE, I don't know ... feminine, I guess. My hair is straight, my clothes are monochromatic; greys, beiges, and navies. I don't wear makeup and I favour flat shoes. She pulled the same trick again with the streetcar driver and he let us off close to our house. She pulled me by the hand as if I were a small child, to work on my "transfor-

---

[10]tavla: backgammon

mation." I was glad there would be no marches or splashes in the bathroom that evening. "Come on" she rushed me up the stairs, "this is going to be so much fun!"

We sat in the dining room, with all her equipment; there was a large makeup kit with brushes and pencils, curlers, a blow-drier that had a nylon tube and a cap stuck to it. You put it on your head with your curlers on, and it was better than a salon job, she said. She brought a small mirror that looked like a magnifier for me to look into while she was tweezing my eyebrows. I could count every pore and blackhead on my skin. I could even see the beginnings of a small pimple that was going to erupt in a week. "Why do you carry such a depressing thing around?" I left it on the table face down, feeling irritable. She frowned as she continued tweezing the area between my brows. "You used to look like Brezhnev, darling, and now you will have two thin arches, like Greta Garbo. It will open up your face, bring out your eyes. You've got lovely eyes, you know." She was really getting into the role of an all-knowing aesthetician. "Where did you learn all this?"

"My mom had a beauty shop," she shrugged. "She did nails and hair and everything. I watched."

Fixing me turned out to be a bigger job than I anticipated. While she had me holding the hair dryer that sent scalding air through the intestinal tube into the puffy cap on my head, she rushed to the kitchen to fry eggs again. If you do something more than twice it becomes a habit, someone once told me. That diet of greasy fried eggs and toasted bread was becoming one really quickly. She rushed back to the table with the steaming teapot then ran to the kitchen to finish the eggs and toast. Within a few minutes she had set the table—not adequately, mind you, but still—I was amazed by her agility and speed. I turned off the noisy machine and sipped my tea and ate my eggs sitting beside her. She stopped me as I was about to pick up the dirty plates. "Let them be, for heavens' sake! Let's finish this and go out. What is the point of all this work, if we'll go to bed right after?"

When she was done I had red fingernails and toes to match the red lipstick. She had glued fake lashes on my eyelids and given me Egyptian eyes with the black eyeliner. I had a smooth bob and was trying on her corset. A tight mermaid suit squishing and puffing my bosom so that her blue and white polka dot dress with the plunging v-neck the gevrek boy liked so much turned me into a sultry vamp.

"I can't go out like this. This is not me."

"Sure it's you, silly. In a different dress and a bit of colour, is all. Don't be a bore. Come, zip me up."

We were out of the house just as the sun was setting.

We met some of her friends—she called them cousins—a group of about seven, men and women combined, and went to a disco on the seaside. In the car, the man who was driving us, Kudret, opened a small flask of scotch and passed it around so we wouldn't spend money on drinks at the bar. Joni Volker he called it. I was the only one who didn't drink. We got out slamming the doors of his new Impala. Kudret got irritated. "Don't slam! This isn't your father's barn, guys! This car costs a fortune." He took a quick petulant walk around it to make sure there were no scratches and we went into the disco. Nuray danced, I sat. One of the men was also not dancing and he tried to strike a conversation with me that went nowhere. I kept asking him "Pardon? What did you say?" over the music, and if by chance I caught the gist of it and replied, he couldn't hear me over Mahalia Jackson and Rolling Stones and whatnot. Then they played the slow music, and he ventured to ask me for a dance. "I promise I won't step on your feet," he hollered. I nodded, tired of all the shouting and rose. He held me in an awkward, distant embrace and forced my body to move in unexpected directions, his limbs apparently unable to gauge the movements his mind prescribed. It was a simple beat, one-two, one-two, and we managed to dance off it. My back started aching from all his unpredictable decisions to move here and there, fast and slow, plus he never got quiet. I can't even remember the things he was saying. Something political. About İnönü. They must have been jokes because he would make a few bleating sounds after he finished the story. I smiled vaguely and looked away so he would take the cue and give my ears a rest, but he kept on going. Someone must have told him he really knew how to tell good jokes and this was the night he remembered them all. As soon as the song ended, I went to the washroom to get away from him. I stood there surrounded by the smell of old pee and new shit, in front of the mirror, dazed from trying so hard to hear the man I had no desire to listen to, and unable to breathe from the tightness of that polyester corset squeezing my stomach.

I left the stench of the washroom behind and wiggled my way through the crowded disco looking for my group. Nuray and her cousins were gulping down Coca Colas, their faces covered in sweat. "Nuray, I want to go home. We have to go to work tomorrow. This smoke is making me ill." I shouted. She nodded and went looking for the male cousin who owned the convertible Impala. One of the girls said, "If it weren't for Kudret, I would never go out. My parents would never let me go with anyone but my own brother and cousins."

"Who is that guy over there?" I pointed to the man who had eaten my ears off all night and had now moved to another table, where he was shouting his jokes into another victim's ear.

She shrugged. "Never seen him before."

On the way home someone explained that he was a regular at the disco and would pounce upon anyone sitting down long enough to hear a joke. That is why none of the regulars ever sat down to rest. It was a kind of initiation; even the shiest girl ran to the dance floor the second time around. They all laughed when I said, "I thought he was one of you, a cousin. Was he not in the car with us?"

When we got home and I finally got rid of that corset, I thanked Nuray for all the trouble she took fixing me up, and told her that I was not too much into dancing. She nodded and closed her door, saying nothing.

The next morning, on the streetcar she broke the silence, giving my usual navy-blue pants and white blouse combination a sidelong glance. "You don't like to have fun, obviously. Not with clothes, or dancing at least...."

We started what I hope will become our Friday night tradition. So far we've seen *To Kill a Mockingbird*, *Spartacus* and *Psycho*, *Cleopatra*, *The Guns of Navarone*, *Breakfast at Tiffany's*, *Lolita* and *A Bout de Souffle*, and many others I can't remember to name now. There is a theatre not far from my house, and there, on Tuesdays we go watch Turkish movies. The open-air theatres in the summer are my favourites. Sitting on creaky wooden chairs in a schoolyard converted into a theatre for the summer, drinking Cincibir[11] and eating sunflower seeds. The entire neighbourhood is there—families, grandparents, friends—having fun. Nuray falls asleep sometimes and snores with her head on my shoulder. If the woman is not talking, dancing, eating, or making a racket in the bathtub, she's sleeping. Going to the movies is her way of making me happy while taking expensive naps. In return, I have decided to go wherever she drags me with her "cousins." She comes alive when her makeup kit comes out of the drawer and she starts tweezing, brushing, fluffing, and painting. Every time she tries to give me that Cleopatra look, with the heavy black eyeliner that goes far beyond the limits of my eyes I feel ridiculous, but I don't have the heart to say it. She says this is the Juliette Greco look. Very fashionable, she says, very "je ne sais quoi," whatever that means. To me, I look like a stout second-rate casino singer who turns tricks between gigs. I hope to God I

---

[11]Cincibir: a Turkish brand of ginger beer from the sixties

won't attract anyone's attention in the discos where she takes me, because they will surely ask me "how much?"

THE NEIGHBOUR FROM ACROSS who's always watching my house, Nalân Hanım, asked me today if Nuray is my sister. She knows I'm an only child; we have lived here since I was a teenager. I told her she is my cousin. When we go out to meet the "cousins" in the Impala, all made up and in tight clothes, I swear those sheer lace curtains quiver all around the neighbourhood. The lady next door to the right who used to ask my father to clip the honeysuckle bush that fell over her wall on account of its migrainous fragrance, has already asked me about the people in the car, with pursed lips and a disapproving gaze. I told her that they were our cousins. We are part of a very large extended family.

"*Hmmph*," she sneered, "how come they were never coming around before? When your sainted father died, none of these people came to the funeral."

I told her this branch of the family had fallout with my dad, a long time ago, and their father had also passed away, so we had turned a new page. I don't think she believes me. She asked if they were infidels. I told her no, they were all Ramadan-fasting Moslems. "What has the world come to?" she shook her head in apparent disbelief as she walked away, her left hand tapping her thigh gently. I never thought I could lie so fluently, but there it is. I'm certain life with Nuray will give me plenty more practise.

SHE SITS, NURAY DOES, LOOKING OUT from the cumba, her arms folded under her chin, waiting for the sun to set on this cloudless late summer evening. I got her into the habit of sunset watching. "What are you scribbling all the time?" she said a few minutes ago, looking bored. When she pouts the sides of her plump mouth go down a little. She is beautiful, with her thick black mane that reminds me of the deepest hours of the night, and she's especially lovely when she doesn't try too hard; but she does try hard often. She puts her heart into looking campy and I don't know why she keeps insisting men are heartbreakers and creeps, when she acts so seductive around them. "Well", she said, "who else am I going to flirt with? Can I seduce you?" She batted her long fake eyelashes at me, "I didn't think so," she sighed. "So, where is the fun? Where is the thrill? You wouldn't know sugar, would you? Because you are not twisted, you weren't born like me, with a cunt—yes, she did say it like that, pa!—that wants to eat the world alive, that wants to take it all in and turn it into cells and blood and magic. Don't cringe! You have the same tasty mussel. But you, dear, wear flat nuns' shoes, plain colours, invisible clothes, and straight hair, not to mention a single thick brow. Do you even know what your breasts look or feel like? You are as far from your body as the Moon is from Earth. I may not like men, darling, but I sure do like my body!" her upper lip had a few beads of sweat on it and her cheeks were flushed. She said all this with a nonchalant shrug and winked at the end. I was flustered and pretended I had to run some errands, so I could get away, catch my breath and feel less shaken. How dare she be so vulgar with me? I thought I was angry, at first. As I walked around the neighbourhood, it occurred to me this may have been something like arousal.

So now, I'm writing about it and she is asking me what I'm scribbling, giving me a sidelong glance with her half-closed dark eyes. "Well," I said, "I'm writing about you." She cocked her head.

"Really?" She reached over to grab the notebook and I pulled it away just in time.

"Nuray, you touch this notebook and I will never speak to you again. It's a promise." I was dead serious. This is the only thing in my life that I will never share. These pages are the pit of my heart. The rest is a muted approximation, what passes for me, a skittish creature guided by fear of censure. Why is it so easy for her to use an obscene word like cunt and ruin a perfectly innocent mollusc that is a mussel so flippantly in the same breath? How will I ever eat the latter again and not think of the former? How come she can say it just like that, while I break into sweats at the mere thought and feel like a social outcast even when no one knows what I'm thinking?

LATELY, SHE HAS BEEN DOING SOME OVERTIME at work, which means I commute alone in the evenings, a situation in which I'm finding relief and comfort once again. My thoughts and daydreams remain uninterrupted. Since that odd conversation, colours seem brighter all around me: Patron's red tie with its dark blue paisley motif, the greyish white dust on the green table lamp on my desk, the maroon varnish over the ancient cracks on the wooden floor in my living room, the stone wall on which the honeysuckle vine crawls with its yellowed flowers. These flowers look like spinsters, don't they? They have that faded countenance; yellow and white, ageless yet old, droopy but scented. It is not that I find the colours themselves richer or more enticing; rather, they seem to have acquired a stubborn hue drawing my eye to the deeper shades where everything eventually disappears into darkness.

I have been unwell. Is Nuray's lack of inhibition to blame, or my shaken propriety? Or is it the sudden realization that I'm already in my mid-thirties and will not become a mother? I will not wed, most certainly. My overdue pubescent fantasies about my boss, the earthquakes ripping my heart when he leans too close to me, all of that is fading to black. There is nothing ahead that was not there before. Is Nuray my saviour or my enemy? I feel tired. I feel a great injustice has taken place, on account of two words. She has removed my dreams and given me commonplace reality.

I HAVE NOT BEEN ABLE TO WRITE anything in this journal for weeks. Last week she started coming home with me again. No overtime, no cousins, no out of town visits. She chatters endlessly about clothes, about girls at work, and politics. I lean my head on the tram window, half-listening. In a way, I'm glad she is back with me. I missed her energy, I suppose. She did the same thing again, this time to a different tram conductor. "Ah, my toes, look at them, look!" she removed her sandal and showed her baby toe and bunion having acquired a deep carmine hue. "Mr. Conductor Uncle, it is such a long way to walk from the stop to my house, and there are at least a THOUSAND stairs to climb still. Would you be so kind as to let me off here?"

The old man glanced at the red-hot bunion and as he was moving his eyes back to the street, he took in her Gigantic Stuffed Breasts in White Shirt and stopped the tram. Just like that.

"You have to stop doing this, Nuray! It's really awful." She giggled and told me to shut up as she waved and smiled at the conductor as if he were our new best friend.

"I got exciting news for you! I don't think I can wait until we climb these goddamn stairs all the way up."

"You're not putting my hair in curlers again." I stopped walking.

"No, stupid," she started fishing in her large purse and giving me things to hold, her wallet, her lipstick and powder case. "Here!" Two train tickets to Istanbul. She fished in her purse some more and took out another paper. A hotel in Moda. By the sea. "I asked them for a room with a view. We're leaving next Thursday. We'll spend Friday and Saturday there, and then we'll take the train back on Sunday. Our first trip together!" I was about to open my mouth to tell her I had to ask my boss for the time off first. "Shh!" she frowned, "don't talk to me about your Patron! I told him it was a surprise for your birthday. He said fine. All arranged."

Never been to Istanbul before. In my mind Dario Moreno's version of *"Istanbul c'est Constantinople..."* keeps replaying. I couldn't help singing it out loud during my bath and even splashed around. As I was looking for clothes, I shouted from my room, "Nuray, did you ever realize that our names mean pretty much the same thing? Moonlit night, moonshine. Did you? We're like sisters, you and me!" She pushed the door open suddenly, as if she'd been waiting there for me to speak, making me jump, underwear in hand. "Get out!" I shouted. "Out!" She shrugged, "Don't act like you have something I don't have. Besides, you've already seen me naked and…" she said as she moved closer, "we'll share the same room. Even the same bed! They have really big beds there. Here!" She started taking off her clothes quickly and pulled my arm to stand side by side in front of the mirror on the wardrobe. "Here, take a good look. Essentially, everything you have, I have bigger." She started laughing with that head-swishing neigh. Our breasts hung there, four large orbs side by side, each a different size with their soft, extended roundness sitting differently on our chests, nipples at various heights. I have more muscular legs and thicker knees and calves; hers have a wobblier look, thinning toward finer joints. She took my hand and made me turn around, so we could crane our necks and look behind us, to analyze our backs and buttocks. "You are really muscular!" she whistled, "and you practically do nothing to deserve it. I'm full of cellulite, look at those thighs! I should lay off all those gevreks and baklava. But, ah, who cares?" She was smiling as she reached for her bra and started putting everything back on again.

No one's ever seen me naked before, except my mother when I was little, and the doctor once or twice. I was mortified. "I can't imagine showing all this to a man."

"Don't worry, darling, someone must have already seen it all, from a keyhole, or a window. Unbeknownst to you." I thought she would neigh again or cackle after she said these words, but she simply slipped on her dress and left my room.

Later in the evening, in the cumba sipping our tea, we sat silently gazing across the street, over the brick rooftops at the bay of Izmir, its thick grey aquatic mass with slivers of yellow skipping here and there trying to stay afloat on the crests of small foamless waves, all unstable and shimmering, a solitary plane tree across the street crowding the left corner of the window, its majestic immobility betrayed by the leaves' intermittent shudders and to the right, a couple of freighters in the horizon looking static, as if simply placed there, cardboard cut-outs from a black and white postcard. A vegetable vendor was pushing his cart, shouting in his sing-song cadence the names of his remaining vegetables, his deep voice echoing up and down the hushed street in the early hours of the evening. A woman at the top of the street shouted at him hoarsely. I could see her bust leaning out from a window, a cigarette dangling from her lower lip, curlers on her head partially hidden by an orange-coloured kerchief tied at the back of her neck, still in her nightgown at dusk, motioning for him to come, her flabby arms waving furiously. She disappeared and reappeared with her basket tied to a rope, asking him for the price of his eggplants. He must have said something, I could not discern it. I could only hear her telling him he had to discount it on account of it being the end of the day. "Where are you going to find another customer to take all those eggplants" she asked with nasal gruffness. She halved the price, blowing smoke from the cigarette still dangling from her lips. The vendor was already loading the long slim eggplants into her lowered basket, after weighing them, muttering his displeasure, and spitting on the ground beside his cart. But she must have been right, or he must have been tired of pushing the heavy contraption all day. She tugged on the rope quickly, her head and the basket disappearing momentarily, and then the empty basket once again descended at the end of its rope, presumably with money. The grocer fished it out, counted it meticulously, and made a sign that all was well when she once again poked her head out of the window. I had a better view of her face this time. She had heavy cheeks that sagged from their own weight and a down-turned mouth, like Churchill's.

The grocer made his way slowly down the slope of the road to get to the stairs, where he adroitly manoeuvred his cart down one step at a time, diagonally, taking care not to move the few remaining peppers and squash until he reached the avenue and disappeared around the corner. I heard his voice, "Fresh squash and delicious green peppers," weakening by the third announcement and then the voice of the woman with the cigarette took over, in echoes, from her apartment father away, "Aylin, get here and give me a hand! Aaylin ... Ayliiin, get here, I said, and make it quick!" Who was Aylin? Nuray and I turned our heads and strained to see, but the open window remained dark. Someone somewhere turned on the radio in time for the evening play, and we listened to the wife's shrill voice confronting her husband over some suspicion of infidelity. There were creaking doors, heavy rain, and footsteps in the following act. Ominous music hinted that the wife was going to be murdered. We sat there, unable to move, listening to a woman's voice screaming in agony until the play was cut by a husky man's voice announcing it was to be continued the next day.

"It was the husband who did it, I'm sure. We have to listen tomorrow."

"No more fried eggs, please, Nuray." I rose from my chair to make a salad. I decided we were going to eat nothing but vegetables until the trip to Istanbul, after feeling the cutting pinch of my panties' elastic around my bloated midriff. "We have shorts to wear and so much waxing to do," I added, the excitement of the trip waning dangerously fast as I looked at the stubble on my legs.

"Are you always like this?" She reclined in the chair and lifted the mass of hair off her nape, twisting it with her fingers. "Ready to turn every adventure into some kind of martyrdom? God almighty! What is wrong with you?"

"My underwear is pinching my guts. I'm worried I won't fit into all those things we will have to wear in Istanbul. Okay?"

"I should have just gone alone!" She got up and stomped to the door, slamming it behind her. I heard her going down the few steps heavily and saw her light up her cigarette as she marched down the street. She blew smoke out of her nostrils and never looked back.

I wanted to run after her and say I was sorry, tell her we could eat eggs everyday, and I didn't give a damn, just come back home, please, but I just sat there, watching her disappear around the corner. I'm not sure how long I sat in the cumba. It got dark; the streetlights came on. People got ready for bed all around the neighbourhood. Lights went out one by one. I rose from the chair and went to my room to sleep with the door slightly ajar so I would hear her entering the house. I must have fallen asleep at some point. In the morning when I awoke she was having breakfast, dressed for work and ignoring me. She took the earlier tram. I got out of the house feeling like a prisoner. Strange how the vastness of the world surrounding you, the thousands of sounds and voices, the ever-changing sights of a city can feel so narrow and stifling when you're jilted. I suffocated and sighed all the way to work, ignored the King of Zippers when he shouted from behind the closed door of his office. "Giritli, I have news for you. Pour us some tea and come sit with me." The King of Zippers is the love of my life. Why do I not care about his news? The thought sent me spinning down the well of melancholy that had sucked and swallowed the world's sights and sounds earlier. My mind was now in that bare room covered with Nile-green semi-gloss paint; a tiny, small, square space with a wooden chair in the middle, surrounded by shiny walls I imagine they must have in prisons to easily wash off the blood or graffiti or other unsightly traces of previous inhabitants. A place to feel abject and forgotten. Her office is down the long hall from mine. Fifty steps, a staircase, and I'm there. If I had the courage to walk the distance and peek in, what would I see? Her head bent over the typewriter, black waves of ink descending from her scalp to cover the down-turned eyes and mouth. If she looked up and saw me there, would her anger turn into a smile? I shuddered standing at the doorway, waiting. Her *clack-clack-clacking* stopped abruptly. I was completely absorbed by the sight of my shoes, prepared for a storm of accusations.

"*Psst!*" she went, "*Psst,* Mehtap, don't stand there looking foolish. Either get in or get back to your office."

It was as easy as that. She giggled and gazed at me with that twinkle in her eyes. "Idiot!" She smiled. I burst into tears.

"Why did you walk out, huh? I was so worried something would happen to you. You're crazy to be walking the streets at night, all alone. And your anger slices into me. Don't ever do this again!"

"I saw how worried you were, snoring cosily in your bed!" She emitted a few neighs, twisting her head. "Next time you ruin my fun, I'm moving out. I swear."

"I can't help who I am. Why are you so harsh?"

"Sit down, sugar." She motioned to the chair with an old broken typewriter on it, moving her wrist furiously, to indicate I should remove it from there.

"The boss was calling me before I got here. I have to get back." I hesitated before moving towards the doorway.

She shrugged, "I understand we should eat more salads, fewer eggs, shave and wax and so on and so forth. But the way you say it, it's like the world was coming to an end unless we did these things. You assassinate the excitement right out of a moment. You know? Here we were having a lovely evening, listening to a play on someone else's radio, dreaming about Istanbul and all was fine. Why couldn't you just get up and make that salad without any announcements, like you're accusing *me* of turning you into a fat and hairy orangutan. Just wax your damn legs and eat your grapefruits all day, why should I hear about it?"

She was getting heated.

"Let's talk about it later," I said and walked out of the room, hurrying down the corridor. I heard her hitting the keys of her typewriter again. Patron was waiting for me in my office.

"Everything okay, Mehtap dear?" he was holding a letter in his hand. Unconvinced by my nod, he kept looking at me, arms akimbo.

"What is in it?" I asked business-like to change the subject. He waved it before throwing it on my desk. "Your bonus!" he laughed, and going "*tsk tsk tsk*." I could see his stomach muscles go up and down under his tight shirt. It was a letter from the Dutch company he had been trying to sell zippers to. They had finally placed a huge order. Patron was single-handedly going to fill the Netherlands with zippers made in Turkey: every hip, bottom and belly would be touched by our very own Turkish zippers made in Halkapınar, right in this very factory. The deadline was tight. Therefore, the Belgian had to send us the machinery as soon as possible. I was to send a telex to ask for a rush delivery of equipment along with the technician who would install them. Our production had to triple within a couple of months to meet the Dutch order. Things had to be perfect, he frowned. "Europeans are picky. One broken zipper and they will call the whole thing off. I can't afford any errors. Come with me. Let's take a walk in the factory together. I'm too excited to sit in my office now. Come. Help me decide how to organize the space." He had two engineers, but I had to walk around the factory with him instead. I suggested they come as well, but he was adamant he didn't want them around yet. He took my arm and rushed me out of the office.

We meandered around the deafening factory floor, his hand still holding my arm, squeezing it a little in fact, passing by workers who nodded respectfully and lowered their heads as we rushed on. I kept shouting "Good morning!" to each of them, while Patron stared, oblivious, above everyone's head, at a spot high enough to be undisturbed by the human element surrounding him, so he could think his thoughts clearly, I presumed. I pulled my arm away from his grip. "Greet them, for heavens' sake! You're acting like they don't exist." I could see the focus shift in his eyes, like he was coming out of a trance and he looked around at all the workers standing immobile bent slightly at the waist in reverence. He wished them an absent-minded good morning, then grabbed my arm once more and rushed me to the spot where he planned to install the Belgian machines.

"Five machines here." He extended his arm, waving it in a sweeping gesture. "Three over here." He turned us around to show me another corner. I will need more workers, won't I? Perhaps I can move some from packing to production. We'll have to train them. Get me Head Engineer Niyazi, tell him I want to see him this afternoon." His face was tense, from excitement mixed with panic. I wondered if he would manage to organize the work on time to deliver the order. If he was successful at this, his business would double in output and profit.

He had once told me it was a question of pride for him, being the grandson of a Cretan who arrived in Izmir with wife and children and nothing but the clothes on their backs in the late 1800s. It was during the uprising that liberated Crete. His grandfather used to tell him the story of their initial destitution when they arrived in Izmir, the dank basement they lived in which had a floor made of packed earth and a staircase so old that it fell apart taking his grandmother down with it. His grandfather was his hero; despite all the hardships he suffered as a young man, he had created a good life for his family out of nothing. I could see the fear of failure in his narrowing eyes as he looked around the factory. If he did not succeed at this, so much more was at stake for him than the disappointment of contending with yet another mediocre year at the factory. He had wanted to make his grandfather proud since he was a child, and this would be the moment, to at least confirm in his own mind that he was cut from the same cloth. His father had never succeeded in this. Patron, as a child, could sense that tension whenever the two were in a conversation, he once told me. There was no overt accusation of failure, yet it hovered between them, dormant in every inattentive gesture, awakening with every mundane word to infect the moment with unspoken resentment. The grandfather, leonine in stature and ego, could not forgive his son for not living up to his expectations; and Patron's father, being a self-effaced master of compromises, spent his life in passive resistance, spending all his energy avoiding confrontations instead of exploring the man he might have been. Patron once told me he grew up hating family gatherings for this reason. He felt like a field mouse in a frozen forest at those gatherings, where invisible hunters were shooting arrows and bullets blindly trying to hunt big game, while he scurried about feeling like the innocent casualty in the cross fire.

I touched his arm lightly and told him his grandfather was proud of him already from wherever he was. "Look at everything around you." He didn't say anything; just looked away after gazing at me for a moment and nodded. He walked back to the office without saying another word. Maybe he had forgotten the things he'd told me; or maybe he was not expecting to be reminded of them. Some days, I'm simply his employee; others, his friend and confidante. Hard to tell which one he wants me to be. For me, he is always my one true love, the one for whom I could sacrifice everything. Even when I make fun of his ego, even when he talks to me of other women he finds beautiful and enchanting. When he gazed at me, my heart momentarily stopped, I think, even though it continued pounding inside my head. I wished he'd embraced me for what I said so I could feel his heart beat into my chest and that would be a moment to cherish for the rest of my life.

ISTANBUL HAS COME AND GONE. Months have passed. Istanbul, the hazy postcard beauty of it, with the sleek minarets and domes facing the choppy waters of the Bosphorus, dots of gulls caught in mid arch, and fishermen's boats anchored in the foreground. Istanbul from eighteenth century engravings, opulent and so ancient even back then, the grand palaces and water fountains and arched alleyways, their stones imbibed with moisture, and lovely women in transparent veils and men in fezzes carrying things, and the minarets and cupolas and large chestnut trees, old walls covered with convolvulus vines, ornate mansions lining the Bosphorus amidst greenery, narrow streets snaking up and down the seven hills. I have dozens of postcards and reproductions to remind me of what Istanbul ought to represent for anyone passing through, what it is to awestruck eyes. The heart of Byzantium. The head of a once formidable Ottoman Empire.

And there is another Istanbul. The one that will never be represented in any pictures of any kind. The one that is mine to keep.

How to talk about it without betraying some sense of—what is it? I don't even know…

Nuray and Mehtap were not meant to be sisters. The two women named after moonlight, took a long journey by train, travelling north through fields and olive groves and more fields and small houses and more groves and some forests to reach Bandırma, where they got off, and took a ferry across the deep Sea of Marmara to Istanbul. Then they took another ferry crossing the narrow Bosphorus, to the Asian side, to the district of Moda where the small hotel by the sea was a few minutes away by taxi. Night had already descended, covering the trees and houses and the sea with its diamond-studded cloak except in some areas where streetlamps created large holes and tears of bright visibility. Couples and families out on strolls by the quay, licking ice-cream from cones, the laughter and gaiety and pretty floral dresses countered by the immense, dark mass of the sea beside them, its silent presence almost malevolent, like something from a horror movie, had it not been for the gentle, soothing laps of water on the rocks beneath them. Nuray and Mehtap rushed out of their hotel room to join in the strolling crowds, taking in the excitement of being in an unfamiliar place. Then there were two young men, who spoke to us as we strolled. They introduced themselves as Ali and Bora. They were both wearing white shirts that were unbuttoned just enough to show a tiny bit of chest hair and their gold chains. One had hair that was brushed back in an Elvis cut, the other with the aquiline nose had curlier light brown hair that fell all around his face. Their skin looked golden from being in the sun all day. Ali was talkative and smiled a lot. Bora was the quieter of the two, but followed the conversations with interest. They told us they lived in Moda, a few streets inland from the quay and invited us to have tea at the teahouse by the water. We sat on wooden chairs with straw seats right by the sea, waves lapping gently below, and our small tea glasses steaming. They were rich boys, we gathered, by their watches and gold bracelets and social ease. Well-travelled, too. They had both graduated from Lycée St Joseph, and spoke French fluently. They were probably in their early twenties, going to university in winter and off enjoying their summer now, strolling up and down the boardwalk and the quay in anticipation of some excitement, something involving beautiful girls. We felt flattered and flirtatious, spending time with the two handsome young men. Our trip to Istanbul had started very well indeed. "Well, boys," said Nuray, "we might return to Istanbul in the fall. You must give us your contact information, so we can meet again." She winked. Ali leaned back smiling. His legs were relaxed and open, his arm dangling behind the back of his chair. At first, I thought he was smiling at me and got nervous, but soon realized it was a smile of beatitude, indiscriminately offered to passers-by, Nuray's jokes, and the midnight darkness of the sea. When we rose from the table, we thanked them for their company and Nuray told them we might see each other on the boardwalk again the next evening. I was pleased she did this; normally her flirtatiousness would get the better of her, and she would say something impulsive, make a commitment, or invite them to go to museums with us. Then we would be stuck with two twenty-year-olds for the rest of our stay.

Nuray and Mehtap returned to the hotel, feet aching from being trapped in narrow shoes all day. Mehtap had never stayed in a hotel before; she marvelled at the small wrapped soaps and shampoos, the white towels and immaculate sheets, with exclamations: "Oh my, look at this!" and "Ahh, how pretty!" Nuray had done this before, it seemed. "It's cheap shampoo in small bottles, don't faint over it," she half-scolded.

She emptied the contents of her suitcase into a drawer without much attention and threw herself on the gigantic bed for two. "I hope you don't kick in your sleep," she frowned, "I'm a light sleeper."

"You'll find out soon enough," Mehtap grinned and went to the bathroom to take her shower. Everything smelled new and clean. From the open window, the warm lit night with its strollers and laughter and distant strains of music filled the room like a promise. Under the shower, murmuring bits of the song that had been playing at the teahouse, from the movie *Breakfast at Tiffany's*, "*Moon River, wider than a mile, lalalalala, two drifters off to see the world….*" Mehtap felt joy as she had never felt before. It was as though she had broken free from her life, her past, her appearance, that carapace of being carefully guarded and fortuitously cultivated to represent her in her own mind. It all seemed random to her, why she was who she was; a compilation of events and decisions some of which were not even her own, that had congealed into this image of her that everyone saw. Her budding revolt rose with every lalalala and bit of song she remembered, her voice getting stronger and louder as the water ran abundantly over her skin. It was perhaps possible to change the course of one's life, to abandon the stifling old rules that had harnessed her being all these years, to live from that impulse which rose through her chest as she sang now, opening up like petals and swirling, making her feel faint and hungry, not for food but something more essential, something connected to breathing and feeling alive and being free.

"I have never felt so happy!" She exclaimed as she left the steaming bathroom in a white cotton burnoose, still drying herself.

Nuray looked amused. "You haven't even seen anything yet."

"It's not the seeing; maybe it's that no one knows me; that I'm elsewhere. And this place, it smells like freedom."

Nuray giggled. "Freedom smells like bleach?"

Mehtap leaned over to smell the sheets. "I love it!" she concluded.

"Tomorrow, Aya Sofia, Topkapı, Beyoğlu."

"I want to spend time here too, swimming...." She took her lilac cotton baby-doll with matching puffy shorts from her suitcase and returned to the bathroom to change. When she came back to bed, Nuray was already under the covers, arms and legs spread out. Mehtap remembered that Nuray always slept naked as she saw the outlines of her body from the sheet covering it. She slipped in gingerly from the side of the bed, making sure she put a lot of distance between them. Nuray rolled toward her, "I don't bite, you know. Get comfortable!"

"Not with you naked. Why don't you wear something?"

"What are you worried about?" Nuray smiled.

Mehtap held her breath.

"Try something you've never tried before. Take off that silly puffy thing, sleep naked for once. If you get cold there is another cover to pull on. It smells like freedom, too." She brought it to her nose to inhale the smell of bleach.

"It feels improper ... I don't know...."

"Honey, freedom is improper. Some would have us commit suicide for not having a thick enough hymen, in the name of propriety. Remember? They would have us slit our wrists, not enjoy a single sexual act. What is freedom to you? Bleached sheets in a foreign city? Please...." She got out of bed, her nakedness filling the room around Mehtap. She went to the small fridge and got out some peach juice and after some hesitation put it back in and slammed the door. She called room service, ordering bubbly wine.

They had quite a lot of it too. Mehtap felt a sensation of warmth rising within her that she attributed to inebriation. Laughter was easy. The edginess inside her was giving in to hilarity, making her roll around the bed in uncontrollable fits of laughter. Nuray lit two cigarettes and gave one to Mehtap. There was some coughing, and more giggling. The smoke was snaking its way toward the open window where the night had emptied itself of all the bustle and noise, leaving the sidewalks to stray cats wailing and hissing in dark corners. The freshness of the sea entered the room moving the listless curtain back and forth a few times before it stopped. Small invisible waves were lapping unseen rocks down below. The "pot-pot-pot" sound of a fisherman's boat crossed the invisible horizon. Then, as Mehtap was wiping tears of laughter from her cheeks with the back of her hand, Nuray reached over and softly kissed her lips.

Mehtap recoiled; "Nuray ... I cannot...."

Nuray did not reply. She took Mehtap in her arms and hugged her for a moment. "We should go to sleep." She cleared her throat and turned off the light, pulling the sheet to her chin.

They remained side by side, one naked, the other in a lilac baby-doll in the dark room, where the window was still letting in unfamiliar sounds and a feeble breeze was trembling through the lace curtains. Farther inland, a guard dog barked at reassuring intervals. Mehtap felt a throbbing inside her that was not letting her sleep and wondered if this was a shared sensation between them. She turned to look at Nuray's profile, the outline of her shoulders and neck, the cheeks glistening with what must have been tears.

We took the ferry early in the morning and visited Aya Sofya and Sultanahmet Mosque. We passed by the church of Aya Irini and walked in the large park with its beige earth and centennial trees providing shade, looking up and down and sideways and walked some more in the splendid Aya Sofya with its domed ceilings and shiny old stones and mosaics, and in the Blue Mosque and saw the obelisk, and walked and walked; bought postcards and engravings and made our way to Topkapı, and visited the various halls, and saw the sultans' clothes, the rubies and emeralds and swords, and the disappointingly spartan harem, then the Museum of Archaeology and made our way to a teahouse nearby with a view of the Bosphorus, and finally sat with our aching feet and reddened heels at a table under a linden tree to have a glass of soda pop. I reached over and held Nuray's hand in mine and thanked her for this lovely trip. We sat there holding hands and gazing at the freighters and ferries crossing the Bosphorus down below.

I thought it would be easier to write about the events that still disturb me, in the third person, as if it involved two other women in a page from someone else's story. And it was, somewhat. But in the end, who am I fooling? This notebook?

By our second night in Istanbul, the tension had continued to grow in silence during all those hours spent together sightseeing, buying postcards and knick-knacks, until we could no longer contain it when we returned to the hotel room. I was moody and annoyed having worn myself out battling sensations of shame and desire. I was curious and angry for it. Mind you, everything a woman could desire is forbidden. Desire is forbidden, isn't it? To be desirable is encouraged, but to desire and seek one's own personal satisfaction, and with a woman at that.... I had broken all the rules. Yet, I also felt that I deserved all my desires. I deserved to live as one who made the decisions, rather than one who moved like a shadow in this man's world, because we do; don't we? They make all the rules, and what does that mean for us? To cater to their desires, to try and eke out some elbow room in a universe they have worked out for themselves using us as mothers or wives or whores. Damn the rules! We sat side by side at the foot of the bed and I started sobbing uncontrollably, fury tumbling out of my chest. She kissed my eyelids and held me close and wiped my tears and whispered she loved me and would always be by my side. I kissed her back. This time there was nothing tentative to it. We made love until we were spent and fell asleep with the lull of afternoon noises; the shrieks of kids swimming, peals of laughter from girls, young men's voices strong and mocking coming from the sea—I thought I heard Ali and Bora among them. Then it all faded all away. The last thing I remembered was the gentle rising of the tulle curtains as Moda's seaside life streamed into our room, and thinking of the distance to the moon for some reason, and how airless it was there despite its faraway beauty. Two women named after moonlight, a place where breezes never blow from the Sea of Tranquility into a room where lovers have wrestled.

"GIRITLI, YOU LOOK ... POSITIVELY RADIANT! What happened to you? Did you meet a handsome guy in Istanbul?" Patron asked as soon as I brought him his cup of Turkish coffee with the daily newspapers.

"I simply rested, Patron," I smiled, "thank you."

"Well? Aren't you going to tell me your adventures?"

"Honestly, Patron, what adventures could a couple of women have? We walked around, saw sights, ate.... What more?"

"There is something you're not telling me. It's all over your face. Are you in love?"

"*Tsk ... tsk....* Patron, I don't ask about your love life, do I?"

"I never wait for you to ask. You're my only trusted friend in this world. I tell you everything!"

"Is that true?"

"I don't know what I'd do without you. Quit standing there. It makes me nervous. Sit, sit...." He motioned to the chair impatiently.

I sat down. "Are we going to write a letter?"

He smiled a mysterious little smile, "Yes, a letter to the stranger in Istanbul who stole your heart. Here…" he pushed a pad of blank paper and his pen towards me pointing his index finger to the desk. "Write: Dear Sir, I have been made aware that you've recently borrowed something very dear to me. Did he simply borrow it, or is this for good?" He wasn't smiling anymore.

"What? I just had a long weekend vacation. Being away from here was really good for me. You already know you're a slave driver. You call me at impossible hours, make me do all this work day and night, tell me about Gönül and all the details of your many escapades, hiding from wife, mistress, and god knows who else. I can't sleep at night thinking of all the dangers you put yourself into. If your wife ever finds out about the things you do, she will take everything you own, everything, and kick you to the curb. But you don't seem to worry. You act like a careless teenager. I do all the worrying, plus all the work around here. If anything, I need more vacations like this one."

"Ahhh! Shame on me for causing you such grief, my good friend! I'm grateful to you. You know this…." He nodded and reached over his desk toward me to pat the top of my hand, "Tell me, why do you do so much for one as undeserving as myself, Mehtap?"

"Because you need it."

"You haven't answered my question," he insisted.

"And I shouldn't have to," I replied with finality, but then something made me continue. "This is what friends do. You'd do the same." I knew he wouldn't. He was selfish.

"Mehtap, you're good for both of us. I'm a hypocrite. No good as a husband, or even as a friend. I couldn't be less deserving of such affection. We both know it."

"Now you're telling me? After I've put up with your craziness all these years? That's it, then. I resign as your friend. I'll continue as your assistant. And, you better make that bonus worth my while. I will need more vacation time, too."

"Yeah, yeah…. You're going to suck my marrow dry." He chuckled.

I nodded.

"Well," he nodded back, "my secretive friend. Whoever he is, you tell him from me he better treat you right, or he'll have to deal with me."

"There is no man, Patron."

"So be it."

Before Istanbul, I would have cherished his sudden worry about losing me. Now, it amuses me.

For many years now, I've been celebrating his birthday at the office. I'll buy a chocolate cake (his favourite) and call all the clerks to my office so we can all sing him happy birthday. I make a big deal of it because apparently his wife forgets to celebrate it, or when she does remember, she invites her friends, not his, and buys a variation of some fruit flan he dislikes, so that he never has a good time. I buy him a present that I give him when we're alone. Every year, I get him one small crystal sculpture, tiny really, the size of a thumb, representing an animal. Last year was an owl, before that an elephant, this year it is a horse. When he receives his gift, he hugs me tight and kisses my cheeks. This kiss, most paternal and un-erotic as it may be, sends shivers up and down my spine. I don't wash my face all day, to keep a bit of his tea and cigarette breath on my skin a few moments longer. The next kiss will be on a religious holiday, my birthday, or the New Year, so, all together I think he plants one of those avuncular kisses on my cheeks five or six times a year. Nuray teases me. She knows of my crush by now. She was looking for a handkerchief in my drawers and came upon the tin box where I keep his cigarette butts. He no longer smokes, but when he did, I used to steal the cigarette butts at the end of the day and took them home to have something that touched his lips. I also have a handkerchief with his initials that he gave me at my dad's funeral, because mine was already soaked. It smelled of aftershave, his manly perfume. I just breathed into it and momentarily forgot I was there on account of one of the saddest occasions of my life. He put his arm around me and rubbed my back as I kept pressing his handkerchief to my face. Then, he held me in his arms, to console me, as the sobs burst once again from my chest into his. He held me for a long time, so that the anguish I felt at my father's burial is forever entwined with the ecstatic sensation of being held in his arms. I begged my departed father to make this man love me back, if he could read my mind at all from the great beyond, as his remains were being lowered into the earth.

His wife was standing farther behind, wearing a stylish black suit with ivory trimmings around the jacket, a rimless hat with a matching ivory ribbon in a butterfly knot on the side, placed carefully on hair teased like some bird's nest, big round sunglasses, and an ivory clutch. This was one of her Chanel moments; standing dutifully with her husband, probably mostly concerned about the sharp heels of her shoes sinking into the soft earth and getting ruined. Or, perhaps not. I tried to imagine myself in her shoes. Would I wear these clothes, have my hair teased, and adopt this look that grazes the top of everyone's head as if everything of utmost interest lies beyond the weeping crowd cluttering the foreground? Up there, above everyone's head, beyond the scene of this burial, was there the fantasy of a chic boutique with fancy clothes or some big expensive thing that makes the heart glad when owned that occupied her thoughts? Whatever she was thinking was aptly hidden by the sunglasses covering half her face. The freshly dug hole in the earth was swallowing my father and despite the exquisite despair of that moment I was able to think all those disparate, inconsequential thoughts about this woman who was oblivious to my deepest, most secret yearnings for her husband, taking in the sight of the crusty grey bark of an old tree across from me on which hundreds of ants were going up and down in single file, focused on bringing food into their subterranean caves, so near my father's new abode, with soldierly determination.

But here we are. His line of questioning was a sort of confession, I believe, that he has come to need me and doesn't want to lose the attention to which he has grown accustomed. I, in turn, confessed to Nuray that he will forever be the immutable love of my life, unrequited, unnoticed, and secretive as it may be. I assured her that my affection for her was deep and sensual, our lovemaking the only kind I knew, and would likely ever know. She asked, "If one day he declared his love to you, wanted to marry you, would you leave me?"

"He never will, Nuray. We both know this."

"Let's suppose he did."

"Yes, I believe I would. Forgive me, Nuray. I can't help it."

"How can you love him so? What do you know of him? You're attached to some teenage fantasy of a man; this cannot be real."

"Well, I know what I feel when he's around me. I know what I feel because of him. For him, I would give everything up. He hasn't done anything to deserve it. But I'm deeply attached and that's how it is."

"So I'm some kind of pastime, some kind of dirty little secret experiment...." A despondent look came upon her face.

"Those are hurtful words, Nuray. You've brought such a sense of adventure to my life. You've given me a glimpse, the only glimpse I will probably ever have, of what it is to want and be wanted, and of all the pleasures a woman can have. What did I know before you? You've opened the doors of existence and womanhood for me. Don't say these things Nuray. I will always cherish your companionship and the life we have together."

I said those things. Or an approximation of those things. I cannot bear to see that sad, dejected look on her face. She is one of the most beautiful women I have ever seen. It is all very clear to me now. The funny thing is, even Patron gives her those lusty stares from time to time, when she passes in front of him at the office, her bosom jutting out in those fitted sweaters and the tight skirts moulding her hips and plump bottom that she swings as she walks, like Marilyn Monroe. It makes me insanely jealous, not only that HE desires her, but also that he desires HER. She has had sex with men before, she's told me. She shrugs it off; says she is mostly interested in having their attention, that is why she flirts so shamelessly. But the sexual act with a man does nothing for her, she said. "Trust me, it is not for a lack of appetite," she swished her head as she laughed. "That whole in-and-out thing is highly over-rated, my dear," she continued. "What I like about men is that I can command their attention. In bed, I find, they don't know what I want, or perhaps they don't care, or perhaps I'm the one who doesn't care." She giggled some more. "Problem with women," she went on, and there was no shutting her up at this point despite my visible signs of discomfort, "is that they won't flirt with a woman they find attractive. Not in the same way anyhow...." She sighed. "It's all very complicated." She was thankfully quiet after that.

I WAS LOOKING AT THE FULL MOON from my bedroom window the other night. Nuray was sleeping in hers. We have an understanding about our mutual need for space. Anyway, I couldn't sleep. And I gazed at the surfaces of the moon, pearly white with grey shadows, wondering why dogs howl at it. Is it because of their fascination for a distant ball that glows night after night never rolling any closer? Is it because it reminds them of the dark and remote universe all around as they toil for a discarded piece of meat, for a warm corner, a mate, some kindness, all the while carrying all that vast remoteness within like heartache? Wouldn't the moon howl back if she could, gazing at the earth day after day, filled with such noise and movement and emotion from which she remains forever disconnected? It is odd to think of those things that do not speak for themselves, that do not live as we do, and do not share our desperation. Beyond the crust of the earth and its atmosphere is the unimaginable silence of perpetuity from that life spares us with its incessant chatter. When stars explode, who hears them?

NURAY IS SINGING OFF-KEY as I write this, not in the bathtub, but in her room, where her Singer sewing machine is making its own kind of rhythm. She has decided to make us some dresses we saw in the *Burda* magazine. She chose a bright red fabric for herself and I chose a greyish blue. She twisted her nose at my lack of exuberance. We had a slight argument while Saim Bey stood there watching us from behind the piles of fabric he had unfurled for us to admire.

"Why do you always want to disappear behind drab colours?" she said petulantly.

"I like *this*. 'Bright colours just aren't *me*!" I retorted with a scowl.

She pushed the fabric I had chosen with disdain. "You will look like a walking curtain!"

"Well, let me worry about that, and you worry about yours! I don't want a damn dress anymore, pay for your stuff and let's go." I turned my back and walked toward the door.

Saim Bey tried to appease us. "Nuray Hanım, I'm sure your friend has a great pattern in mind that will make this a very good choice for her. Don't you, Mehtap Hanım?" he said encouragingly. I shrugged and replied I wasn't sure I wanted to buy anything anymore, and I that had a headache.

"Trust me, it will all work out! And I will give you a very nice discount. An Aspirin, too. You'll come back to thank me when everyone compliments you on your choices." He proceeded to measure, cut, and package the whole thing before we could change our minds. This is how our visits to the cloth merchant are generally concluded. He pats our shoulders and calls us his daughters, assuring us we will not regret this good bargain. We go home, with me sulking on the way. She is strategically quiet until we get home. Then, she attacks her Singer machine fiercely, and sings loud. I leave the house to run errands, or just wander around not to hear her singing. Mostly, I go to the cinema, which I did today. I watched *Belle de Jour* with Catherine Deneuve. The theatre was full probably on account of it being advertised as the most shocking movie of the year. It was about a beautiful housewife who loves her husband but has no sex with him while she develops a secret life as a prostitute in an exclusive brothel in Paris. At the end, the patient and loving husband is shot and paralyzed forever by one of her obsessive clients and she spends the rest of her days taking care of him. There is more to it but this is the general idea. I dislike the fact that the loving if bland husband who is utterly deprived of sex must also get shot on top of finding out his cold wife doubles as a whore when he is not able to even walk to the bathroom let alone walk out on her, as if his misfortune was already not profound enough. Many scenes must have been cut, deemed too outrageous for our censorship board, so I can't say that I understood much. As I was leaving the theatre, I overheard people heatedly talking about how they too understood absolutely nothing and was relieved that I was not alone in my ignorance. I was glad this happened on a Saturday instead of a Sunday, because Sunday movies are a melancholy affair. There's nothing else to look forward to but eating and going to bed before work the next day.

   I came back home and found her still busy at her sewing machine. She is adamant that she will wear the dress tomorrow. I turned on the radio in time for the evening news. Dr Barnard performed his second heart transplant in Cape Town. In Ankara, they transplanted a heart into a dog only to put him down a few minutes later. Dubcek is now the Communist leader of Czechoslovakia. American soldiers massacred more civilians in Vietnam. The Turkish government is the first one to recognize the military junta in Greece. Everywhere students are demonstrating.

I turned my parents' prized Grundig radio off, cutting the speaker's phrase midway. It came with a record player, encased in a large pine wooden frame containing the circular speakers and standing on four slim legs angled outwards with metal casings that looked like small hooves. The records were in the buffet, behind the bottles of banana and mint liquor. I took out some of the newer records I had bought. My mother used to love Tino Rossi songs, so there are a couple of records by him, then some Greek songs, of course, and *Madame Butterfly* featuring Maria Callas. I pushed all the large records aside to reach for my 45s. Yaşar Güvenir's, "Seni Uzaktan Sevmek,"[12] my favourite song. It smelled like ripe bananas. I put it on, turned up the volume. In the softly sung tango, he asks, "*What is happiness without you? I haven't tasted it, I wouldn't know.... You were etched on my forehead.... Loving you from afar is the most beautiful of loves. I've grown so accustomed to your absence; if you were to say, 'Come to me' I don't think I could find the way.*"

In my maudlin state, I didn't notice that the noise of the sewing machine had stopped. Nuray was kneeling beside the armchair where I sat with eyes closed. She gently caressed my limp hand that was hanging off the armchair before placing a kiss on top of it. I looked at her. She said nothing; kept caressing the top of my hand gently.

SHE IS DEVOTED. My inability to reciprocate that particular generosity despite trying to be the best person I can be, adds regret to the sentiment of failure I carry within. She is clearly the one I'm convinced I should love, yet I can't seem to reach that exalted assurance. Like Roxanne in *Cyrano de Bergerac*, I'm fascinated with the other one, the scintillating but lesser version, not the one whose soul is noble and vast. In stories, awakening happens at the precise moment when action has become

---

[12]"Seni Uzaktan Sevmek": "Loving You from Afar"

irrelevant. In my story, I am Cyrano to Patron's Roxanne, and Roxanne to Nuray's Cyrano. Nuray, however, is no Cyrano, at least physically. At the snap of her fingers, she can have her pick among dozens of men. Yet she couldn't care less about them. For me, Patron is an anomaly; the only creature man or woman who sends my heart into that frenzied rhythm. Otherwise men leave me rather indifferent and I prefer the company of women: their warmth, their shapes and manners, the doughy smell of Nuray's sweaty mound of Venus, especially. So how does this get defined in the world of accepted notions in which I'm finding myself less and less complicit? Indecisive lesbian or reluctant heterosexual? Since this will be the secret I hope to take to my grave, I shall not concern myself with the World of Accepted Notions. Easy to say.... Inside my head, in my dreaming and waking life, even in the moments preceding sexual climax when I feel Nuray's soft, naked flesh mixed with mine and I almost entirely forget who I am, my somewhat Christian mother, my somewhat Moslem father, all their pious ancestors, my grandmother, and the neighbours watching my every move, Gülbahar Hanım with her fascist dross are all frowning from the ceiling, index finger pointed in accusation for deviating from Accepted Notions and warning me of expulsion from their midst.

I am worn out from the constant effort to conform to these notions so I won't be perceived as a half-breed, a foreigner, someone who half-represents the enemy, the child of immigrants, the potential infidel and traitor, and now, the lesbian. Did my parents give me this moon-related name anticipating I would feel like an alien all my life?

I HAVE GROWN FOND OF SUNDAY AFTERNOON naps with Nuray, especially in this unseasonably warm September, with the heat pressing down on us so that we can hardly move all day, every thought and limb struggling against some thick mud of torpor to budge in the tiniest increments. I keep the windows of my bedroom wide open. The tulle curtains swell and part in two soft arcs with the hot draught streaming in, bringing plaintive echoes of *manés* from some faraway record player sung by sorrowful, birdlike female voices. A few ever moving patches of sunlight scatter on the white sheets crumpled around our perspiring naked bodies as we lie side by side, content in our indolence. Nuray puts on her bathrobe and leans out the window when she hears the gevrek boy on his afternoon rounds. She lowers the basket from the bedroom window, just like the neighbour up the street, and we eat our gevreks with slices of tulum cheese, scattering sesame seeds all over the sheets. We talk about this and that, or read the papers or just sit propped by pillows quietly waiting for the sun to set and the house to cool down. I cannot imagine doing this without Nuray. I suppose breaking the biggest rules makes the smaller transgressions insignificant. I owe her these carefree moments. She is reading the newspaper as I write these words. One of my wide golden bracelets she fished out of the top dresser drawer moves back and forth on her forearm. On my wrist is an identical one. She asks me how come I got two identical golden bracelets. I ignore the question. I tell her they are from Crete. Family souvenirs. She carefully observes the embossed figures on it and asks me what they represent.

"Look," she exclaims, "there's a guy with a bull's head, here!"

"It's the Minotaur. You know, from Greek mythology. An ancient Cretan story."

She had never heard of it. She clapped her hands, her lovely breasts shaking with them. "Tell it to me. Tell it to me like a bedtime story. I love those. You should start with 'Once there was and once there wasn't. In the days before time, when the sieve was in the straw, when flees were barbers and camels were town criers…' you know, like that!"

She had transformed into a child momentarily, begging to be taken back in time, to those days when every story told was real and wondrous, opening an enchanted path toward places one could visit someday, places filled with magical creatures and adventures, where words like impossible, unlikely, illogical didn't exist. I caressed her sweaty cheek.

"The story takes place on the windy mountains of Crete, in the Mediterranean where two imaginary lines, one from Anatolia and the other from Greece, cross on their way to Africa." I started a bit professorially, imitating my geography teacher from high school as Nuray dropped her newspaper and settled comfortably on her propped pillows.

"No!" She raised her hand to stop me, the bracelet swinging a little before moving toward her elbow. "You must start properly, the way all good stories start. Once there was, once there wasn't...." She nodded encouragingly.

"Once there was and once there wasn't. In the days before time, when the sieve was in the straw, when fleas were barbers and camels were town criers, there was an island called Crete."

"Don't tell me anything about Crete, I know it; just tell me the story," she interrupted.

"Is this your story or mine? Settle down and listen or I won't tell it to you. So ... where was I? The island, back then, was home to the terrifying Minotaur who dwelled inside a labyrinth and ate children."

"Where did he come from?"

"Shh! You know Zeus?"

She didn't.

"The God of Gods. Ancient Greek. So this Zeus had a habit of transforming himself into different animals when he wanted to make love to beautiful women. Make love is an embellishment. He pretty much raped them disguised as an animal. He did this partly to hide from his jealous wife who was always on to him. When the beautiful Europa caught his eye, he immediately transformed himself into a bull to kidnap her from Phoenicia where she lived —that's Lebanon—and bring her all the way to Crete. Once he brought her there, he made love to her in the shade of a plane tree and got her pregnant. That is why plane trees don't shed their leaves, by the way. Then he arranged for the king of Crete to marry Europa, so that all the sons Zeus had with her would become kings."

"Did the king know he was a cuckold?" she interrupted.

"I didn't ask," I snapped and threatened to stop talking. She promised to keep quiet.

"When the king of Crete died, the three sons were happy to rule the island all together for a while, until Minos, Zeus's favourite, decided to banish his two brothers from the island and declare himself the sole ruler.

"Once he took the throne, he prayed to Poseidon, the god of the seas, asking him to send him a white bull, to show that the gods approved of his decision. In return, he promised to sacrifice the animal in his honour.

As soon as he had uttered these words, a magnificent bull appeared on the shore. Spotless white, larger-than-life.... A marvelous creature. Minos, enthralled, couldn't bear to sacrifice such a beautiful animal. He had a handsome bull of his own killed instead, to fool Poseidon. But who can fool a god? Poseidon was livid, and decided to punish the conceited Minos where it would hurt him the most: his wife.

"Minos adored this woman of legendary beauty. He lavished presents and all his attention on her, to keep her happy. Besides his kingdom, nothing mattered to him more than the love of this woman. When he boastfully showed her the gorgeous white bull sent to him by Poseidon, however, she suddenly got feverish with lust. She started dreaming of having sex with this powerful and magnificent animal and couldn't get this desire out of her mind no matter how hard she tried. To hide her infidelity from her husband, she asked the architect Daedalus to build a big wooden cow, as a monument to honour the bull. At night, she secretly led the white bull into this big wooden heifer and did it with him."

Nuray opened her iridescent brown eyes wider, the irises quickly overtaking the colour like bottomless wells. "Go on!" she ordered, annoyed by the pause.

"Nine months later, she gave birth to a freakish monster, something neither animal, nor human. In appearance, he was half-man and half-bull. He ate human flesh. To hide him from sight and protect his kingdom, King Minos had Daedalus build a labyrinth and they imprisoned him there. As for the steady diet of human flesh to keep him pacified, Minos had a shrewd plan. He sent word to the King of Athens, that in return for a shipment of seven young boys and seven virgin girls to be sacrificed every nine years, he would leave Athens alone. Not having the strength or the army to fight back, King Aegeus of Athens acquiesced. Thus, boats carrying innocent children to their cruel deaths sailed from Athens to Crete every nine years to feed the Minotaur, black flags flapping on their masts.

"This went on for years until Theseus, the Athenian king's son, decided to put an end to this horrible pact and volunteered to go on the boat as the fourteenth youth. On the way to Crete, he kept looking at the dark banner flailing with the violent slaps of the poyraz winds, wondering if he would ever return home. Before boarding the boat, Aegeus, his father, tears flowing down his bearded face, said to him: 'My only son, my gold, I will be waiting for your arrival, standing on that cliff. Hoist a white flag to tell me you're alive and well, so I can rejoice when I behold your ship in the horizon.'

"When Theseus arrived in Crete and got off the boat, Princess Ariadne, the daughter of King Minos, who had a habit of going to the port to see boats come and go, became intrigued by the youth's regal demeanour. She approached him and they talked briefly. Theseus, not knowing she was the daughter of Minos, whispered to her that he had come on this boat with the intention to slay the monster. Ariadne retorted, 'Not so easy, bold Athenian. Let's say you slayed him; you still wouldn't be able to get out. It's full of dead ends and wrong turns. You'll die of thirst and starvation.' Theseus was valiant all right, but not very clever. He didn't have a plan to get out. 'So be it,' he replied, 'at least I will have rid the world of this horror once and for all.'

"Ariadne admired his readiness to sacrifice himself to save others. 'I will figure out a way to save you, brave Theseus.' She held his hands and felt the pounding of her own heart in her palms squeezing his. 'I want a promise in return.' Theseus had all that adrenaline pumping, thinking about the next morning when he'd be entering the cave to go to his certain death with all the whimpering children by his side. Truth be told, he thought Ariadne was a naive young girl who had an evident crush on him judging from those doleful eyes and sweaty hands. He didn't believe she could do anything to help.

"'If I save you,' she continued with a firm tone, 'promise me you'll marry me and take me with you on that ship.' At that moment, the guards came to take all the virgins away to their dungeon and Theseus, knowing this would be the last time he'd see a fine young woman with such soft eyes again, gave her a gentle kiss and whispered, 'I promise.'

"Ariadne, elated, went home and shut herself in her room, thinking of ways to save him. She sat at her spinning wheel weeping from frustration at not finding a solution hour after hour. Then, in the middle of the night she had this brilliant idea looking at the yarn in her basket. I think a goddess had something to do with this, maybe Aphrodite, I don't remember....

"The next morning, she rushed to the dungeon gates waiting for the heartbreaking procession of lamenting youths being led to the Labyrinth. As soon as she saw Theseus, gaunt and sad with his face unshaven and his hair crimpled after a sleepless night in the dungeon, she got close to him and stuffed a ball of yarn into his belt with her free hand. 'Unravel the thread as you walk and you will find your way back out. I'll be waiting for you near the entrance. I'll arrange your escape. May the Gods keep you safe.'

"What had seemed like a suicide mission to Theseus suddenly turned into a hopeful one and he imagined sailing back to Athens into his father's proud embrace as a living hero. 'Thank you, clever girl,' he whispered back, 'I will take you on my ship, I promise.'

"As soon as he got into the grotto he took out the yarn and put one end of the thread under a rock, slowly unravelling it as they advanced in the light of his torch. He told the children to be quiet and follow his instructions. When he arrived and saw the sleeping Minotaur from a distance, he hid the children in a corner, told them to wait for him there holding on to the thread and not move until he told them to. The stink of rotten flesh and refuse was so overpowering that they couldn't help retching and vomiting, making sounds that awoke the Minotaur from his sleep. The monster rose. Theseus, sword in hand, ran towards him, and before the Minotaur could shake the sleep off his eyes, swung the sharp blade at his jugular. From the monster's gashed neck sprang a fountain of blood, splattering all over Theseus. He swung it again, and severed the head. The body of the headless monster ran about the cave and the children screamed with horror. Finally it collapsed in a twitching heap and expired. Theseus, legs still trembling with fear, picked up the heavy head from the horns. The eyes were wide open with frozen surprise. He shuddered at the sight before lifting it high and shouted, 'Children, I'm taking you home!'

"When Ariadne saw blood-splattered Theseus stealthily emerge from the cave, she ran to him. They secretly boarded the ship taking them back to Athens. A couple of days into the trip, when Theseus slowly came back to his senses, he looked at love-struck Ariadne and in his heart nothing stirred. He felt gratitude and admiration but no love. He realized he could not marry a woman out of gratitude and admiration alone, and so he asked the captain to make a stop at an island so they could replenish their food and water and spend the night. They all got off. At night, as unsuspecting Ariadne lay sleeping, Theseus quietly gathered his crew and the children and set sail for Athens, leaving her behind. It was a cowardly thing to do and Theseus felt awful about it. In that brooding state of mind, he forgot to hoist the white flag to announce his victory.

"His father, standing on the cliffs, saw the black flag and knew that all was lost. He threw himself down the precipice into the sea. Grief-stricken Theseus named the sea that swallowed his father's body the Aegean Sea, so that Aegeus would forever be remembered by all."

Nuray did not even stir; she was so engrossed in her own vision of the story. She sat there pensive, propped by her pillows for a while and finally asked, "What happened to Ariadne?"

"She had betrayed her own family and kingdom, had her brother (he was a monster, but still a brother) killed for the love of Theseus; yet, he had abandoned her. She was disconsolate. The Muses took pity on her, whispered into her ear that she was going to know divine love, a love far greater than anything Theseus could have offered. Not long after that, Dionysius the god of wine and ecstasy, who was passing by in his golden chariot, his head crowned with vine leaves and his eyes the colour of grapes, took one look at her and fell in love. As a wedding present he gave her a crown of stars in the heavens; the constellation Corona. He was unfaithful, though…. Very."

Nuray nodded absentmindedly, turning the bracelet around, scrutinizing the embossed figures. "Who gave you these?" she asked.

"One is from my mother's mother, and the other from my father's mother," I replied.

"Do all the women there wear these?"

"I don't think so."

"Maybe the jeweller who made them was obsessed with this story," she shrugged as she removed the bracelet to put back into my drawer. "I like the way you told it," she smiled.

"My parents used to tell me they met where the legendary

labyrinth was said to exist. There was a cave there. I've never told this story before. I've never shown my bracelets to anyone either," I added reluctantly.

"I think," she said, "you ought to write Cretan stories instead of writing what you eat and do everyday, not to mention what I do." She swung her head and whinnied in her usual horsey fashion before rising from my bed and swaying her hips on the way to the bathroom to run her singing bath. I wrote about it all as she splashed in her bath and sang my favourite love song off-key. It was an assassination, there is no other description for it; she simply demolished the tango.

Strangely, I find myself cheerful and upon rereading what I just scribbled I thought perhaps I ought to do it. I ought to write the stories I never told anyone.

Notebook II. The Cretans

On the windy hills of Crete was a village where two Greek children lived, born on the same day to different mothers. One was a boy and the other, a girl. These two always knew each other, the way everyone knows everyone else in the countryside. The boy's name was Mehmet. His father, Mehmet the Great, was a portly, fearsome man with a yellowish-white moustache shaped into curlicues on each side of his mouth, a headscarf, and big muscular hands embossed with multiple calluses. He owned acres and acres of lush vineyards. The wine he produced was so sublime that whoever tasted it once couldn't help getting drunk on it. This included Mehmet the Great himself, who, after a sweaty day in the vineyards settled down at his drinking table with his friends to collapse hours later right there on the floor until the next morning. He never went to bed, preferring the concrete surface of his vast terrace overlooking the mountains and the Mediterranean Sea. Some said he feared the ghost of his wife calling him to bed every night for having missed her final moments while delivering Little Mehmet. That night, while she groaned and screamed and pushed the boy out of her belly, the story goes, he was with his mistress, tasting her wine. "Mehmeeet, where are you? May the devil take your soul and that whore's too!" she screamed, as the boy finally came out of the narrow canal. And those were her final words.

It surprised no one when Mehmet the Great did not remarry, choosing instead to loan his son to married sisters, his own mother, and whoever would offer to take him in. The only women who dared enter his house occasionally were his mother and sisters; and they did so with great trepidation, knowing the irate soul of his deceased wife was lurking in the shadows, waiting to pounce upon them at the slightest provocation.

When he was not drunk or busy working, which was not very often, Mehmet the Great tried to be an adequate father. A man of few words and fewer gestures, he limited himself to patting Little Mehmet on the head, the usual hugs on religious holidays. He even visited the school teacher once, when she sent word that the boy did not attend classes frequently enough. "Should I belt him?" he asked, with genuine concern and eager to show her that he did not take his responsibilities lightly.

"No, no, parakaló, kiryo Memetis,[13] just have a conversation with him. Convince him of the benefits of education," she pleaded. Paraskevi, the teacher, was a skinny young thing from Heraklion, a kopelitsa,[14] who was quickly losing her lofty ideals and patches of that shiny brown hair adorning the pretty head that contained them, trying to teach the unruly children of this village how to read and write.

Little Mehmet did not get the belt. His father called him to his side gruffly after a bottle of wine, and with his booming voice warned, "If I hear from your teacher again, you're getting your bottom whipped." The intimidated boy nodded and kept a low profile during the winter months. But in spring, the scent of freedom started blowing in through the open windows of the classroom, carrying the shape of meadows filled with red poppies and the fragrance of dirt roads on hills that smelled of pine needles, oregano, and lavender, beckoning as he sat restlessly at his old wooden desk. Before long, he was playing hooky once again. He sat in the meadows amidst bright yellow buttercups and daydreamed of nebulous, sun-filled fantasies, his heart unable

---

[13]"parakaló, kiryo Memetis": "please, Mr. Memetis"
[14]kopelitsa: young woman

to contain the delightful sensation of freedom from Kyria Paraskevi's monotonous dictations, the sight of the decrepit classroom and its chalky blackboard, and the smell of rancid farts embedded in seats with familiar signatures of garlic and lamb.

One such day, as he was aimlessly wandering toward the stream behind the trees, he saw Maria sitting there gazing at the shallow water eddy and froth around rocks. She had her chin resting on her knees, her arms wrapped around her shins, humming something he could not quite hear.

Maria lived with her mother; both shunned by the villagers on account of her being illegitimate. No one knew the father, and Maria's mother never uttered a word in that regard. Maria was teased and taunted in the schoolyard, and her mother was scorned by the villagers who called her *putana*.[15] Needless to say, the girl looked for every opportunity to miss school. She sat by streams, played in the hills, wandered aimlessly in the streets of the village, and even walked to neighbouring towns on sunny days. Her mother did not bother with the belt or other such correctional measures as she had bigger worries of her own. So, it was a matter of time before Mehmet and Maria recognized each other as friends and started spending stolen time together. Mehmet, who did not miss as many school days as Maria, was more advanced in his studies and took it upon himself to teach the girl how to read and write. Sometimes, Maria would hold his hand and whisper, "Come, let's get lost," the softness of her husky voice making his skin prickle all over his body. They knew the area too well to get lost; still, they pretended to be wanderers, hiding in familiar caves where they reluctantly exchanged chaste kisses at first and as the years passed explored bolder ways to extinguish the fire in their adolescent bodies.

By the time the First World War arrived, further pitting Christian against Moslem on the island, Mehmet's idyllic life had already come to an abrupt end. One morning, his father was found stark naked

---

[15]*putana*: whore

and dead on the matrimonial bed he had been avoiding since his wife's passing. The doctor who was brought in from the nearest town determined it was likely due to a massive heart attack, but no one in the village believed his post-mortem involving blocked arteries, myocardial infarction, hepatic necrosis, and other nonsensical words. The ghost of his wife had lured him to bed, first seducing him—his crumpled clothes at the foot of the bed proved the theory—and finally, killing him for being a philandering drunk.

Almost everyone, with the exception of his drinking buddies and his mother, agreed that it served him right, too. "Alas, the poor child" they said, momentarily softening at the thought of Little Mehmet. They quickly buried the man and boarded up the house after accompanying the boy to take his clothing and effects from there.

Soon enough, Mehmet's many uncles and aunts started squabbling over this considerable inheritance that could be possessed by taking guardianship of the boy. Two of those uncles were Orthodox Christians, one aunt was a Catholic, and a couple of others were Moslem, all having been born to different mothers, which further complicated the squabbles. He lived with whichever uncle temporarily won the argument; sometimes, in the heat of such tug-of-war he was taken to the mosque on Friday and to church on Sunday by relatives eager to show him the straighter way to heaven. Mehmet was equally comfortable in the three traditions as a result, and partook in ceremonies heartily especially when feasts followed piety. An advantage during Ramadan, he discovered, was that he could eat with his Christian relatives during the day and break the fast with his Moslem family at night, eating twice as much as a result. When such excesses occasioned vomiting in the middle of the night, his aunts would scold their husbands, "The poor boy has a weak stomach; he shouldn't be made to fast." Although it was clear to everyone that the boy took advantage of the situation, no one dared call him out on his hypocrisy, from fear of losing his affection and the vineyards that may eventually come with it. He was left to do as he pleased, and to roam free, meeting Maria here and there, now that the danger of getting whipped had passed entirely. He sensed he was the absolute monarch in his own story, and that his uncles and aunts would defer to his every wish, hoping to sway his opinion in their favour. He nonchalantly gave each one of them hope, without ever agreeing to sign his name on the documents slipped next to his bowl of soup with equal nonchalance by the grownups. He was deeply anxious at the same time, not knowing how long he could keep up the charade in a world where the rules were set by adults.

Mehmet never got to make his decision. With World War I, vicious unrest came to the island. Venizelos, a Greek hero and native of this rebellious island was dreaming up grand ideals that roused the Greek nation as it gained force against a weakened Ottoman Empire that had dominated the region for centuries. Parts of Anatolia were controlled by the British, the French and Italians, and the Greeks had captured Izmir and a large part of the Aegean region with the help of the British. Kemal gathered an army in central Turkey, and thus began the war that was to rage for a number of years, before ending with the burning of Izmir in 1922. By 1923, the Treaty of Lausanne had been signed, spelling out how peace would now look for the new Turkish Republic. The process of population exchange had begun on both sides of the Aegean. The considerably large Greek Orthodox population in Turkey had to be absorbed by Greece, while the Moslem minorities in Greece and the Balkans were expatriated and migrated to Turkey.

And this was the point where Little Mehmet's young life had taken a turn for the worst. His father's house and vineyards were confiscated and ordered to be given to Greek Anatolians who had just arrived in boatloads from Turkey. The uncles and aunts stopped squabbling and put the boy on a boat headed for the coast of Turkey at the first opportunity. They promised to follow. Under his shirt and in a pouch sewn into his pants were hidden a dozen golden chains with rings passed around them. The jewellery his father had given his mother, over the years, many of them in return for forgiveness. There were dozens of bracelets for dozens of *indiscretions all padded into a cloth belt to be worn close to his belly for the voyage.*

Maria, being Catholic, could have stayed, but wished to leave. Her mother, too glad to see her child abandon this cursed island that had ruined her own life, sewed her own set of bracelets into a belt for the girl and sent her off. The youths boarded the old creaking boat that carried a Turkish ensign, destined for the port of Izmir.

Approximately four hundred and ten kilometres, or two hundred and twenty-one nautical miles away was the city of Izmir, a port they would reach after a day and a night. The two teenagers stood side by side, knuckles whitened from clasping the side of the boat taking them away from home, surrounded by hundreds of exiles like themselves, sailing towards unknown shores, a place they were assured was their true motherland, from the tinny echoes of the speakers on the boat. The captain's deep and mellifluous voice was advising them in Greek and Turkish of the formalities to expect once reaching the shore with Turkish military band music blaring through the same speakers intermittently. The brassy cadence was intended to elevate moods and instil a sense of national pride in their new Vatan, the place that was going to offer them a new life and where they would never again feel persecuted. Without the music layering its cheerful mood on the visuals, the refugees only had to glance around and see their neighbours' anxious faces to feel desperate and weep. As Crete disappeared from view, the band music appropriately intensified in decibels. Small children started running back and forth on the boat encouraged by the festive music, giggling and screaming with glee. An old man with a headscarf could be seen sitting on his luggage, leaning on his walking stick, counting his worry beads. Portly mothers were screaming at kids, double-checking their suitcases and papers, feeding their brood meatballs, olives, and bread. There were groups of gloomy men smoking and talking in circles, scattered around the deck. A rooster had somehow made it on board and was monitoring the deck with its majestic gait in his newfound coop surrounded by water. He paraded haughtily across the wooden surface, roosting to gather the stray hens he could not see. A boy started throwing bits of his bread for the rooster to eat; within minutes all the children were doing the same, one giving up his meatball to throw at the bird which fluttered his helpless wings and squawked in anger before running after the projectile rolling off the swaying deck. Seagulls had sensed food was near and were floating alongside the boat, waiting for their turn.

Maria had grasped Mehmet's cuff and was twisting it as her face soured into a grimace. She buried her head in his chest finally, sobbing into his shirt as he nervously patted her back to make her stop. "Shh ... shh ... don't do this, Maria. I'll take care of you, I promise."

She looked up at him eventually with a tear-drenched, melancholic face that made his eyes sting. "But you've never worked a day in your life. And we're not even married. What if they don't let me get off when we reach the port?" To these good points, he had no answers. He gently disengaged from her embrace and told her he would return shortly.

The old man with a cane who was still slouched on his suitcase, was now rolling a cigarette. Mehmet thought it wise to approach him. "Kalimera, papoulis,"[16] he said in a subdued voice. The old man nodded taking a deep puff of the cigarette he had just lit, eyes fixed on the horizon.

"So," continued Mehmet awkwardly, "do you know anyone over there?" he moved his chin toward the Anatolian shores.

"No."

"And what are you going to do when we get there?"

"Find work, God willing."

Mehmet nodded soberly. "What kind of work?"

The old man shrugged. "All those people who came to Crete from there, they left work to be done, I reckon ... there has to be something for me too. If not...." He looked up at the sky as if expecting a reply to come down.

---

[16]"Kalimera, papoulis": Good morning, grandpa"

"Do you know if there is a hodja[17] on board?" asked Mehmet.

The old man nodded and took a deep drag of his cigarette. "Over there, you'll find one."

Mehmet had to negotiate his way across the deck through the crowd of meatball-throwing children and the angry rooster, the fidgeting mothers and the smoking men who stood gazing at the commotion impassively. Finally he found the hodja on a bench, sitting with his wife and quiet children. "I need to get married," he blurted after greeting him. "Can you do it?"

"What's the rush?" smiled the portly man.

"We want to be married before we arrive there."

"Where is she?" The hodja moved in his seat, ready to get up.

"She is Christian."

The burly man scratched his neck. "Maybe that'll be a bit of a problem."

"I think she would be willing to convert, though," threw in Mehmet, wanting the hodja to get up.

"What do you mean 'I think?' Is she or isn't she?"

"She is, she is."

"Has she made up her mind on her own accord?"

"Yes, yes."

"Good, let's go," said the hodja, amused by the prospect of a wedding in the midst of this bleak adventure.

They were unceremoniously wedded before nightfall. At night, the waters got choppier when the poyraz[18] started blowing from the northeast. The couple settled on a wooden bench inside the ferry, lying face to face on the narrow plank, their heads propped on folded coats. Children were throwing up their digested meatballs here and there in acrid-smelling brownish puddles, occasional adults could be observed to heave from the sides of the boat leaving trails of yellow bile on the white sidings while those with hardier stomachs tried to

---

[17]hodja: educator, wise religious man
[18]poyraz: wind

sleep, using suitcases and bundles as pillows, ignoring the confused cock that kept roosting every half hour through the night.

When they reached the shore at dawn, the sleep-deprived travellers could see many boats such as theirs already docked, with crowds streaming out, clogging the entrance to the port. Officials in striped uniforms were directing them into a building with yellow walls where they were to submit their papers prior to being ushered onto the Quay of Izmir, the wide cobblestone avenue with mansions on one side and the sea on the other. The building was noisy and stuffy, with echoes of all the sounds getting trapped within the tall, bare walls and patchy ceilings intensifying in pitch. Maria was reassured by the sight of the rooster walking beside the queue; unlike the refugees, he was hopping alongside them with the short-sighted assurance given to his kind, chest pushed out, carmine comb wobbling proudly on his small head, the multicoloured feathers on his tail erect and fluffy. He may have been as anxious as his fellow travellers waiting in line holding their yellowed, folded papers in hand, sweat oozing from their hairlines, Maria mused, but he was not showing it.

A short and skinny official in a brownish khaki uniform a couple of sizes too large was keenly observing the line up, his dark irises rolling to and fro in their white eyeballs like marbles, occasionally raising his arms to fence the crowd into a straighter line while blowing the whistle nestled between invisible lips under a thick brown moustache, in an effort to establish order. The effect was quite the opposite. Babes terrified by the shrillness of the sound began to wail, the cock roosted to chase a potential rival away, all this causing the exasperated official to blow his whistle even harder, at which point the bird suddenly lunged at him in semi-flight and pecked his thigh, sending the surprised man and his whistle tumbling, arms folded over his head to field further attacks. Giggles turned into bursts of laughter in the queue. The official finally managed to straighten himself, dusting his pants and cuffs with irritation, using the tip of his shoe to distance the cackling animal from him. "Who's the owner of this damned *horoz?*" he shouted in Turkish. There were *baffled murmurs in Greek travelling up and down the queue. The burly hodja who spoke some Turkish stepped forward, apologizing with half a smile, and squeezed the unwilling bird into a tight embrace, trying to keep him still. The rooster apparently upset, defecated on the man's coat; half-digested meatballs in a watery mix now running toward his shalvar pants. The crowd started laughing again. "Hold him upside down!" shouted someone from farther up the line. The hodja shook his head sternly at his giggling children. His wife took out a handkerchief and attempted to wipe away the mess, suppressing a guffaw.*

One can only imagine the first impressions of these refugees in those early days of the republic when the fire that reduced Izmir to a pile of ashes was still fresh in the locals' memory whenever they stepped onto the quay, and their noses twitched remembering the smell of cadavers and smouldering cinder, and their pitiless ears replayed over and over the blood-curdling screams of those jumping into the sea and suffering countless other horrors. The ashes had been swept away in one year, and the mansions and houses that were spared from the fire were being restored. Saplings were planted here and there, and those who saw an opportunity in such catastrophe started rebuilding the city and made their fortunes.

When Mehmet and Maria finally passed customs and took their first steps on the cobblestone avenue named Kordon, weighed down by their bags and an old suitcase, luck smiled upon them in the shape of a pleasant, tubby, middle-aged woman holding a cardboard panel on which the words "Welcome to Smyrna" were written awkwardly in Greek alphabet. They were immediately drawn to her, knowing she spoke Greek and could direct them as to where to go. They had heard it said on the boat that the Turkish government was placing refugees in houses left behind by the Rum[19] who had been deported or had escaped during the war. There were promises that everyone would have a house to live in, and that those who were farmers, or

---

[19]Rum: Anatolian Greeks

had vineyards or olive groves in Crete could take over the abandoned lands in Ayvalık and other coastal towns and continue to do what they knew best. The desire to go on and survive had suppressed the homesickness that tormented their hearts on the ferry. The grey-haired lady introduced herself as Inez. She was a Franghisa, a Levantine, and invited them to rent a room in her house until they found a place of their own. The two teenagers readily agreed and followed her through the narrow streets where blocks of houses with rubble in between reminded them of an infected gum line with missing teeth. Kirya Inez was prattling on, giving explanations about the fate of such and such a house or the absence of one, and what happened to those who had lived there, as they walked along. The words came out in torrents from her cracked lips. Once in a while she tightened the kerchief around her chin as she walked and nodded to a few other pedestrians.

The two-storey house with an extended bay window on the second floor was in one of the narrow back streets of Alsancak, within walking distance from the port. The couple settled on the second floor, in the bedroom with the bay window. Inez provided them with towels, soap, and other necessities, leaving them to unpack their belongings undisturbed until suppertime.

After freshening themselves up and placing the few things they had brought with them into drawers, the young couple descended to the kitchen hesitantly, the creak of each wooden step accentuating their feelings of awkwardness in the new space they were to call home. The bowls of steaming tarhana soup and slices of fresh bread invited them to the kitchen table where Inez was already sitting, waiting for them. She motioned for them to sit and eat, which they did while she recounted her stories: the husband who died years ago as a soldier in the Balkan wars, the young daughter who perished from a bout of dysentery before the fire, the desolation of her solitude when the war and subsequent fire came to Izmir, the ships that left the harbour gorged with refugees, her flight to the hills of Bayraklı with countless others to escape the fire, and her return weeks later to find her house miraculously intact. She crossed herself a few times at this part and moved her lips quietly in prayer. By the time she had gotten through her stories, the soup had already been finished, the bread had disappeared, and the wide-eyed teenagers were focused on this chapped mouth that was producing chains of stories, one more tragic than the other. She sighed at the end, feeling despondent and became quiet. Maria reached over to gently rub the woman's cuff mumbling that they would now be her family if she wished, as they were both orphans in this strange land in need of someone they could trust. They promised to take care of her in return, and the woman nodded and patted the girl's head. "I reopened the haberdashery my husband used to run. It's a small shop, not much business. But I can find you ironing work, if you wish." She told Mehmet of an acquaintance, a carpenter who was looking for a trustworthy apprentice, a Cretan like themselves. "I will take you there tomorrow," she continued, "and God willing you will have a job."

Mehmet got his job as a carpenter's apprentice in Halil's atelier at the far end of the market street, not far from the French school for boys called Saint Joseph. He learned how to use hammers and planes, and various saws and dovetails under the close supervision of his master. Orders were brisk; the city was being rebuilt and there was no better time than this to be a carpenter, the boss confided to his helpers. There were two other Cretans working at the shop, both having arrived at different times of the population exchange process. They commiserated about their circumstances and the ache of being torn from their homes. They hummed Cretan songs while they worked and soon enough they all discovered to their great pleasure that there were plenty of people in Izmir who spoke Greek. Some had arrived from Crete, others from Salonika, the local Levantines and remaining Rums, some other islanders.... Finding this community in exile gave them enough encouragement to envision an adequate life in the first few months of their stay. Mehmet was relieved to have a roof over their head, and a job, all thanks to Kirya Inez whom Maria believed to be an angel sent to them by the spirit of Mehmet's mother.

 Not everyone who was forced to leave Crete ended up in Izmir. Some went to Bodrum, Ayvalık, and other less fortunate ones were directed to more remote regions of the Mediterranean coast that were swampy and malaria-infested. Mehmet got word that some of his family perished from malaria soon after they arrived there. Remembering the particular aunt and uncle who had fed and clothed him when his father died triggered an avalanche of tears. Although he did not realize it at the time, to this sadness was mixed the grief of having irretrievably lost his childhood, his sense of belonging to a particular world with its own textures and colours that would never again be reproduced in his life except for fleeting approximations. He wept in Maria's arms up in the bedroom on the second floor of Kirya Inez's house, seated on a small worn sofa on the creaking floor of the cumba surrounded by windows, which had become their universe, their small island in this half-perished city haunted by missing houses and lives. Maria whose lovely soft cheeks smelled of plums held him close, and caressed his head murmuring love words that took him back to their afternoons in the caves. The more he sighed and inhaled the smell of her, the calmer he became, entering once again the cool grottos that hid them from the world, that universe of their own creation made of hasty unbuttonings and slow caresses in the damp earthy shade.

 Life continued its steady uneventful course until one day upon his return from work, Mehmet found Maria with swollen eyes, sitting with Inez in the kitchen, having tea. She wouldn't tell him what was wrong. She just kept staring at her glass of tea, and shaking her head to suppress sobs. Inez found an excuse that took her away from the kitchen, leaving them alone. After much begging and cajoling, Mehmet managed to understand that someone on the street had heard her speak Greek with a vegetable vendor and followed her home, calling her an infidel, a dirty Rum, and other words she couldn't bring herself to repeat while he spat on the street to show his disgust.

"I was a putana's bastard, over there. An infidel, here. I thought he was going to kill me." Copious tears followed, with some trumpeting sounds from her nose blown energetically.

"Get dressed" Mehmet ordered, "We're going out."

"No!" Maria exclaimed, her reddened eyes wide open. "I'm never going out again."

"Get dressed. You'll take me to the place where you saw him. I'll make him swallow his damn tongue if I get my hands on him, I swear." His wavy brown hair was standing on end around his reddened forehead looking like a halo, making her fear for his life.

"Shh, calm down," she scolded. "What will I do if they kill you or put you in jail?"

He would not be dissuaded. Maria put on her coat and they started retracing her steps in the cold, darkening streets, the smoke of burning coal from chimneys filling their nostrils. Vegetable vendors were covering the produce on their carts with large tarps before slowly pushing them through the narrow streets to disappear from view. Storeowners were pulling down the creaking rusty metal blinds for the night. Stray cats with full bellies who had skulked about butcher shops and fishmongers all day could be seen stealthily retreating from the main avenue toward smaller darker streets. Dogs' barks were coming in saccades from a distance to echo upon darkening walls, increasing Maria's sense of desolation.

"He started following me somewhere here, in front of Ali's shop" she said. "See? There's no one in the street anymore; let's go back."

Mehmet was still seething inside, wanting to harm. He walked into a side street, looking up and down the houses.

"We should learn Turkish," she whispered and pulled his arm, "I'm tired, I want to go home."

The year was 1928. All around the city, on walls, were glued off-white posters advertising the stern dictum in black ink: "Citizen, speak Turkish!" Inez who spoke broken Turkish herself, started teaching her protégées whatever she could. The end of the year came with a new alphabet law, making the Latin script official. Efforts *deployed by the government to make the transition successful were monumental. Newspapers had to change from the Arabic script to the Latin one within three months, creating a flurry of feverish activity in print shops and newspaper offices across the country. Aside from prohibitive measures put in place to ensure adoption of this new alphabet, a number of national schools had opened across the city to teach the population how to read and write Turkish with these new letters. Mehmet, Maria, and their Cretan friends enrolled in order to learn the Latin alphabet hoping to advance their command of Turkish, as well. They would come home late in the evening with their notebooks and chewed pencils, writing and erasing with greater assiduity than they had ever shown as pupils in Paraskevi's class.*

It was during one such evening that Maria rushed from the table where she was struggling with homework to the washroom where she remained locked up for some time. Inez who was ironing clothes in the small adjacent room, knew. She called out to her as she was leaving the bathroom looking blanched and shaky.

"What's wrong Maria?"

"I don't know ... I vomited yesterday, too."

"I'll take you to my iatros.[20] He delivered my baby."

---

[20]iatros: physician

Notebook III. Autobiography

From my mother's stories, I retained the hodja's rooster on the boat taking them to Izmir, her nuptials at sea, and the man who insulted her on the street for speaking Greek. She used to tell these frequently. And although I knew them by heart, I tried to imagine, with each repetition, a slightly different scenario, to be able to appropriate her events, and make them come alive for myself. Once in a while an unexpected element would rise to the surface of that sea of memories she carried within, something she had never told me before, and she would just let it float there, among her well-rehearsed repertoire, without any apparent need to integrate it, the way a seahorse may suddenly appear in the path of a determined swimmer.

One such detail was the story of the golden bracelets from Crete. Both my parents had their mothers' jewellery sewn into cloth belts for their voyage to Turkey—their only fortune. The story that I knew well was that once her pregnancy was confirmed, my mother unstitched them and sold a few of those bracelets to buy baby clothes, furniture, and a fancy baby carriage imported from Germany the likes of which very few mothers owned in Izmir due to its exorbitant price. It had an ivory-coloured leather body with a shiny chrome structure and springs to gently rock the baby during long walks. "Only the best for my daughter," she would smile and say.

While she was removing the many bracelets from the belts, my mother noticed that two of those were identical. She thought it curious that two unrelated women would have the exact same bracelet. However, she reasoned, both women were from the same village in Crete and it was likely that the same jeweller sold these bracelets that ended up on their respective mothers' forearms. The bracelets were each an inch wide, and felt heavy in the palm. They were the loveliest pieces of handcrafted jewellery she had ever seen. She decided to never sell them, saving them for me, instead.

On her deathbed, she told me more about them. A secret she wouldn't take to her grave.

Notebook II. The Cretans

THE GIRL WAS BORN IN 1929, on the second floor of Inez's house, after much pushing, screaming, and sweating on Maria's part, while Mehmet was relegated to pacing around the living room downstairs for the seemingly endless hours it took the child to arrive. For all the commotion she caused, the girl appeared scrawny, with a head full of straight brown hair pasted to her forehead, swollen eyelids and rosy thighs that were sagging from lack of fat. When Mehmet held her awkwardly in his arms, an inexplicably pleasant ache spread in his chest gazing at her small defenceless frame, a hand the size of a walnut around his finger and the gradually reddening forehead as her toothless mouth began to wail. He sat next to Maria on the bed and observed his wife's face, swollen and tired from all the effort, and somewhat sad too, he imagined, now that the movements inside her belly had stopped and she had lost what must have felt like a permanent entanglement of two souls in one large body. She was left with only the large body now and the baby was latching on to the nipple with blind and relentless hunger. Mehmet was not entirely sure if the sadness was indeed Maria's or his, feeling left out of this tangible new bond, a mere spectator and secretly resentful.

Sensing his sudden change of mood, Maria looked at him. "What name shall we give her?"

"You'll decide in the end, anyway, like you always do," he grinned. "How about your mother's name?"

"I want a Turkish name. She will be everything she is expected to be."

"How?"

"I mean that she will grow up feeling Turkish, speaking Turkish, and no one will ever think otherwise. I think her name should start with an M," she ventured, "like yours and mine."

"Like Minotaur? She's about to rip your breast out." It wasn't a smile that accompanied this statement, but an imperceptible jerking of a jaw muscle, like a cramp.

"You don't care!" she pouted, turning her attention back to the nursing baby in her arms.

"Like Mehtap," he replied quickly. "Moonlight. Remember the olive grove? The moon that hung in the sky like a ripe melon. The night you rushed to me like a river, and carried me off like a drowning man." He stopped, surprised by his poetic formulation. "Scariest moment of my life. After this one…" he smiled. "Do you like it?"

For the next couple of years, the baby had an evil eye pendant permanently attached to her clothes with a tiny golden diaper pin and a golden Maşallah in Arabic script hanging right next to it. Those who dared say she was beautiful had to pretend to spit as is the custom, and those more cautious said she was indeed an ugly baby so as not to awaken evil eyes.

Maria who had spent her childhood roaming freely, untouched by the drudgery of housework, had to quickly learn how to care for her child. The never-ending piles of diapers to wash and boil and wash again, her chapped bleeding hands from so much washing and hanging in the cold winter days; the baby who needed nursing, the engorged breasts, and the sense of being constantly attached to another being so entirely dependent on her all contrived to change her outlook on life. She found herself disheartened as she went through the motions of her days. There were mornings when she woke up to a wet pillow, having wept in her sleep. Mehmet observed the sadness that had come over their lives; his wife's red eyes and uncombed hair, her recoiling from him toward the edge of the bed at night, the lack of appetite and curiosity. She wouldn't go near the baby carriage she had chosen with such great excitement. He felt lost in his new life. One night when he tried to caress her in the hopes of rekindling the passion that was so bafflingly lost between them, she removed his hand from her rump and without turning to face him declared that she never wanted "to do it" again.

"What's happened to you?" He was leaning on his elbow, waiting for an answer.

Her body started shaking with hidden sobs; she put her pillow over her head to muffle the sounds, and drew her knees close to her chest.

"You're going to drown us in your tears, woman. Stop it. Say something...."

"I ... cannot ... tell you." She managed to say, taking deep breaths between the sobs.

"Is it the baby?"

"I don't want it...." Her sobs had turned to wails.

He turned her forcefully towards him. "Shh ... you don't mean that. It's a sin."

"I'm her slave. She is constantly in need of something. Stuck here.... You go to work every day. You have your friends. You go for drinks. You come back home and you find your supper on the table, the child in bed. If she cries, I run. If she throws up in the middle of the night, do you clean it? Look at my hands! They're bleeding. I don't have any friends. I can't speak the language properly. Every time I open my mouth I'm afraid someone will call me an infidel. I hate this place. I hate being a mother; I should have never gotten on that cursed boat." She wiped her nose with the sleeve of her nightgown, turning her back to him once more, hiding her head under the pillow.

"Go to sleep, Mehmet. Leave me alone." She hugged the pillow tighter over her face.

"Shh, let go of the pillow. You'll smother yourself."

He managed to pry her away from the pillow she was squeezing to *her face and held her in his arms until she fell asleep. He spent the night thinking about her words. The next morning, he took extra care not to awaken baby and mother, tiptoed out of the room and had tea with Inez in the kitchen. They whispered for a long time over their lukewarm glasses of untouched tea.*

Notebook III. Autobiography

INEZ RAISED ME. While my mother took care of her haberdashery, she took care of me. A woman came to wash clothes once a week and an old man brought goat's milk every morning for me to drink. She taught me songs in Italian and Greek, and took me for very long walks on the quay on cloudless afternoons. We threw pebbles into the sea; she was the one who taught me how to skip stones on water. Bought me vanilla ice cream in the summers and roasted chestnuts in winter, kissed my knees when I fell and made me dresses and bonnets with her sewing machine. It was black and shiny, with golden vines encircling it. I used to turn the handle for her while she guided the cloth with her expert hands as the needle hurried in and out on a straight or curved line. Sometimes I turned it very fast, sometimes I stopped abruptly to see how she'd react. She never got mad. She'd simply laugh and caress my cheek.

When the time came for me to go to school, Inez woke me up with a surprise. She was holding a handmade cloth doll with painted eyes and long eyelashes, a button nose, and a small red pout. Her hair was made of yellow yarn, braided on both sides of her face. She wore a black school uniform with a plaited skirt and a white collar; an exact replica of mine waiting to be worn at the foot of the bed. She said, "She'll be going to school, too, just like you. See?" They dressed me up and took me to an immense concrete building filled with noise. Children in uniforms were running and shrieking in the schoolyard. A tall man with crane legs and curly white hair greeted us at the door and bent all the way down to face me. He said a few words of welcome, asked for my name which I could not remember from terror. He patted my head.

"The school principal," my grandmother whispered as we walked on to find my classroom. I was squeezing the doll into my cramping belly.

The classroom was filled with children, lots of them, maybe fifty. The teacher, Gülbahar Hanım, was a stern-looking and tall woman with pockmarked cheeks, whose brown dress with small buttons going up to her chin had chalk stains all across her bottom. She wore black stockings and flat shoes that squeaked whenever she walked up and down the isles. Her dark eyebrows were thick and knit together on the bridge of her aquiline nose. Long, grey-streaked hair was tightly rolled into a bun close to her nape. She had a small samovar on the coal stove in the corner of the room and served herself fragrant tea in a tiny glass. She gently lowered two cubes of sugar, one by one, with her miniature teaspoon and then vigorously stirred it, making frantic "ting ting ting" sounds in the quiet and stuffy room. While stirring, she asked us one by one whom we loved most in the world. It was an easy question, everyone shouted their answers. Some said, "My mother" others said, "My parents." Caught in the excitement, I exclaimed, "My Granny!"

She shook her head with a frown. This will not do!" Her voice boomed and the clinking of her spoon stopped. "You must love God first, then the beloved father of our republic Mustafa Kemal Paşa," she raised her hand with reverence toward the framed photograph centred above the blackboard, "then your parents, and then, your grandparents!" Her eyes were on me when she said "grandparents" and I knew that from all those wrong answers, mine was the most offensive. The girl sitting next to me leaned over and whispered in my ear. "What about a brother? Is he before or after grandparents?" I shrugged and whispered back, "I don't have one."

Later, in the grey schoolyard where I was wandering forlorn and anxious, clutching the doll, an older boy ran by me and grabbed it out of my hand. I ran after him, but he was too fast. With a smirk, he pitched it high over the wall and out into the street. I cried to the point of losing my breath and collapsing. A young teacher supervising the schoolyard came to ask if I was hurt. I was unable to respond, having lost my breath from all that wailing. I kept pointing at the wall. She didn't understand anything.

At the end of the day, when my grandmother came to pick me up, her smile shrank and fell when she saw my swollen, tear-drenched face. I rushed her to the other side of the wall to find the doll, but it was too late. She tried to console me saying she would make another one just like it; but I said no. I did not intend to return to this horrible school ever again. She hugged and shushed me and kissed my wet cheeks. "How about you come home with your old granny and see the surprise she has for you at home?"

We walked hand in hand, slowly through the busy market.

"I'm not supposed to love you first," I burst out.

"What do you mean?"

"I'm supposed to love God, Atatürk, Mother, then Father and you, last. The teacher hates me because I said I loved you first."

She shrugged, "I'm sure she doesn't hate you."

"Anyway, she can't read my mind." I let go of her hand and climbed on a low wall separating a garden filled with fragrant roses from the sidewalk and walked on it till the end. Then, I jumped down and started skipping and by the time we got home, I felt better.

She had made a cake for me. It took forever to make cakes in those days. You beat the eggs and sugar with a fork until they were white and smooth and frothy. It hurt her shoulder, so

Granny rarely made them. I ate a few pieces of the soft, spongy yellow cake and my mother took out my notebooks and books, laid them out on the kitchen table and got to work. She had to cover them in paper: red for notebooks, blue for books. I had already written a third of the alphabet in a notebook and it looked awful. The page was littered with small greyish holes, mostly around the thinning B, the grotesque G, and some other places from erasing over and over. I wept again when I opened the notebook and saw this mess, anticipating Gülbahar Hanım's screams over the ting-ting-ting-ing of her spoon, this time, for being inept. My tears softened and curled parts of the notebook, and the grey holes surrounding the B and G grew.

"I need a new notebook!" I wailed. My mother ignored me. I stomped my feet. "I want a new notebook!"

"Settle down or else," she said, but I was already far gone in my tantrum and couldn't stop, so I got a spank that left a burning sensation on my right buttock. She had lifted my skirt up before slapping my bottom; she had a way of doing all this at lightning speed. My mind suddenly emptied out in shock. I ran up the stairs and hid under my bed, where she couldn't reach and wailed some more, until I got hiccups, feeling lonely and unloved. I knew that if I hid there long enough, Granny would make her way up the stairs in her slow, deliberate, huffing and puffing cadence and sit on her bed without even attempting to look for me and say: "Mehtap, are you in the closet?"

And then, "Mehtap, my lovely moonlight, are you in a drawer?"

She would wait a while and try again. "Mehtap, my gold, are you hiding in my denture glass? If you are, better get out now before you end up in my stomach...." She would hear me giggle and make the sign of the cross, touching forehead, chest and shoulders, her eyes raised to the ceiling and say, "Thank you, Lord, for protecting this naughty child from danger once again." I would creep out from under the bed. She would continue talking, ignoring my smile. "Good, you washed and dusted the floor again. I hope you didn't miss any spots. You should act naughtier and get yourself spanked more often. I won't have to kneel and clean under your bed...."

She had a way of making me feel stupid and happy at once.

Between our beds was a night table that held her denture cup and rosary, the framed portraits of her daughter and her husband. She would blow a kiss to both after praying with her rosary beads every night. I loved the sound of her snoring because it reassured me she was fine and alive and I was safe in the world.

There was no getting used to Gülbahar Hanım's wrath, however. Gülbahar, the elusive spring rose. The flower that was supposed to adorn this mass of thorns had evidently never bloomed. And like all names that mean something, this one was beyond immense disappointment. It was a crime.

In her class, we sat row after row, with our tightly wound braids in white ribbons, our black uniforms and white socks, our gums missing a few teeth and our sharpened pencils. Our main subject was obedience. I had heard a few parents saying, "Eti senin, kemiği benim" to Gülbahar Hanım, "The flesh is yours, the bone is mine." My parents thankfully did not understand this idiom, because it appeared that Gülbahar Hanım was taking it to heart. If she called a boy a "Donkey, son of a donkey," he had to reply "Yes, Gülbahar Hanım," and look at his feet. If she hollered, "I will break your legs if you get the multiplication table wrong," I replied, "Yes, Gülbahar Hanım," and tried to hide the fact that my teeth were chattering from fear as I started reciting two times two. "Yes" became a dreadful word, but it was very useful considering that it protected against having your head slammed on the blackboard, or your legs, palms and fingers whacked with a metal ruler.

Next door was Nergiz Hanım's class. We heard laughter and melodious children's songs seeping through the peeling walls while we sweated in our seats. It was like being lost at sea in the night and hearing mermaids. Then the metallic sound of a spoon hitting the small tea glass would awaken us to Gülbahar Hanım's shrill voice asking us to open our notebooks and pay attention.

Nergiz is another spring flower; the fragrant narcissus. Elegant, delicate, dressed in bright fashionable dresses with matching hats and high heels, Nergiz Hanım would make her rushed entrance into the schoolyard just in time for the national anthem which was hollered off-key by hundreds of children for the benefit of the entire neighbourhood. She had shiny black hair in tidy curls under small hats. Her wide mouth and almond eyes over high cheekbones made us think of movie stars whose smiles were perpetual. Hers shone when she sang, or said serious things, or even when she scolded her pupils. She never told them whom to love first. Everyone in school was in love with Nergiz Hanım, whose fiancé was a pilot; he had flown one of the dozen bomber airplanes the Ottoman army owned during World War I. Once in a while he would wait for her outside the schoolyard, smoking a cigarette in his striped uniform and cap. He was quite older, but very slim, blond and dashing. We would rush to the windows to spy on them. They never touched in public. He would flick his cigarette as soon as she appeared and greet her with a boyish, somewhat naughty smile, lifting his cap ever so slightly and she would respond with that lusty red-lipped smile we knew well, and they would quickly walk away, side by side, still not touching until they disappeared around the corner.

We wondered where they went and, most importantly, whether they kissed. Mustafa, the bright-eyed boy in my class who was beaten almost daily by Gülbahar Hanım for not doing enough mandatory things and having too much fun, decided to follow them, to elucidate the mystery of Nergiz and her pilot. He did not have anything very interesting to report the next day when we all swarmed him to get details. They had gone to a house, she had removed the key from her purse, opened the door, and they had both disappeared inside. Someone asked if he had spied through a window. He said no, he didn't want to get caught.

Tahsin, another boy who liked to spy on girls when they undressed in the locker room before gym class, offered to do this for us and asked Mustafa to show him the house. He was a show off; his father was a locally known politician and Gülbahar adored him. If he made a mistake, she would say, "Don't be nervous son, take your time," and if he still didn't get it right, she would make him sit down, encouraging him to review the subject at home and to give her regards to Muhsin Bey, his father. There were no beatings for him, and he was clearly not genetically related to donkeys like the rest of us. So when Tahsin did his spy work and returned to school saying that they had actually kissed in the living room in a really disgusting way and appeared to be living together without being married, no one believed him.

Notebook II. The Cretans

MARIA CONSIDERED HER DAYS at Inez's narrow store, now renamed "Mehtap Tuhafiye," on a street adjacent to the market, the best in her life. She dressed with care every morning, put on silk stockings, removed her curlers and styled her hair, wore high heels, makeup, and a hat, and off she went after kissing Mehtap goodbye. She enjoyed the sound of her heels clicking on the pavement, and the smell of the sea enveloping the city just before it awoke to the bustle of streetcars and vendors. Early in the morning she would roll up the metal blinds, turn on the lights, buy her glass of tea from the tea boy who showed up at the same time everyday with his swinging tray filled with dozens of trembling and clinking tea glasses, and get to work. She liked to start by repairing stockings. Then she dusted the shelves and placed the new merchandise, waiting for the women to start coming in. Some were returning from the nearby church, from morning mass and stopped by to pick up whatever was being repaired, some buttons, or try a new bra. There was always an excuse that made certain women stop and say hello, have a chat over tea, and move along. If one's husband got a promotion at the bank, or her mother-in-law gave her a hard time, or so-and-so got a new fur, Maria knew all the details before anyone else. She gossiped without malice, passing innocuous information back and forth. The heavier subjects of daughters getting pregnant out of wedlock, men cheating on their wives, money troubles that were discussed in her store in confidence did not make the rounds.

She remembered her own suffering as a child in Crete and stopped short of repeating such tales.

Her own mother's absence in her life grew as time passed. She tried to chase away the painful thought that she would never be able to see her again and sometimes, despite the vivid memories of rejection and ridicule suffered as a child, she let herself sink into the deep, soft mud of regret for having followed Mehmet to Izmir. Maria's mother descended from a once-wealthy Genoese family that had settled on the island a few centuries before; they were seafaring merchants who purchased a title of nobility and were once part of the ruling class. Her mother grew up in a mansion where servants did everything for her. When her father died, the remaining wealth slowly eroded and things were sold piece by piece, including the lovely mansion, until she suffered the misfortune of an accidental pregnancy. There was no money to send her abroad to carry the baby to term away from wagging tongues, there was no groom for a rushed wedding, and Maria's mother had to endure the now brazen scorn of townsfolk who, until then, had merely whispered their disapproval of the rich family fallen from grace.

Thinking back to her childhood days in Crete, Maria came to the realization that she had not loved her mother as a child but had instead felt deep resentment for having brought her to the world under such circumstances, and for doing little to protect her from its harm. Eighteen years with a woman who looked harsh and acted broken with those uncombed, frizzled blonde strands of hair trying to escape from the tight kerchief. A woman with a hardened look in her eyes, who imposed on her child an oppressively silent life allowing no questions, providing no answers; a gloomy shadow who went through daily chores with absurd tenacity. There were no affectionate gestures; on the contrary, whenever she spoke to Maria her voice resounded with exasperation, as if unbearably painful efforts had to be summoned from her depths for the task. Maria did not miss her mother as such, but since having a child of her own, she couldn't help but wonder if the relationship could have been improved, begun even, and the silence ended. Without Inez's timely intervention, she could have very well been a bitter and despairing mother herself, treating her own child like an affliction. This thought took substantial form and glued itself to the recesses of her mind so that she never acknowledged it in words while it informed her deeds. She put all her youthful energy into looking like the women who came into her shop, practiced Turkish words in front of the mirror at home so as to sound local and not shame her daughter in public. At home, she spoke Turkish to Mehtap while she continued to speak Greek with Inez and Mehmet. She forbade the use of Greek on the street so that whenever they would be out as a family and someone ventured to say something, she would turn and whisper, "Shh, not in Greek, they'll hear us." Mehtap, who grew up hearing this admonishment, became terrified of this unwanted language that was better left at home. It was her mother tongue and was spoken with ease within the confines of Inez's house, but she was not allowed to speak it, nor was she allowed to acknowledge what her father or Inez had told her, even though she understood perfectly well.

One morning, following a parent-teacher meeting attended by her mother the day before, Gülbahar Hanım called out her name in class. Mehtap rose ready to solve the math problem on the blackboard.

"Mehtap, what is your mother's native tongue?"

Mehtap's eyes darted to the closed door and the windows in panic while she said almost inaudibly, "Turkish."

"How can she be Turkish yet speak it so badly? Where is your family from?"

Mehtap cleared her throat, tears stinging her eyes, "From Crete, my teacher."

Gülbahar Hanım turned around to face the class and snickered. The class, as if on cue, followed suit. Mehtap stood in this ever expanding moment of shame, her hands grasping the sides of the wooden desk, tears streaming down her face until Gülbahar Hanım asked her to be seated with a dismissive gesture. The girl sitting next to her gently held her hand and whispered as soon as the teacher's attention had returned to the blackboard, "I'll always be your friend."

It mortified Mehtap even more to hear this declaration, as if she had been afflicted with some awful, contagious disease and her best friend had to sacrifice her own interest to prove her love. "I don't even want your friendship. I hate this class," she replied sullenly looking down at her lap until the shrill ring of the recess bell. She gathered her books, put them into her school bag, and left the school.

Inez who was cooking in the steamy kitchen, her attention taken by the pots boiling on the stove, was startled to hear Mehtap's voice behind her. She turned around to find the girl standing there, her shoulders jerking up and down with the force of her sobs.

There were a few trips to the principal's office. Maria went in her Sunday best, accompanied by Inez whose indignation seemed to add a few inches to her height. Mehtap was taken along. She walked beside them, unable to fight a sense of profound dread making her feel faint and sweaty as they approached the schoolyard.

In the first meeting, Inez had impressed the principal with her invented connections. She knew people in high places, army officials, and would not mind passing the story of the incident along for the betterment of our Republic, she said, nodding her head. The principal was entirely committed to the betterment of the Republic himself, he assured her. There was only one other class where a spot was available and that was Nergiz Hanım's. She was one of the young teachers, the principal added, anxious to resolve the issue, and a very enthusiastic one. Inez and Mehtap looked at each other. The next day Mehtap was a pupil in Nergiz Hanım's class.

Notebook III. Autobiography

As I sat next to a boy whose name I did not know, in this new class that had an entirely different smell and appearance, I kept thinking of the other side of the wall and my familiar classmates waiting for Gülbahar Hanım's humourless early morning entrance with various stomach aches and hidden sweats under their starched white collars. There was a sweet citrus smell coming from the coal stove in Nergiz Hanım's class, where a white enamel bowl with a blue rim held fresh orange peels. On the wall were drawings: houses with purple roofs and red walls, birds with green beaks and orange eyes. I wanted to cry remembering the time I had made a picture of spring. There were multicoloured kites in the sky attached to children with strings, all of them smiling on the ground, a round brown mountain in the distance, and a house that had a neon green roof and aquamarine walls, a single window and a red door. It was one of those rare art classes we had, pure indulgence, probably due to the teacher having run out of math problems and grammar to drill into us.

I had smiled as Gülbahar Hanım approached my desk and hovered above me while I put the finishing touches. She told me to rise and go to the window. She followed me there. "Look around," she ordered.

"Any houses with green roofs?"

I nodded once backwards, meaning no.

"What colour are they?"

"Red." I didn't think they were; the tiles had more of a peachy-orange hue, but I knew the answer was "red."

"And the walls?"

"Whitish."

"Any green tree trunks?"

"No."

"So what are you supposed to do now?"

"Do it again with the proper colours."

"You'll sit through recess, since the next class is math."

But I was in Nergiz Hanım's class now and it smelled of oranges. She entered with a perfumed smile and beautiful shoes. The kohl around her eyes made her look like an Egyptian princess. Her hair was pulled into a ponytail and she wore an emerald green suit matched by small emerald earrings. She asked us how we were feeling and if we had had a good nights' sleep. "Who wants to have slices of orange?" Then she announced to the class that they had a new friend. She asked me to rise and say my name and made everyone in the class do the same. We then sang a folk song called the poplars of Izmir, the story of a beloved bandit and a favourite of Atatürk's apparently, and opened our math books. She spoke slowly, deliberately, writing on the board and waiting for everyone to copy into their notebooks before erasing. She was politeness personified and I felt I needed to moderate my joy with some deep suspicion that perhaps this was a show. But every day brought new confirmation that she was not only beautiful and elegant, but also polite and kind. I gradually accepted that I was in elementary school heaven and Nergiz Hanım was a woman of distinction.

THERE WAS A NEW BOY in class named Bahtiyar. He came in the middle of the school year and was extremely shy and quiet. He sat in the back, with his shaven head down, kept to himself and carried with him an air of poverty and heartache. His notebooks and books were not covered in blue and red, and the soft covers and pages curled upward like crashing waves. He walked up and down the schoolyard during recess and did not participate in any games or conversations. In class, he never raised his hand to speak. He often seemed absorbed in a realm invisible to us, yet more tangible to him than our presence.

The day I decided to approach him and invite him to play tag during recess, I started walking behind him in the schoolyard as he made his solitary rounds. It wasn't a spontaneous decision. I had been thinking about it for days. I quickened my steps and called out his name. "Bahtiyar!"

He did not look at me.

"Bahtiyar!"

He stopped and looked down, waiting for me to go on.

"Come play tag with us. Over there. Come!" I pulled him slightly. His body did not resist, but from his eyes I could tell he did not really want to play. He was a good runner though, and before long he tagged Tahsin from Gülbahar Hanım's class. Tahsin, who was a bit on the heavy side, had difficulty tagging anyone else until the bell rang.

I knew Tahsin's strategy in the schoolyard. He would recruit one or two girls who could not run fast so that he could tag them easily. By the time the bell rang, there was usually a desperate and sweaty girl running around unable to tag anyone else. He once made the mistake of asking me to play tag, thinking I was easy prey. He regretted it, needless to say, and from there on, ignored me. The other boys did not, however. They knew that I was fast and kept asking me to play. The day I asked Bahtiyar to join us, Tahsin had not had a chance to find a prey to keep busy until the end of recess. I saw a glimmer of hope in his eyes when I approached the group with Bahtiyar trailing behind me looking uninterested. "He's playing," I announced.

Tahsin ended up being the tag for a while. When the bell finally rang, he was red in the face with beads of sweat crowding his angry forehead and upper lip. As we all ran toward the building to get back to class, he hissed "Infidel Seed" as he passed me, and then "Dirty Gypsy" to Bahtiyar, who without missing a beat turned around and replied, "I'm a Kurd and you're a pig." It was probably a good thing that Bahtiyar was not in Gülbahar's class. Insulting her protégé would have resulted in a few headers to the blackboard, some epithets from the domestic animal kingdom, and lousy marks for the rest of his life. Tahsin stuck out his tongue in fury and ran to his class.

In those days, Kurds were described as Mountain Turks. Someone had once told me, I don't remember who anymore, or perhaps I had read it somewhere, that Mountain Turks got to be called Kurds because of the snow going "kard kurd" under their boots in the mountains. Since everyone, even the Sumerians and Etruscans, were originally Turks from Central Asia according to the Sun Theory, so were the Kurds, naturally. They settled in the mountains in eastern Anatolia. I asked him if it was true about snow going "kard kurd" after our friendship had evolved enough to exchange some words in between tag games. He looked at me with blank eyes and said, "I've never heard of it."

"Well then, you go ask your parents if they have," I said to him.

When my grandmother came to pick me up I asked her about it, too. She said, "I don't know about that. I know Kurds are Kurds, Armenians are Armenians, Laz are Laz, Rum are Rum…"

"Yes, but do you know where they all come from?" I cut into her pointless enumerations.

She shrugged and winced to show I was giving her a headache. "From their villages and provinces. Where else?"

"Granny, don't you know that everyone comes from the Taklamakan Desert?" I felt extremely proud knowing something she didn't. "We're all from there. Even Cretans must have been from there and so this makes me pure Turkish once and for all. And," I added, so she wouldn't feel left out, "I think Italians also come from there, so you know, you're also a Turk, in origin."

She chuckled, shaking her head, "I've never heard of this. But if you're learning it in school who am I to argue?"

Social anxiety coloured my entire childhood. I came from everything weird; all my family associations, my adopted grandmother with the un-Turkish name of Inez, not to mention my mother with the name of Maria—thankfully she went by the name of Meryem, the Turkish equivalent—the censored Greek mother tongue at home, and our lack of religiosity, the fact that I was registered as Moslem but accompanied granny to church on Sundays where I learned to say prayers in Latin, all those things that just did not fit in with being Turkish demanded a need for secrecy and lies. I lied about my origins, about my grandmother's name, and asked Inez to say her name was Huriye if asked when she came to pick me up from school. I would drill her on the way there to make sure she wouldn't forget her new name. One morning she finally said, "Lying's no good, Mehtap. Sooner or later, the truth comes out. Besides, I like my own name. Why are we changing it?"

"Because it's not Turkish."

"But aren't we all from the Taklamakan Desert anyway? You told me yourself."

"That was too long ago. You didn't even know anything about it until I told you. Nobody knows it. Only the book says it."

"I can say 'I'm Inez, originally from Taklamakan. And you?'" She put on her mocking little grin.

"It's not funny."

"It is, too. Listen, child. I can't change my name for anybody. I was baptized Inez and will die Inez. Stop calling me Huriye."

I sulked all the way to the gate, and told her I couldn't wait to be old enough to walk to school alone. She looked crushed when I didn't wave at her.

I was around nine or ten at the time, I believe. Bahtiyar and I had become a tight team in the schoolyard where we made sure to get Tahsin to sweat a little every day. He hated me for siding with my new friend, but he had no recourse; he could not get Gülbahar Hanım to do anything to me since I was no longer in her class and whenever he protested I simply told him to stop playing if he didn't like it. He never stopped, though, and I was glad because I would have not enjoyed myself as much in the schoolyard without Tahsin to annoy.

    As the months followed one another, I got to learn more about Bahtiyar's life. Mainly, that he did not have much to say about it. I knew he spoke a different language at home, just like I did. He spoke Zaza and I spoke Greek; because we could only speak our mother tongues in the privacy of our homes, we were both not very fluent in them. After making me swear not to tell anyone he told me his family was from Dersim. I did not know where it was so he showed me on the map a spot near the source of the Euphrates River. He said his family all died there and he was living with his aunt and uncle in Izmir now. I had no idea why this had to be a secret, but I respected his wishes and told no one. I thought perhaps the fact that he was an orphan, and poor at that, was a source of shame for him. Long after elementary school was over and we had lost touch completely I heard some stories about what took place in that region in the couple of years preceding his arrival in Nergiz Hanım's class. Another thing struck me many years later, as I was reading an article in the newspaper.

Notebook II. The Cretans

THE DERSIM UPRISING TOOK PLACE in the years 1937 and 1938. In the mountainous region mostly inhabited by Kurds, there was a feudal system resistant to change and modernization; the Aghas of the region did not want to relinquish their power over the peasantry and an uprising against the Turkish state was fomented, which was then successfully suppressed by the army. This was the version that became common knowledge through the newspapers and school books, etc. God knows, in the early years of the Republic there were many uprisings, many opposing forces wanting the pull the country backwards into the darkness of religious superstition and feudalism, and this was Atatürk's biggest challenge as he tried to pull the debris of an old empire, now reconstructed as the Turkish Republic, into modernity, laicism, and enlightenment. There were stories that went around if you knew someone who knew someone whose uncle perished or was a soldier.

Through the years, Mehtap had vaguely heard those whispered insinuations and the hush-hush tone and the don't-repeat-this looks but had not given it much thought given the lack of support and evidence. They came to her ear in the same breath as the story of the woman in such and such a village who gave birth to a two-headed serpent, from the mouth of her talkative cleaning lady who swore it was God's truth.

The newspaper article that Mehtap was reading with some difficulty, using her magnifying glass as she sipped her tea in the sunny cumba on the second floor of her house, confirmed that a massacre had taken place; it involved mass graves and aerial bombardments on innocent villagers. It was the object of a state-issued apology and some political upheaval. There was mention of Atatürk's adopted daughter Sabiha, celebrated as the first Turkish woman pilot, being implicated in the aerial bombardment of the villages back in those days. Heroes and heroines of old were falling from grace, crashing down. Mehtap took off her glasses and pushed the newspaper away.

In her school years she could not have known this, nor could she have guessed that Nergiz Hanım's handsome fiancé had been one of the few pilots flying the handful of fighter planes owned by the army in those days. Her teacher's dashing lover stopped coming to meet her outside the schoolyard around the time that Bahtiyar joined the class. These two seemingly unrelated events were connected for Mehtap as two facets of the same incident even many decades after the fact. It was perhaps a bomb released by Nergiz Hanım's fiancé that vaporized Bahtiyar's entire family and caused him to move to Izmir where relatives took him in. When this idea took root in her mind, Mehtap shed tears of inconsolable sorrow for her long-forgotten childhood friend Bahtiyar over the pages of the newspaper she was reading in her solitary old age, sitting by the bay window of the cumba on the second floor of her house.

She saw in her mind, the pilot being called for a top-secret mission and taking leave from the beautiful Nergiz in Izmir, promising to marry her upon his return, and Nergiz gracing his departure with her luminous smile. The sinewy pilot in his sharp uniform being given the mission to bomb insurgents hiding in mountain caves only to find out after the fact that the cave he had targeted was inhabited by fearful elderly people and children who had run up to the hills for protection. She imagined Bahtiyar cowering in some corner of a closet, surviving the attack and then being sent to Izmir by some kind-hearted person who found him in the ruins, perhaps even a soldier who could not live with himself after following the order to kill unarmed villagers. After putting the child on the train and *giving him pocket money, she imagined this very soldier going back to the barracks and hanging himself with his own belt. She wept and wept imagining Bahtiyar's childhood buried in a mass grave along with his parents, grandparents, and siblings. She understood the sorrowful silence enveloping the boy like a tattered coat in the schoolyard. What happened to Bahtiyar? She wondered about this for a long time and dreamt catastrophic scenes involving the boy with whom they had shared the secret of secrecy as children.*

Nergiz Hanım lost her radiant smile around the time Bahtiyar came. It wasn't due to Bahtiyar's presence, of course, but to the inexplicable withdrawal of her lover's affection. He returned from his secret mission a changed man, one who awoke screaming from nightmares and would suddenly start shaking and sweating in mid-sentence for no apparent reason. He could no longer work as a commercial pilot and was fired for incompetence and alcoholism. He stopped coming to visit Nergiz altogether a year after his mission and withdrew his proposal to marry her, telling her he was a broken man, unable to support her and unworthy of her love. She started coming to school with her eyelids swollen and her once impeccable clothes frumpy, her beauteous smile and movie-star looks forever gone. Many years after her graduation from elementary school, Mehtap encountered Nergiz Hanım on the quay walking alone. She kissed the top of her teacher's hand and touched her forehead with it to show respect. Nergiz Hanım asked her about her parents and grandmother, in her usual affable politeness. Throughout this exchange, Mehtap kept trying to find her beloved teacher in this now somewhat swollen, pasty face and heavy trunk. The eyes that used to light up from inside had a matte, dead-fish look to them. She told Mehtap she was still teaching and invited her to visit the school one of these days. This was the last time she ever saw her teacher and after taking her leave, Mehtap walked away heavy-hearted, carrying the crushing disappointment of witnessing the transformation of her heroine into someone utterly banal, lost in the crowds.

Notebook III. Autobiography

WORLD WAR II HAD ALREADY BEGUN when I started middle school. It was a time of deprivation, even though we did not enter the war. There were dinners of chewy bread, grapes and weak tea, most days. That is what I remember. And the Wealth Tax that ruined my grandmother. In November of 1942, a law was passed enabling the state to collect this tax from all business owners, estates, property owners, and so on. It was devised ostensibly to fill the coffers of the state in case the country had to go to war against Hitler or Stalin. It was also a way to push all non-Moslem minorities' influence out of the economy and transfer their assets to Moslem, and therefore "pure" Turkish hands. The Armenians, Jews, Greeks and Levantines were taxed severely, and many lost all their assets. Those who couldn't pay the tax were sent to a forced labour camp in Erzurum. Some of my grandmother's acquaintances, tradesmen all, were sent to Aşkale to break rocks, for being unable to pay the exorbitant tax imposed on their fledgling businesses. My grandmother's haberdashery, still run by my mother to keep her busy, had been generating just enough income to keep it going till then. But when the tax came, Granny had to sell the house we lived in to pay the tax on the haberdashery. Mehtap Tuhafiye closed its doors. I remember my grandmother sitting on her bed, holding her prayer beads. She couldn't pray. My mother who sat beside her, was rubbing her back, telling her we were a family and not to worry, that just as she took care of them when they got off the boat, they would now take care of her. Her tears kept streaming down her face as she mumbled incoherently. "Spared from the great fire. I was born. Gave birth ... where my baby ... all my memories.... Why do this to an old widow? We make next to nothing with this shop. Why?" And so it went. She sobbed, and my mother wiped her tears reminding Granny that she was a brave woman and would come out of this stronger. I suppose there is only so much the heart of a brave woman can take. For my grandmother, this was the breaking point.

We moved to the house where I now live, in Karataş. A Jewish family was renting it out after having moved in with relatives to pay for the tax. A decade or so later, my father was able to buy the house with his savings when the owner decided to move to Israel with his family. My grandmother's health and spirit were forever altered by this event. She didn't know the new neighbourhood, and made no effort to acquaint herself with it. She had the room where I now sleep, which was the sunniest and most spacious in the house, but spent her days in the small cumba in her armchair, sitting in the exact spot where I'm writing these words today. She stopped teasing me, and did not enter the kitchen to cook a single meal until the end of her days. My mother had to learn to cook. It was a most unhappy time for us all. Mom, who saw herself as a businesswoman running a store, looking fashionable and trendy, had to contend with the role of a housewife in a frilly apron, making uninspired meals that had a bafflingly absolute lack of taste. My father would take a forkful during supper and make a face behind my busy mother's back that made me smile in complicity. Granny did not participate in our secret. She ate impassively and thanked my mother for feeding us at the end of the meal with polite indifference. My dad and I would join her dutifully in the thanking, and he would then carefully venture, "Next time, a touch of salt and pepper would make it even tastier." My mother would get defensive immediately and snap, "I'm sorry I don't know how to cook better. You can try your hand at it next time if you wish."

He would cautiously retract, "No dearest, it is very good; I was just making a suggestion, to be helpful."

She punished us for the events that took her out of Alsancak and changed her daily routine to one that stuck her in this old kitchen with steam from pots frizzing her hair and giving her pimples. My father secretly begged Inez to start cooking occasionally to give Maria a break from the kitchen and most importantly to give us a break from her atrocious cooking, but Granny wouldn't give in. She said the inspiration and desire were gone from her and the food would turn out worse than Maria's. "Trust me, nothing you could ever cook would turn out worse than this. If not for me, do it for Mehtap. She is still a growing child and is losing her appetite." There was no budging my grandmother. We forcibly developed a taste for bland, loveless dolmas, chalky pilav, and fat köftes.[21]

In my young eyes, the aftermath of the Wealth Tax became forever associated with the withdrawal of affection and inspiration from the two women in my life. To this day, when this hereto buried piece of history is resuscitated and aired in newspaper articles or television shows, I experience the same melancholy twinge I used to get watching my once dynamic grandmother sit idly by a window day after day looking old and disconnected, and my mother's deep personal dissatisfaction manifesting itself as what my dad had nicknamed "Furious Food." Around that time, he suggested I meet him at work after school so we could eat fragrant kokoreç[22] sandwiches from street vendors on the way home before submitting to Mom's angry cuisine.

We ate and strolled side by side, my dad carrying my school

---

[21] dolmas, pilav, köftes: stuffed grape leaves, rice, turkish meat balls made of lamb
[22] kokoreç: grilled lamb intestines

bag through the busy market street in Alsancak, pausing here and there to look at store windows, while we wolfed down our quarter-bread sandwiches. I found out about his childhood during those walks: Mehmet the Great and his curly big moustache, Kirya Paraskevi's one classroom village school, the vineyards and mountains of his beloved Crete, the terrace on which his dad would stand, legs planted wide, to admire his days' work down in the vineyards, sipping red wine from a tall glass. "Life," he said, "is a lot like skipping rope. One handle is your birth, the other your death." It just made sense to him, the way you keep turning the rope and jumping, the repetition of days and the surprise of each turn, one slow, one fast or wobbly, the part you play in your destiny while it puts a pebble here, a wall there and throws your rhythm out of whack. I don't know if he meant this image to be soothing, but it had a terrifying effect on me, and I stopped skipping rope thinking of death and birth making everything go round and round.

"If they were to give your vineyards back to you and allowed you to go back and live in Crete, would you, Baba?" I asked one day. Perhaps I shouldn't have asked. His face darkened under his frown. "Why should I waste my time thinking about such impractical things?"

Notebook I. The Journal

THERE ARE EVENTS IN OUR LIVES we are sometimes too embarrassed to acknowledge, even to ourselves; I say "we," assuming it is part of being human, but I ought to take ownership of this particular embarrassment, even as I speak of it to myself. Nuray has gone away. She quit her job, too. It has been a few years, now. I found out from a mutual friend that she got married soon after she left me, and has a daughter named Mehtap. Plunging the dagger even deeper, this common acquaintance of ours innocently told me she had never seen Nuray so happy before. "I can imagine," I smiled as we stood chatting on the sidewalk one sunny January morning. There were frozen puddles where the tiles of the uneven pavement had sunk in a little. The weather was penetratingly frigid, and her hurried phrases came out of her mouth wrapped in warm pockets of steamed breath. She kept rearranging her beige handknit scarf as she spoke, tugging it this way and that, fixing the stylish knot covering her neck with gloved fingers that refused to remain still in that cold weather.

"What about you? Are you still working at the zipper factory?"

I nodded, the smile I had put on earlier still frozen on my face. "Yes, I'm still working there. You should come over for tea one afternoon." I proposed vaguely before saying goodbye and she acquiesced waving those previously frantic fingers.

It is a painful story to tell. Despite my best intentions to avoid it, I can't help going over it at night when the world becomes still.

In fact, I try hard to find ways to distract myself, but it creeps into the current of my thoughts, surreptitiously, on its flow to some innocent destination that doesn't know her name. Alas, every word I use, every thought or image that crosses my mind knows of her, and there is no escaping this. The other night I tried to find a thing that I imagined completely safe to focus on, so I could finally sleep. *Wood*, I thought looking at my dresser.... How can the woman be conjured by thinking of it? And yet....

There was a bookcase in my room, she had brought it when she moved and took it with her as she departed. A bookcase made by some uncle or friend of her mother's, I don't quite remember. It had ornate trimmings with hand-carved roses at the top of the bookcase and was riddled with tiny holes borne by woodworms. She had few books, mostly comprised of translated romance novels or such. On the shelves she had arranged picture frames of her mother and her brother who had passed away very young. She asked me to place my books there as well. Once or twice, we made love leaning on it, making the frames collapse. I have learned, thanks to Nuray, that there exists no such thing as an innocent word. They are, all of them, guilty of presenting us the world in the particular way we attempt to shun it.

One day she came and told me something I had missed at work. It had been going on for some time, by then. My boss had been lusting after her; that, I knew from the way his eyes would latch onto her rear end whenever she came to talk to me at the office. Apparently he made his moves one day when she was at work after hours, and she had an affair with him, all the while knowing my feelings for him. He left his mistress Gönül as a result, and almost sent his fashion-obsessed wife packing. That was the extent of his infatuation. She didn't like men, she had said; she only enjoyed their attention. This man's must have been especially important to her, I later surmised, because he stood in the way of our relationship. Why did she feel the need to punish me so?

And, why had I been so oblivious?

I called her a traitor and a tramp. She packed her suitcase and slammed the door. A week or so later her cousin with the Impala came to take her furniture and the rest of her things. He wouldn't talk to me about her, only confirming she was fine. As he left, he shook my hand, eyes fixed on the concrete tiles of the pavement as if to conceal some embarrassment, "Nuray has always had a fiery temper. But she isn't too proud to admit when she is wrong, either. We need to be patient with her."

He must have imagined we had a jealous tiff over a man—which we did, but not as he imagined—or some friction over living arrangements. No one knew we were lovers. How could they?

I've been going over the past in my mind, trying to find the clues I had missed. Perhaps it started the day she said not to wait for her because she was doing overtime and came back home long after I had washed the dishes and put away her supper. Why did I not look out the window that night to see if someone had driven her home? And why did she buy me the gold necklace with the letter "м" a few weeks before her confession? She knew she was leaving me. Did she enjoy his kisses and caresses? How did it feel? Was he a gentle lover? Was she lying to me when she had assured me she preferred women?

Hell is the place, much like a theatre, where those betrayed are made to watch the scenes of their betrayal re-enacted ad nauseam with minute variations. Sometimes the lines change, or the décor, or the gestures. I don't know about betrayers; I have never had that experience. She got married, had a child by my name; never once called, wrote or even passed by to see how I was doing after she left. While she did all those things, I was sitting in the cumba, a frozen version of myself, wondering what I could have done differently. If I had told her I didn't love Patron, would she have still seduced him? She destroyed me for not loving her enough in theory. If he had loved me, would I have left her? Patron could have never loved me. Therefore, I would have never left her. I gave her an insane answer to a stupid question that has become the cause of my deepest regret. I remember asking my father about Crete, and whether he would return if they gave him his vineyards back. He never bothered to answer. It was a waste of time. Why could I not see that?

There is another hell hotel at which I am a permanent resident. In this particular place I'm the only one I know or see, or speak to. I'm provided with many tools of torture with which to hurt myself, on condition of being absolutely silent about it. No one knows, or will ever know, I loved a woman, gazed at her, was aroused by her while I was deeply, desperately infatuated by a man.

I used to worship the man. I did everything I could so he could deliver his damn order of zippers that made him rich. I got my bonus. Then, he wanted to tell me about his mystery lover. I didn't know yet that his mystery lover was Nuray. He would ask me to field calls from Gönül, "Aydın Bey is busy with a client. May I take a message?" or "Aydın Bey is on a trip with his family. Is there a message?" She would slam the phone down. The woman called me a liar and a harlot one day, screaming into my ear. I put the receiver beside the typewriter while she spewed her poison and continued typing my letter feeling smug. Finally, the unreturned calls ceased. Then his wife started calling; to check up on him I suppose. Perhaps he had started being careless with Nuray. "So where is he again?" She would question irritably. "He said he'd be at the office." I found excuses, dutiful as ever. I knew another conquest had replaced Gönül, but I figured she was a woman from some strip joint he frequented. I was his confidante. "She's got black hair," he said once, "opulent and so soft. Sometimes, I keep running my fingers through it while she talks and talks. That is all I want to do. The hair alone makes me swoon." I despised every minute of his heart-to-hearts with me. My fault alone. Not his. What man speaks so openly to a woman about the mysteries of his heart? What Turkish man? There is no one like me in his world, man or woman. No one. Should I derive some satisfaction from this? If only I could escape this tyranny they both exercise over me.

I don't have a thick black mane. My hair is thin, brown, and straight, with an oily disposition unless I wash it often. Why couldn't I have hair to make him swoon? I wanted those cheekbones, that rump, those equestrian ankles, and that cold, calculating heart. Why did she make me repeat, "*I'm yours, I'm yours*" when I climaxed? Callous. Bitch.

THERE IS STILL THE RIDDLE of her daughter's name. Mehtap. She must be uttering it constantly, every day, torturing herself, wanting to get to me. Why has she thrown us down this path strewn with broken pieces of us, the irreparably divided reflections we have become?

THE LONG CORRIDOR THAT LEADS to what used to be her small office at work: In measured strides to steady my pounding heart, I walk those fifty steps every day, like a pilgrim who has memorized the path to a miraculous spring that will not cure her, for no other reason except to feel the returning ache of anticipation as I approach the doorway with its crusty bits of old ivory paint and peek in to find some other smoke-shrouded female face sipping tea and pounding the keys of the large electric typewriter in the weakened hazy sunlight that has seeped through the dusty blinds, fallen on the maroon tea glass for a lacklustre lick before skimming over a plump wrist choked by the leather strap of a watch, to disappear into the half open drawer of the grey file cabinet across the room. I walk the fifty steps back to my office thinking of the light in our hotel room in Moda after we first made love, the golden bracelets shining in the morning light on our wrists, her spilling bosom in the gaze of the tramway conductor and her hand on my hip, on the roundness I never knew contained so much pleasure for me. I sit back at my desk. Patron will call me shortly to take notes in my steno pad. He, too, has also been abruptly abandoned by Nuray, although it has been long enough now that he has returned to his steady old diet of Gönül and his wife. He still hasn't admitted to me that Nuray was his lover; perhaps she's asked him never to tell—as if I wouldn't find out. We don't talk about her resignation, or the nights he slept on the couch in his office after she left him, not wanting to see his wife or anyone else. He knew we were housemates, but he never asked what happened, where she went. I never asked him either.

And so it is. I write letters to prospective zipper buyers, take notes, water the plants, inspect the factory, meet with union representatives, meet with the engineers, inspect the kitchen, listen to complaints, take notes, meet with lawyers, take more notes. Aydın has deferred almost all this work to me while he travels to Europe to meet customers, attend conferences, and so on. He brings me back silk scarves, Mont Blanc pens—so I could take more notes, I suppose—chocolates, and once a bottle of perfume identical to the one he got his wife, and also Gönül; I know because I had to wrap them for him. It was Fleurs de Rocaille by Caron. Whether he is at home, or with his mistress, or at work with me, Patron is surrounded by the very same flowery fragrance of Fleurs de Rocaille. Was it on purpose? Was it due to laziness? "Give me three of those." I imagine him gesturing at the saleslady at the airport duty-free shop and winking at her with that naughty flirtatious look.

He has asked me to call him Aydın. "Enough with Patron this and Patron that," he said when I woke him up one morning as he lay on the leather couch in his office fully clothed, soon after Nuray left us both. "Call me Aydın, except in front of all the others and my wife. They won't understand. Simply Aydın. Can you?"

I told him I would try. He added, "I'm the one who should be calling you Patron. You've been practically running this place all by yourself. And better than I ever have. You should be the general manager." He said this, but never changed my title or my salary. He simply let me run the place disguised as his personal secretary. I still bought and wrapped his wife's and mistress' presents, called the gardener every spring for his roses in Çeşme, fielded both women's phone calls to him, and bought plane tickets for Gönül to meet him in various European cities: Vienna, Rome, Paris, Amsterdam, Cologne. She had done very well for herself, I thought. I couldn't bring myself to say, "Listen, I'm doing all this for you. Why can't I go on a trip too, once in a while, see the world a little?"

I practiced at home in front of the mirror. I was confident and assertive. I demanded. I folded my arms with feet slightly apart as I waited for his reply, sort of like Yul Brynner in *Anna and the King*. I put on lipstick and mascara. Tried again. Finally, I worked up the courage to have this conversation with him as I rode the bus to the office one day. There was a fair in Germany. I'd found it among the brochures we regularly got. I would say: "You remember how you once told me I ran this place so well? I have done some research and found a fair that we could participate in; I have already written to them. This time, I would really like to be the one going, if you agree. There is a friend I would like to see also, while I'm there. Can we do this?" I repeated this a dozen times until I stepped into his office. Nice and clear, I said to myself, be nice, be clear. Start with. "Aydın…."

He was shaven and wore a white shirt. This meant he was in good spirits and felt in control that day. When he felt in control, he acted generous. It was a good prospect.

"Aydın, merhaba!" I started with a sunny smile. The lipstick was there and the Farah Diba hairdo I had paid for dearly the day before. I practically slept sitting down all night not to mess the upward bun. "Are you having a good morning?" I asked him cheerfully.

"Yes, I am. What's the occasion? You're all made up."

"Nothing special. Just felt like it. Listen, I have a great plan…."

Half an hour later I was calling the travel agent to book my ticket and his. Yes, his. He said he would attend the first couple of days of the fair and then return while I went on to visit my friend. I was disappointed to have him tag along at first. He wasn't in my plan. I reminded him that there wouldn't be anyone to mind the factory. He said there was always Head Engineer Niyazi, and he couldn't do too much damage in a couple of days. He assured me he'd carry back all the samples and things from the kiosk so I wouldn't have to bother with them at the end of the fair. That was a good thought. Slowly, I began to imagine having supper with him, going out perhaps; just the two of us in another location that held no reminders of Nuray.

I WENT SHOPPING FOR CLOTHES yesterday. The visa has taken a long time. I had to fill out so many different forms at the German Consulate. Aydın had no problems. As a wealthy businessman who owns a factory in Turkey there is little fear he will disappear underground and remain there illegally, I suppose. I wrote to Kerime to advise her of my arrival. She will meet me at the train station after the fair. I chose a few bright coloured dresses, remembering Nuray's complaints that I always went for drab colours and shapeless pants. I packed the corset to slim my waist and push up my bosom. Leaving in three weeks!

Notebook II. The Cretans

*N*EITHER MEHMET NOR MARIA *ever returned to Crete for a visit. They were afraid of travelling and remained profoundly suspicious of Greek and Turkish border officials. In the late fifties, when trips to Greece became possible for Turkish citizens, the couple categorically rejected the notion from fear that something would go awry between the countries during their visit and prevent their return to Turkey. Disputes between the two neighbours always seemed one island away. They imagined being stuck in Crete with nothing but a suitcase, having no friends, no acquaintances to take care of them, strangers to their birthplace or adrift in the Mediterranean, unclaimed by either country. "Worse than strangers," Mehmet would insist, with that particular shade of bitterness that infects the memories of those who have suffered profound injustices in their youth. He never spoke of enemies; he seemed to have none. Although he knew himself to be Greek and Turkish, he could acknowledge neither fully in his mind and he felt like a mongrel that had been groomed to pass for an acceptable breed, thus living his days with an omnipresent sense of dread which, like a gas leak, permeated his universe, emanating a deep suspicion of ideas, governments, convictions, and neighbours. Obsessed by the thought of toeing the line at all times, Mehmet would become taciturn, self-effaced among friends.*

Maria died of miserere, a disease by which the intestine self-strangulates, gets tied in a knot and makes it impossible for the feces to move through the bowel resulting in a push upward, through the oesophagus. There is absolutely nothing about death that has any sort of redeeming value, even though it happens in the hundreds of thousands every day around the globe. It is ugly. Eyes stare into space, the breath rattles. The air goes out of the chest like a leaky balloon. The skin gets sallow and rubbery. It smells of rot. In a nutshell. Childbirth is hard, sometimes a mother dies, but hope is born. Illness can get cured. The amputated get artificial limbs. Maybe they write books or tell stories of redemption. The blind may sing, or the deaf invent theorems. In death, all that was beautiful and moving becomes hollow. Hundreds of thousands of holes are dug each day around the earth, like groundhog mounds, the totality of which would be invisible from space, or anywhere in the universe where the Almighty is said to reside. Many minuscule holes are dug, and equally miniscule corpses are placed and then covered. It is an insignificant, abject daily occurrence from which we derive the greatest despair and sorrow, tears burst forth and sobs tear through our bodies. To what avail? Someone else may write a poem; someone who will also end up in a little mound invisible to the blindness of space permeating the galaxy. It is so. Maria died of miserere. Mehtap could not witness that final departure. She ran into the bright street filled with the smells of exhaust and noises, she ran from the hospital as fast as her legs allowed her, tears flowing into her nose, spilling into her shirt collar, and sat on a park bench facing the port in time to see the ferry disgorge hundreds of people onto the concrete pier like beetles on a hot sunny day.

Notebook I. The Journal

I AM SITTING IN A HOTEL ROOM in Düsseldorf, not far from the train station and the Rhine. Greyish fog hovers over the river, a sinking cloud, covering church steeples and tall buildings in its path. I feel out of place. I also forgot to water the plants at the office before leaving. Is Head Engineer Niyazi sitting in the boss's office now? Would anyone there think to water them? I should tell Patron to do it when he returns. Every tile and handle in the bathroom shines with cleanliness and luxury. Plush white towels hang from racks, on the bedside table is a small bar of milk chocolate, a telephone. The bedcover is a pastel green satin quilt. Small etchings framed under glass adorn the walls covered with beige wallpaper. They represent the German countryside, I presume. There is a church steeple marking the tip of a triangle on top of a distant village, next is a small path among trees in what must be the Black Forest. I ate the chocolate as I unpacked. In a couple of hours I will have dinner with Aydın. I fretted about my clothes and double-checked if I'd brought my dressy shoes before taking my shower. They have plastic caps in small cartons if you don't want to wet your hair. I have never had a tête-à-tête dinner with him. What do I want? How do I act? I write these words to still my nerves. As soon as the thought of this dinner enters my mind, my intestines cramp up. I've run to the bathroom four times since he called my room to tell me he's taking me out to a posh restaurant tonight. I don't know why I'm so nervous. Of course he'll take me out, and he will probably talk to me about the Belgian or the Dane, metal versus plastic zippers, the technology required for the new cheaper models; all that dross. This is what a boss talks about with his general manager who also waters his plants and tells lies to his wife. This is nothing but an expensive business dinner. No need to run to the bathroom as if I was attacked by dysentery. Go tell my guts. My bum hurts from incessant wiping. Two hours left, and I don't know what to do.

I'M WAITING FOR MY TRAIN. Three days have passed since my arrival in Düsseldorf. The fair is finished. Aydın has boarded his plane back to Izmir. I reminded him again to water the plants. I'm sitting at a café at the station, waiting to board the train that will take me to Cologne, to see Kerime.

He never talked about work; not even remotely, that night. He came and knocked on my door. I thought I would faint when I saw him standing there in his black suit, grey wavy hair brushed back with gel, the softness of his closely shaven fifty-something skin with fine lines around his smiling eyes, his hands in his pockets, that playful half-smile I have always imagined him offering other, more beautiful women. There he was, covering the doorframe like a man waiting for his date. And that night it was I, Mehtap, the invisible woman who wears navy blue pants and white blouses, who doesn't know how to apply makeup or fix her hair; I, the wearer of practical shoes and writer of business letters who was going out with this man, the seducer of women as beautiful as movie stars.

I did put a lot of effort into my appearance in those two hours of waiting. The corset that cut my breathing and all those grapefruits I ate last week did take off some waist circumference. I wore a night-blue dress with a black bolero top, a simple pearl choker. Hair was teased into a bowl shape. I was careful with the mascara and applied wine-red lipstick for dramatic effect.

A touch of rouge on my cheeks, and silver pumps matching a silver clutch. Small, clip-on pearl earrings. Fake, of course. In my entire life until that night, I had never worked on my appearance so carefully. I wore the imitation fur coat I'd borrowed from a friend and the Fleurs de Rocailles perfume he had given me, hoping he'd remember. And he did, even though (or because) he gave his wife and mistress the same and made me wrap them. He said, "I know that perfume, is it the one I brought you?"

We sat in a restaurant the likes of which we never even dream of back home, a large hall with mirrors framed in rococo gold alternating with still lives (dead animals next to randomly spilled bowls of fruit) from another century, and tapestries representing hunting scenes. Large bouquets of exotic flowers in hand-painted porcelain vases representing men with white wigs and silk jackets kissing the dainty hands of seated women with tiny, pointed shoes peaking out from underneath layers of shiny, bejewelled dresses. Waiters, impeccably dressed, gliding to and fro to the music of Bach. I was trying very hard not to seem provincial, remembering to keep my mouth from hanging open as I glanced around. I truly wanted to gape. Aydın had clearly seen it all before, and I realized for the first time that he belonged in this world of gallantry, he knew exactly what to do and how. When the sommelier came, he exchanged niceties in German, tasted the wine, swishing it around in his mouth and approved. He chose every single course for me and himself from the menu. When he picked up a fork, I picked up the same, in a choreographed lag, hoping it would seem nonchalant instead of inept. He was a consummate gentleman that evening, doing everything he could (so it seemed) to enhance my elegance, rather than emphasize how gauche I felt.

I wondered if Nuray ever travelled with him to such places. I wondered what they did, how they made love, while I listened to Aydın's anecdotes of his various travels to Europe. Did she neigh like a horse swishing her head around when he told her those very same stories? Did everyone in the restaurant turn to look at that tangle of bouncing black curls and unsuppressed laughter? He must have had such a marvellous time with her charmingly indecorous manners. He must have gaped at her with awe and admiration, not to mention lust. The three of us were there suddenly, Aydın and I bewitched by her irrepressible spirit. I continued nodding and chuckling at his stories, asking for details, my eyes focusing on his mouth as words came out of them, bits of teeth peeking from his moving lips, the gestures of his hands as he made flourishes in his pursuit of a punch line and the way his eyes creased when he emphasized something in his story.

What did I experience that evening? Regret and jealousy over Nuray? Seduction? Half listening, half-poisoned by my own reveries, I sat there, feeling numb. A few years ago I would have bled for such an opportunity to sit face to face with him, with no one else around. Now, I wasn't even sure what I wanted to get out of it. In the midst of a story of how he got lost on his way to The Hague, I blurted that I had something to confess to him. Did he promise to be my friend after my confession? He looked bewildered.

"What did you do?"

It was like a bump had made the record jump and scratch, bringing the graceful moment in the restaurant to a discordant halt.

"Actually," I started, "I have two confessions."

He leaned forward on his elbows, clasping his hands.

I leaned forward and clasped my hands too.

"You won't fire me?" It came out more tremulously than I had intended.

"Did you steal from me?"

"No."

"Did you tell my wife about the others?"

"No."

"Then?" he frowned.

"Do you remember the day you interviewed and hired me on the spot?"

He nodded impatiently.

"I've been in love with you since that day. Terminally. I mean, I will probably go to my grave with it."

He froze. I could see the white of his eyes all around the irises.

"Why else would I put up with you?" I added.

He grabbed his white linen napkin and shoved it into a pile beside his plate. "What's to happen now?" he whispered after some hesitation.

"Nothing. Nothing at all. What could happen?"

"Why did you just tell me this? Why now, after all those years of making such a fool of myself in front of you? Any sane woman would have been cured of it already."

I knew I had crushed him with this confession. What could the man say, how could he save himself from the embarrassment of unreciprocated love? In the same reckless and abrupt manner in which I cut his La Hague story, I blurted: "And, I'm also a lesbian."

"My God, woman! Are you trying to kill me?" It came out louder than he had intended; the effete waiter gliding to Bach turned and raised his eyebrows before continuing toward the kitchen and Aydın proceeded with a lower tone. "I don't understand anything. Are you making fun of me?"

"No. It's true. Nuray and I were lovers before…."

"How can that be?" The waiter returning from the kitchen with steaming plates glanced our way once more. "That makes her a lesbian too."

His eyes were moving around in their sockets following the befuddled thoughts in his mind. "So you both like men too?"

"I can't speak for her. You're the only man I actually feel attracted to. What does it matter?"

"Sorry if I seem dense! One moment you were Mehtap, my

friend and manager extraordinaire at the office—the next, my secret admirer and ex-lesbian lover of *my* ex-lover. You expect me to say it doesn't matter? I look at you and think, oh my God what a fool I've been. The woman's loved me all those years. All those stupid confessions I made about other women! I recoil with shame. And then, she's a lesbian. Maybe I should uncoil, but then, who is this woman? Who are you? Why tell me all this?"

He cupped his forehead in his palms and sighed. "Your timing is pretty awful, Mehtap."

The dessert was still sitting untouched in our plates.

"I'm sorry. I don't know what got into me. I think it's the dress and makeup."

"Why in the world have you become a lesbian? Did something…?"

"No. Nothing. Just a feeling inside."

"Always?"

"I guess…."

"When did you realize?"

"What does it matter? I mean, I can't help how I am, can I?"

"Maybe if you see a doctor…."

"You think it's an illness?"

"One of my friends, he was caught in bed with a man. His wife made him see a psychiatrist … he is still with her."

"Is that good? I don't need a doctor. No one knows about it except you. You must not tell anyone. Promise me."

"Maybe you haven't met the right kind of man."

"I shouldn't have told you. Now, you'll always be thinking of that. You'll start acting funny around me."

"You mean I wasn't before?"

"Like I have the plague and only you know it."

"Do you still want this dessert?"

I shook my head no. He paid the waiter and rushed me out. We walked on the moist sidewalk along the river until my shoe got stuck between two slabs. He had to crouch and remove the slim heel gently so it wouldn't break and offered his arm which I took and held the rest of the way, feeling the hard softness of his muscle through the fabric of his thick coat. He played soccer in the summer, in the backyard of the factory. At lunch time, I would see him running, wiping his forehead, flapping his arms and shouting; no more zippers and dull telephone calls, no wife or mistress, eyes focused on the ball, free.

"I love watching you play soccer."

"I feel entirely like myself around you," he said, "but you know. You know the worst of me." He patted my hand resting on his arm.

"That, I do." I chuckled. "But you don't know the worst of me, and that's fine."

"I can imagine you and me growing old together, somehow, now thinking of it. I could never imagine this with my wife, or Gönül. Not even Nuray."

I felt a twinge when I heard her name. "Well, you're not in a romantic relationship with me. Me, I could imagine growing old with Nuray."

"My wife..." he stopped in the middle of the street. "She's like the control tower of a prison. Lights on, full blast. No escape. Always has a plan, some sort of senseless obligation she visits upon me. And Gönül, I just want to run away after sex, you know, she starts talking and talking. Half the time, I don't even know what she's telling me. Endless stories about insignificant things. As for..."

"Don't talk about Nuray. I don't want to hear it."

"As for you ... you are the perfect companion."

"You're still my boss. We're not equals. I was looking at you in the restaurant. I don't know which fork to pick. Your friends could never be my friends. We could never grow old together. You're mistaken in that."

"Do you think either one of us will give a damn which fork

we pick when we're old?" He burst into laughter, his eyes creased into small slits with many puffy grooves converging on them.

"Well, anyway, it will never happen. You'll get old with your wife, in your big house. And I'll grow old writing my memoirs in my old house in Karataş. Also, poems of unrequited love." I was making light of it when my smile just slipped away. I saw my life fall apart ahead of me because of my stupid confessions.

He stopped walking. "Nuray or me?"

"Both." I pulled his sleeve so we would continue walking. Something was breaking in my chest and I didn't want either of us to hear it.

"Look at me." He didn't budge. He pulled up my chin that I had sunk into my chest. "Look here." He removed his handkerchief from his pocket and dabbed my cheeks before kissing my forehead. Then he pulled me close into a hug. We remained enlaced for a long time. He caressed my back through muffled sobs and hiccups I buried into his wool coat.

"I want to go back to the hotel," I managed to say after a while.

"No, you don't. Trust me. Let's walk some more and we'll find a club, listen to some music."

We continued walking aimlessly for a while; then, he remembered a place. "It's not far from here," he said, looking jovial. There was a pink neon sign and a bouncer outside. He paid the entrance fee and we went down the stairs into the smoky basement. There were booths all around the dance floor and two singers on stage, both of them women, one brunette in a red boa feather get-up, the blonde, in a white tux, Marlene Dietrich-style. Only after we sat down at our booth did I realize the couples in the bar were homosexuals. Aydın and I were apparently the only heterosexual couple there. He pointed his chin at the singers, urging me to watch them. I didn't understand at first. "They sing well," I nodded. He was looking at me insistently.

"Are they men?" I asked feeling sheepish.

The singers were making asides in German during mid-song

pauses. People laughed at the jokes, Aydın smiled, I looked around feeling lost.

"Have you been here before?"

He nodded, still paying attention to the singers on stage. "Once, with a couple of friends. It's fun. Isn't it?"

He smiled politely at Marlene Dietrich who had come near us to continue her song. The boa-feathered singer would continue the song in counterpoint when Dietrich stopped, in melodious conversation. From up close, I noticed the grey of her closely-shaven beard under her skin and her Adam's apple moving up and down. She was singing, "*He can't cut the mustard any more*" or something like that.

"You're just saying it for my sake."

"I was a teenager. There was this classmate, exceedingly smart, very handsome. We were good friends. Close your mouth." He took a sip of his cognac, looking at me sideways. "I've never told anyone. This is the night our secrets come crawling out." He made me pick up my glass of Grand Marnier and we made them clink.

The singers finished their song and left the scene to absent-minded applause. Aydın asked for a second drink. The disc jockey played a Bossa Nova and couples rose to dance. We watched them absentmindedly for a while; then he asked me. I told him I wasn't any good at it, but he insisted and led me toward the dancing couples, his hand lightly holding my waist all the way there, and we started swaying gently to the music. One hand was on my waist, the other holding my hand close to his chest. I felt awkward, keeping my body stiffly apart. As the song progressed, the distance melted away. Nobody else seemed to care what went on between us. I let go of my shyness or whatever it was that kept my body rigid and soon we were twirling a little. My chest was pressed to his, the smell of his aftershave in my nostrils. The only other time I had him so close was at the cemetery, during my father's burial. His gold wedding band glimmered on his slender finger. He caught me looking at it. We were not ourselves, not our familiar selves at any rate. They were playing an American song that went, "*In dreams, I walk with you.*" In dreams, everything is possible and bittersweet. In dreams, the dead hold you and your boss is your lover. His sex was hard, pressed to mine underneath our layers of clothing. Desire was spreading into my thighs, making them ache. His cheek touched my temple, his hand moved down my back.

"Promise me there will be no consequences when we return." It came out of my throat in a subdued croak.

"I promise you I'm not thinking of our return." He bent toward my ear, whispering. "Shall we leave?"

"Not yet." I imagined the cool air outside slapping our faces, instantly dislocating this exquisite turmoil and leaving behind the grotesque shell of an unrealized dream, something painfully vulgar, a boss and his secretary in a Düsseldorf hotel room if he so much as opened his mouth to call for a taxi.

We danced glued together for another song his breath making the hair on my neck rise. Lust was going up and down my throat like heartburn. I wanted out, I wanted in. I was in that state of utter paradox, every second split within itself, polarized between wanting and wanting not to. He caressed my back and wanting was at the essence of it, I realized, even wanting not to was wanting after all. Wanting him, wanting not to make love to him, wanting not to let him go, wanting not to be alone, wanting not to see him naked, wanting to see his sex, wanting not to awaken to any other kind of life that had no trace of this man who for once, exceptionally in Düsseldorf would give me the love, his love, that I craved all those years. Wanting not to awaken. Wanting the moment, split as it came.

He ordered another drink for both of us. We sat very close, our thighs pressed together. "May I kiss you?" His voice was hoarse.

"No." I pulled myself away.

He did not insist. He hung his head down, looking at the floor and took a few sips of his drink, nursing the glass in his hands, distracted. Wanting, wanting not to. I regretted the word as soon as it had come out of my mouth. I had not wanted to lose control; my countenance, my painfully earned ... something.... What? Acceptance? By whom? By those who decided what mattered and what didn't, who passed and who failed, who could speak and who couldn't, what could be said and what couldn't be mentioned.

"If you kiss me," my body trembled as I spoke, "if you do, it will never be the same between us again. We won't remain friends. I will suffer so much more every time I have to wrap presents for your wife and mistress, every time I have to speak to them. I can't bear to suffer more. And you will suffer too, every time you talk on the phone with a woman, with a new lover and you know I may be around. You will hide, you will become false with me, and see me as a burden to carry like the others, and I cannot bear that."

His lips twisted into a half crescent of a smile, "I'm afraid it is already too late. Maybe we're already better friends, Mehtap. You know what there is to know about my petty life, my stupid habits and lies. I'll never make any promises I cannot keep."

We continued sitting there immobile, silently watching dancing couples swaying under the dim smoky lights.

"I knew I was an in-between guy for Nuray," he started after some thought. "Perhaps I was someone she picked up to spite another who broke her heart. I knew she would leave me, but not so suddenly. She just disappeared one day...."

"Yes, she did. Maybe one day, I will run into her on the street. I run into all sorts of people, why not her? And perhaps I will meet this child who has my name."

My heart was thumping in my left hand sitting on my lap; I felt the pressure and the rhythm of it and thought it peculiar. My heart in my hand, beating. We were sitting like sphinxes, facing the dance floor, not looking at each other, mouthing some words as the music changed and got louder, the couples pulled apart gyrating until the entire dance floor was covered by rubber men twisting this way and that, one's face drawn into a frozen rictus, his partner's in a pout with eyes closed. I envied their rubber limbs and freedom, sitting there heavily, my guts trapped in a corset, my breasts in a bra that I now realized was one size too small, my toes glued together in the narrow shoes. Aydın was saying something. I leaned over to hear his words.

"Do you think the child is mine?"

I pulled back, unable to answer.

By unspoken accord we both rose to leave. Cold air hit my face, the way I expected it would, but there was no magic left to slap away. We were both reflecting on Aydın's possible child with Nuray. I wondered if I would be able to tell by looking at her features. He said, "I wonder if she looks like me." The streetlight was hitting the top of his head casting long green shadows that deepened the creases around his nose, aging him as he stood there in the cold.

"Well," I said reluctant to leave the reflective mood I had sunk into, "I suppose we should walk back to our hotel now."

We did so quietly, along the Rhine once again, surrounded by the city's peculiar night drone. A couple passed us engaged in a heated debate. I was glad there was water nearby. The noises of a city that is near water are softer, it seems to me. You hear the barely audible lick of water on stone. Perhaps it is the smell or the humidity in the air that touches your skin. I don't know. Something familiar from Izmir in a foreign land. I wondered how Kerime felt day after day being so far from home. I suppose I will find out soon enough. He took my arm and pulled me closer, hinting we could shut out the others, for one night. We walked, our breaths forming miniature clouds ahead of us and I leaned my head on his shoulder. He leaned his head as well, placing his arm around me in a protective gesture. I was nauseous with desire. I knew if I turned my face toward him he would kiss me. I could already anticipate the wet softness of his lips touching mine. I turned my face, my legs shaking.

I have no idea why I let it happen. I had every intention not to, in my mind. Not from a sense of propriety, no—maybe from fear of self-destruction. That this kiss, this touch I had craved for so long was going to be the end of me, was going to bring the world as I knew it crashing down, like some immense and heavy mirror embedding shards of glass into my eyes and face and limbs, or a giant wave filling my orifices with its salty mass as it carried my helpless body into the depths of an ocean. Desire feels like a death wish with the wanting, wanting not to that keeps playing out its loop. We struggled through the door of his room, the boxers and slip and the torn nylons falling like pieces of discarded skin. My skin—my skin before him. I saw his sex for the first time in that struggle of semi-darkness, that ferocious thing, erect and blind and seeking. Perhaps we were growling. His hands and fingers and teeth. I pulled his hair hard, gasping in pain, both of us there on the floor, not having even made it to bed.

I'll be boarding the train in fifteen minutes and so must stop writing.

I AM IN IZMIR. It has been almost two weeks now. Kerime's life was not at all as I imagined. She lives in a small, bare apartment, two rooms separated by a small kitchen and a bathroom in the shape of a long corridor. Small cast iron coal stoves, one per room, into which she expertly shoves pieces of coal every evening to heat up the place. I felt miserably cold all the time. One night I even slept with my socks and a wool hat on. She must have gotten used to it; didn't seem to appreciate how unhappy and clenched my teeth were in their efforts to stop from chattering. She doesn't have a boyfriend, in fact she tells me she has separated from him. She keeps two jobs, one cleaning offices at night and one as a shopkeeper by day. Kerime looks worn out to me. I tried to convince her to come back and live in Izmir. I offered to put her up in my house, with all the space I have, and told her I could arrange for her to have a decent job, right away. She will not return, she says; likes her life in Germany. Perhaps it is a matter of pride, or I simply don't understand the sense of freedom she gets from living there. "No one cares what I do, no one watches me. I belong to myself. Can you say that about your life? If you weren't living in the house your parents left you, do you think you could have rented an apartment as a single woman? No way. Do you think you can come and go with a man if you so wish? The neighbours will spit on you, and call the police to arrest you for running a brothel from your house."

"But Kerime, you don't have a lover now. You're wearing yourself out with two jobs. Where's your pleasure? Do you have friends?"

She said she did—some German girls and another Turkish one from Elazığ, from her office-cleaning job. "Well, invite them and let's have a party. I will prepare everything. Just leave it to me. It's the least I can do to thank you," I said.

She agreed somewhat reluctantly. I went to the supermarket down the street and bought food to make a Turkish feast with mézé[23] and everything from home she would be missing; dolmas, eggplant salad, piyaz,[24] green beans in olive oil, the works. I even found rakı and kaşar cheese. Her friends trickled in one by one. Two of the girls didn't speak anything else but German, so we spent a lot of time bobbing heads and smiling as we gingerly ate our mézés and took small sips of our rakı. The girl from Elazığ wasn't very talkative either, and when she did talk, you could almost smell the musty scent of nostalgia wrapped around her words. Maybe it wasn't even the words, maybe just her body language; shoulders hunched forward as if wanting to make herself disappear by some act of prestidigitation and awaken elsewhere.

---

[23]mézé: appetizers
[24]piyaz: Turkish salad made with dry beans and onions

I don't know; perhaps that is how she always was. There was one friend, her name was Betta and she lived across the hall from Kerime's apartment; vivacious and very pretty with long blonde hair and strong thighs in tight blue jeans. She spoke English, so we were at least able to converse. Apparently, she and some of her friends from university had hitchhiked through Greece and Turkey in 1963 or thereabouts, and they bought horses somewhere near Kars on which they rode all the way to Afghanistan. It sounded incredible to me, like a fairy tale. She was working as a criminal lawyer now for legal aid, defending petty thieves who couldn't afford to pay lawyers. Betta seemed to like the taste of rakı which she kept calling ouzo, and took large gulps, eager to finish her glass to start another, I suspected. I was worried she'd turn out to be one of those drunks who plugged the bathroom sink at parties, at first; but soon enough it became apparent she could hold her alcohol well despite her slight frame. I asked her if she went on that incredible trip with a boyfriend. She got close to me, winked "I'm a lesbian, dear," and gave me a toothy smile. It was all quite surreal, the selection of friends Kerime had gathered over the years, and this party where I only understood ten percent of what was being said at any given time.

When everyone left, Kerime and I continued talking as we washed the plates and put the food away. She opened up to me about a man named Franz she was with until a few months ago. They had been together for some time; she was half-expecting a proposal which she dreaded at the same time, she told me, because of her family back home. They would be absolutely against it, what with his being a foreigner and all that. The only reason they didn't mind her living in Germany by herself was because she was sending money back home. "Anyway," she sighed, "it is no longer a problem."

"Why did you break up?"

"His family didn't like me, being Moslem and Turkish and all that. They kept putting pressure on him to leave me. I suppose he found it easier to let me go than put up with their fuss. Christmas gatherings were a nightmare I won't miss."

She sounded matter of fact. This was the reason her apartment looked so bare. He had moved out recently and I felt all the more responsible to make her life more festive while I stayed there.

Still, despite her diminutive quarters and hard life, I could also begin to see how she had succeeded as a woman in ways many of us fail back home, which is to have an independent life and by that I don't mean economically—I am independent and successful; but socially, I mean she is free to define herself as she pleases, without the constant worry of how she will be judged by others. It is a blessing to live in an environment where you don't feel shackled by tradition. Mind you, it is perhaps not the environment itself, which has its own particular traditions, but the fact that you don't belong to them. There is another side to this, Kerime reminds me, lest I go back with a romantic notion of her life in Europe. "There are shackles here as well; every time I search for a job, or open my mouth to speak, I'm not a social equal to someone born here. I am die Gastarbeiterin."[25]

I enjoyed my time with Kerime. She has no artifice, no self-deceptions. We wept profusely at the airport thinking we may never see each other again. Kerime, my very best of friends from high school. I told her about my time in Düsseldorf. Only that. Only because she knows no one in my social circle and is open-minded. I couldn't tell her about Nuray. I suppose I could have told Betta, if I had spent more time with her.

IT'S HIS BIRTHDAY SOON. We have returned to our usual routine. What happened in Düsseldorf is locked up in that hotel room, forever, and in this notebook which no one else will ever read. He looks at me with tenderness in his eyes. His hand may linger on mine when I give him a letter or a folder. He kisses my lips

---

[25] die Gastarbeiterin: guest worker

lightly when I take my leave at the end of the day if no one else is around at the office. And he has offered to drive me home, something he has never done before, even on a rainy day when I used to wait at the bus stop. He would honk the car and wave without stopping. So things have changed a little after all. I accepted the offer to be driven home, of course. How many chances would I get to be alone with him again?

He asked me how I was and how I felt, on the way, concerned for my well-being after Düsseldorf. I told him I was fine and not to worry.

"I'm not lingering, if that's what you're worried about. We stole one night from fate. I have no further expectations."

He wished to see more vulnerability, I realized afterwards. Perhaps he had hoped for an extended affair that involved work trips together so we could spend time as lovers and I could be his Number Three. Flighty Aydın, who could never resist the thrill of an entanglement, an escape, a chase! As soon as he secured Number Three, he would be ready to move on to a fourth, or go back to his favourite nightclubs in search of amusement.

He nodded when I told him I was fine. We drove the rest of the way in silence. He turned up the volume of the classical music playing on his radio. A feeling of peaceful well-being came over me. Music, driving through Mithat Paşa Avenue to get to my house, inhaling his cologne, occasional glances that brought a flock of memories from Düsseldorf.... I had him near me. I had made love with the man I had pined for all those years. I was not in need of repetitions.

"Düsseldorf will always be my one of my favourite cities in the world, now. Not that I know many...." I smiled after he stopped the car to let me off. I was thinking of Istanbul. The other one. He caressed my left hand and placed a kiss on top of it as I opened the car door. He pulled me back slightly so I wouldn't leave and said, "Can you imagine favouring other cities in the future?"

"Goodbye Aydın, I'll see you tomorrow," I managed and left the car quickly. Sure I could imagine favouring other cities, and being far from this narrow world of ours, and away from everyone else. Indeed, I could imagine this so clearly! What I couldn't imagine was being left behind. Becoming one of his discarded conquests. *You must leave him before he leaves you*, I repeated to myself going up the stairs of my street. *You must, while you're still in control.*

Naturally I want the opposite: to travel with him, with hopes that this affair may turn out differently than all his others, since I am a different kind of woman, one to whom he relates on a deeper level—so he said. Why not take a chance? What have I got to lose now that I haven't already? What am I afraid of? Solitude? Heartache? I know how that voracious worm eats its way through the heart, all its bites and squeezes, the breathlessness that precedes sobs, the blank stares fixed upon the ceiling when the rest of the world sleeps. Nuray has taught me all this. So why not take a few more trips, feel cozy and pampered a little before I'm taught the same lesson again? Why not?

It is six in the morning. The fragrance of jasmine rises from the neighbour's yard, tickling my nose into a sneeze as I write these words in the *cumba* sipping my tea. A tiny, lone rowboat is zigzagging up and down in the distance, lifted and crashed by tall, frothy waves. I wonder what has compelled its owner to go out on such a windy day. Perhaps he too had a sleepless night enduring a futile battle between pride and desire. Perhaps he too knows such battles won't yield victories. Nuray's departure has gutted me. Aydın's would diminish me, and I refuse to be so reduced. Soon the doves will start cooing in the neighbouring trees, the sun will climb a little higher losing its reddish glow. There's the jasmine scent again. I should get dressed for work.

Notebook II. The Cretans

*U*PON THEIR ARRIVAL FROM CRETE, *when Maria unpacked their suitcases and bags in the bedroom given to them by Inez, she had chosen not to remove the jewellery from the cloth belts into which they had been sewn, for safety. Instead, she had stuffed the two belts into a cloth sack which contained some lace doilies and fine tablecloths that her mother had given her as family heirlooms. The pieces remained forgotten in that cloth sack for some time, until the day she found out she was pregnant. She wanted to buy the finest of everything for her child; especially the carriage that she had spotted in the window of a shop where only imported European goods were sold. It had large wheels that imitated elegant horse drawn carriages. She had walked past it a few times, lingering in front of the window, and taken Mehmet for walks that deliberately led there, so she could tell him she wanted this and nothing less for their soon-to-be first-born. Some of the jewellery would pay for this, but she had to convince Mehmet it was a good buy. "It will last a very long time and we can reuse it for all the others to follow this one." The sound of that declaration pleased him; it meant they would raise many children and become rooted here. He told her to use the jewellery as she saw fit.*

As soon as she arrived home, Maria unbundled the heavy cloth belts. First hers, with the gold chains and crosses, the medallions depicting Virgin Mary and her mother's small childhood rings with blue stones, all remnants of an older, opulent lifestyle to which Maria had never had any access. There was, of course, the large embossed wristband of a bracelet depicting the story of the Minotaur that would fetch a handsome sum due to its weight and artisanship. She laid them side by side on the bed and went to unstitch Mehmet's belt. There were multiple narrow gold bracelets, she counted a dozen, and gold earrings with blue stones encrusted in them. There was also the very same Minotaur wristband. When she uncovered the identical bracelet, her chest constricted. How was it possible that two unrelated women from such different backgrounds owned the very same bracelet?

She sat down, turning them around one by one as if doing so would reveal the answer to such a mystery. It could have been a coincidence, she reasoned. Two women making the same purchase at the same jewellery store, very possible.... Still, she pursued the thought further: that could have been the case for Mehmet's mother; they were wealthy. But her own had been reduced to poverty in adolescence. She could have never purchased it. Inside the bracelet was the engraved karat. Beside it she read the letter "M" and the year 1906. The two women got the bracelets in 1906, the year when she and Mehmet were born. The letter "M," she realized was for Mehmet the Great—her husband's father.

Mehmet the Great must have been her father too—the secret lover whose identity her mother had kept a mystery. It made sense now. In her complete ignorance, she had married her own brother and was having his child. She repeated this to herself trying to grasp the full import of her words, hands shaking uncontrollably.

Unsure of what she should do with such a thought, she rushed to Mehmet's atelier. He was in the midst of putting together a large dresser and asked her to sit down, have some tea. Her pale face and the fingers that kept wringing the purse handles alerted him. "Why are you so pale? Are you in pain? The baby?" He stood arms akimbo, his forehead in a frown.

"I have to talk to you," she whispered, "not here. Finish what you're doing, we'll go outside."

"I can't finish anything with you in such a state." He called the young apprentice to his side, giving him precise instructions before leading his wife out the door.

"Our mothers had the same bracelet," she whispered.

"So?"

"Exactly the same."

"What is your point?"

"They are both engraved with an 'M' and the year 1906. We were both born that year. 'M' is for Mehmet. You see?"

She waited for his thoughts to lead to the same place. He wasn't saying anything.

"Two women from the same village who didn't know each other much," she continued. "One was rich one was poor. They both got the same bracelet. Your mother cursed your father for not being there when you were born. Do you know why he wasn't with your mother? Because he was probably with mine! My mother was the *putana* your mother cursed with her last breath. You see? Mehmet the Great and my mother…. That makes us brother and sister, Mehmet. That makes us…" her voice trailed off.

Mehmet stood silently, hands still planted on his hips, head down, eyes focused on the pavement as if looking for a lost object.

"What are we going to do now?" Maria's voice was barely audible. Her lips were trembling; soon the tears would flow.

"Shh. Not in front of all those people and my work. For heavens' sake don't cry." He lifted his shoulders. "You'll go and sell some of that jewellery to buy the carriage. I will go back in and finish the dresser. We'll talk when I get home."

"Do you think something will be wrong with it?"

No." He said with finality. "Nothing's wrong with it. Stop fretting. We're both healthy, why should it be otherwise? Look, we didn't have a clue. How can it be a sin if you don't know?" He nodded encouragingly and reached over to pat her on the back. It was all the affection he could show, in front of the shop, on the street. "It will be all right."

She nodded, unconvinced, and walked away. Mehmet waited for her to put enough distance between them and uttered a curse. He lit a cigarette and leaned his arm on the stucco wall of the building, still looking down at the pavement. He took a couple of quick drags and threw the entire cigarette down squeezing it hard with his foot, uttering another curse. The sidewalk was moving from under his feet, trees and pedestrians swinging this way and that with the entire street rocking like the deck of a ship caught in a storm, daylight dimming around him. He crouched on the pavement wanting to retch. Why? His stomach brought up a taste of bile. He spat and rose slowly, holding on to the wall, unable to stop the world from rocking all around him. He crouched back down, to wait it out. The apprentice was looking at him from the doorway when he looked up.

"Are you ill, brother?"

"No. Felt a bit light-headed. Get back in. I will join you in a bit. Go on!"

He went back to work his face chalky and his stomach unsettled. His existence which had thereto been filled with hope and anticipation was suddenly spiralling into a kind of vertiginous descent that could only end in a catastrophe. His entire being was sucked into this frantic vortex. He was married to his own sister and was about to become a father-uncle. He cursed the bracelets, the day his father chose them, and his oversexed father's shenanigans. No sooner had he uttered these curses that he repented and apologized to Mehmet's memory for injuring it. But he wasn't entirely finished, letting out a few more involuntary blasphemies as he went back to working on the dresser. There was no forgiving his father, or her mother, especially her mother, for keeping their relationship a secret. Why did she not realize, in a small village such as theirs, that a tragedy of this sort was bound to occur?

"We shall never speak of this again," he said that night when he returned home drunk. "We will never tell the child or anyone else. It will get buried with us. What difference would it make to this baby, anyway, living so far away from our village in Crete? None! So we will just never mention it again." He removed his shoes and let them fall by the side of the bed with a thud and lay with his clothes on, unable to focus his thoughts.

"You're drunk!" Maria observed with disdain. "I was crying my eyes out here, waiting for you, but you went and got drunk. This was the best you could come up with? Hear this: You won't ever get to decide what I tell or not tell my daughter! Now, go to sleep."

"How do you know it's a girl?"

She shrugged and turned her back to him.

He fell into a deep, dreamless slumber occasionally disturbed by Maria's pushes. "Shh. You're snoring! Stop it!"

When he awoke the next day she had already gotten out of bed and was downstairs in the kitchen with Inez. She stiffened and turned her face away when he tried to kiss her cheek as he was leaving for work. He was not going to be forgiven for his misstep for a long time to come. "So be it," he thought, indignation rising within him. "I'll give it right back to her."

Miserable days of silence ensued. They would not utter a single word to each other directly, using Inez as an intermediary for the most trivial observations until the woman rebelled. "Leave me out of your childish games. I have more important things to do than run silly messages back and forth! The child will have a bitter disposition because of your stubbornness."

APOLOGIES TOOK LONG TO ARRIVE, but they did, somewhat tangentially; he bought her a hat, she gave him a reluctant smile. He carried the crib he had made at the atelier all the way home and placed it in their bedroom. Maria decorated it with sheets and cushions she had painstakingly embroidered. They stood side by side imagining their child in it. He promised he wouldn't get drunk again. She reminded him they were in this mess because of their father's boozing. He wasn't so sure drinking was to blame, but he did not challenge her opinion. Mehmet the Great had a gargantuan appetite for life, like Zeus or

Dionysius who indulged in their pleasures carelessly leaving mere mortals the task of toiling in their sloppy wake, struggling to right those wrongs that threatened to destroy their trivial lives. Except that his father—their father—was no Aegean deity. There were no altars to his name. His legacy was a secret that had to be suffered in silence, an awful darkness that neither he nor Maria could endure to visit in their thoughts.

As the pregnancy progressed they found a way to dull the shock of their discovery by keeping busy and avoiding the subject. Maria thought Mehmet was right in his drunken assessment; they could simply take this to their grave. They would not have more children, certainly. And being half-brother and sister wasn't as awful as being full siblings in terms of heredity, she consoled herself. She had banished the thought of ever making love again, at first. But that thought also dimmed in importance with the passage of time; they had never had an inkling of any other connection when they fell in love, how could they simply erase all their history together? It was absurd. The nine months of gestation gave them time to absorb this new reality and discard in it what stood in their way. Maria continued to speak of Mehmet the Great as her husband's father; she could not bring herself to use the possessive pronoun "our" without an ominous sense that this word alone had the power to destroy her life.

Notebook III. Autobiography

It WAS A SUNDAY AFTERNOON. Bored at home, I decided to go to Konak, take the ferry across to Karşıyaka for a leisurely walk along the quay there. Strolling along the water on that side of the city always lifted my spirits when I was younger, and I hoped it would have the same effect that Sunday. Aside from boredom, which usually found me on Sunday mornings right after breakfast as if by appointment, there was also that hollow feeling of loneliness I was trying to dispel. The same sparrows that chirped daily by my bedroom window when I awakened, for some reason, on a Sunday morning, reminded me of all the absentees once present in the house. My grandmother Inez, my parents, Nuray… and Aydın, of course, who entered my thoughts like a wily thief able to unlock every door, open every window to steal the little bit of peace I managed to save. I opened my eyes and there he was with his aftershave in my nostrils, his stubble on my skin and his lips upon mine driving daggers through my heart. All my ghosts. I had to get away.

An hour later, I was taking a stroll in the sun, beside the wall separating the sea from the sidewalk, admiring the beautiful houses and mansions on the other side of the street anticipating my favourite one, with the rose garden in front and the statues rising among the flowerbeds, marble women in contrapposto covered in drapes, and naked youths with vine leaves covering their sex looking over chiselled shrubbery. I was walking with my head turned to the side, so that I would not miss that vision and bumped into a man. I apologized and looked ahead to make sure there were no other oncoming pedestrians, when I noticed, a few dozen metres away, the back of a woman walking between a tall man and a girl of about three who was skipping once in a while and took a few running steps to keep up with her parents. The three of them were walking ahead of me. My heart skipped when I recognized the woman's silhouette, from behind. That walk, those wide hipbones moving as though they were trying to overturn something with their swing, the fine calves that reminded me of Arabian horses in flight. Then she swung her curls and laughed and I knew for sure. I was losing my breath just standing there, whispering "Nuray, oh my God…." I crossed the street and started running as fast as I could on the other sidewalk, hoping the flow of traffic would block me somehow. I ran and ran until I could no more. I was a good five hundred metres ahead. I waited to catch my breath and dabbed the sweat on my forehead hoping to look composed, debonair, took a deep breath then crossed again so I would be walking toward them. I took a diagonal path thinking it would seem more nonchalant and went straight to the crumbling wall by the sea pretending to look at the water, to be doing something that could seem oblivious. Gazing at the sea, then the horizon, I stood there watching the ferry making its way toward Alsancak followed by a small cloud of seagulls at its tail, the shrill squawks coming toward the land in broken echoes. That day in Moda, standing in our hotel room beside the tulle curtains, facing the Sea of Marmara. The seagulls brought it back. That day when the sun and the sea conspired in another geography, another seaside to set me free. My cheeks were ablaze. After gazing at the water for what I felt was a sufficient lapse of time, I turned toward them to continue my leisurely stroll. We were less than a few paces from each other. She looked straight into my eyes. A wave was building up in my chest. She didn't smile or acknowledge me in any other way. I stood there frozen and they passed me by. She took her husband's arm as they did and the little girl turned back, to size me up, having noticed that I had stopped moving. I had to act fast. I walked after them, "Nuray?"

They stopped. She let go of his arm and turned towards me. "Yes," she said looking at me politely. Her eyes were shining with anticipation, a tinge of mockery.

"Mehtap. From work. Remember?"

"Oh! My goodness! Mehtap how have you been?" She opened her arms and rushed toward me for a hug. When her arms enveloped my waist, the joy of reaching home, of finally arriving at the place of such unbearable longing rose into my throat. I squeezed my eyes shut to prevent tears and held her tightly in my arms. The tickle of her black curls, the familiar smell of her neck. She knew. Her hand caressed my back before pushing me away slightly. A glimmer of tears caught in the long eyelashes was dabbed quickly with her manicured fingertip. "What a long time it has been, my friend! And to say we almost walked past each other. Such absent-mindedness! This is Mehtap, an old friend from work," she turned to her husband with a bright smile. He reached over to shake my hand. Tallish fellow, hollow cheeks, dark eyes.

"Enchanted," I murmured and turned to the little girl. "And who would this be?" I asked with a smile.

"My daughter, Mehtap," she put her hand on the girl's shoulder. "Say hello to Auntie Mehtap." She pushed her a little toward me. I crouched down so the girl could look me in the eyes.

"Merhaba Mehtap Teyze," she grinned showing tiny white teeth. Some of her hair was pulled back on top into a small ponytail, the rest in soft brown curls around her neck. "How come she never comes to our house?" she asked her mother.

Nuray smiled. "We lost touch. But she will be coming over now that we have met again, I hope…." She opened her purse and took out a card. "Please do call," she said, "you must come over for tea. We live not far from here at all." She waved vaguely ahead, with her hand.

"Oh, so you live in Karşıyaka, now? How lovely," I nodded and opened my clutch to insert the card in its inner pocket. "I shall certainly call on you one of these Sundays. So glad to see you again. Goodbye." I smiled at all three and waved at the little girl, then turned my back and walked away. I overheard her asking, "How come her name is Mehtap, too?" The father said something, but I had been walking too fast to catch it.

As soon as I had put enough distance between us I looked for a place to sit. The scenery was moving upside down, my ears filled with persistent ringing. I slumped on a bench with my head bent down for a long time. An old lady holding a shopping bag and a cane approached me asking if I needed help. "Just got a little dizzy … I'll be fine," I replied to her unconvinced nod. As she walked slowly away turning back once in a while to check on me, I sat there, crumpled, trying to still my racing heart, the madness in my head with thoughts jumping here and there incoherently. What was her husband's name? I couldn't remember. How could I ever visit her without fainting, or dying of a weakened heart, or bursting into sobs? The child didn't look like anyone in particular. Maybe not Aydın's. On the other hand, maybe not this fellow's either. She didn't even look much like Nuray, except for the curls. Nuray hadn't changed much. Did she look better? Happier? Did she miss me too? I saw the tear she wiped away quickly. Did the fellow wonder why? How could she do this to me? How could she leave me and go on to be happy with a man, have a child, when she said she didn't like men. Perhaps, I thought, she had said this to make me feel at ease. Perhaps she was like a hungry octopus. Tentacles moving here and there to grab any prey passing by. An oversexed Aphrodite. After all those years she reappeared to remind me those wounds were still bleeding and nothing had healed. I was as devastated—no, more devastated—than the day she had slammed the door and left.

She had replaced me with a child. She had become a housewife. How could that woman be a housewife? The towels everywhere, the military marches splashing in the bathtub, underwear on the floor.... How did that gaunt man take it? As I got up from the bench, I dared imagine she would leave him to come live with me, with her child, now that she saw me again, I dared imagine she realized how unbearably much she had missed me in her life and was going to come to me after slamming the door on him.

By the time I got on the ferry, the afternoon sun had already paled, heavily falling westward on its sinking path into the sea. She would not leave her husband. She would never do that to her child. The ferry was moving faster toward the setting sun as if to reach it before falling, or to fall with it yonder and I gazed absent-mindedly at the horizon where everything disappeared under an oppressively cloudless sky thinking of a world before Galileo where such thoughts must have led desperate sailors to set course toward the ends of the earth, wishing to fall off and be gone.

I got off the ferry and took a dolmuş[25] that left me not far from the stairs going up my street. The gevrek boy was sitting beside his empty platter, smoking a cigarette. "Iyi akşamlar hanım teyze,"[26] he smiled proudly blowing his smoke. I got near him, snatched the cigarette off his lips, threw it down and gave it a violent stomping with my shoe. "What a pity to see you here, filling your lungs with such poison! When will you go to school, huh? You will become a proper man by hitting the books, not by standing in street corners smoking these poisonous sticks. You're so proud but you look pitiful." I went on, couldn't stop myself. "Don't ever let me see you smoking again!" As if he were my son. "Don't you have a mother to go home to?"

He barely whispered, "No, Auntie. She's dead."

---

[23]dolmuş: shared taxi
[24]"Iyi akşamlar hanım teyze": "Good evening, madame auntie"

And I couldn't take it anymore. I started weeping and fumbling in my clutch for a handkerchief. My shoulders were shaking and the boy, whom I could barely see from the curtain of tears, reached and touched my shoulder saying, "I'm sorry Auntie, don't be so sad. I promise I won't smoke again. Don't cry." All this sympathy made matters worse until I blew my nose and was done with it.

"Where is your dad, then?"

"Working," he said. "He starts in the afternoon and comes home the next morning."

"Have you had anything to eat, yet?"

"I finished the last gevrek on the platter."

"Come, you'll have dinner with me."

"My dad says I'm not to follow strangers."

"You sit at my doorstep and I'll bring dinner out to you then. You see me every day and sell me gevreks, I'm not such a stranger, am I?"

He shrugged and sat on my doorstep. I kept the door open as I walked in, so he wouldn't feel alone and went straight to the kitchen, put on my apron and fried some eggs with lots of butter, à la Nuray. The boy walked in after a while, leaving the street door open, standing in the hallway observing my house. "Come in and close the door then, get us some plates." I pointed at the dishes in the cabinet.

"Where is the other lady who used to live here too?"

"She got married and had a little girl."

"She was nice."

I placed the eggs in the plates, cut slices of fresh bread and tomatoes and filled our glasses with lemonade I had made the day before.

"Sit down and eat. What's your name?"

"Emin."

He was sponging the soft egg yolk with the bread and eating with his head dangerously close to the plate, smacking his lips.

I almost told him to straighten his back, but bit my tongue. There was no need to make him feel smaller, after the cigarette incident. I noticed the shadow over his mouth. I waited until he had cleared his plate and asked, "So, how old are you now? Fourteen?"

"Something like that," he nodded.

"Have you ever gone to school?"

He clucked his tongue and shook his head backward to mean "no."

"Can you read and write?"

"A bit."

"Listen, when you're done selling your gevreks, you're welcome to come here and have supper with me. I will teach you to read and write, a little bit every day, if you wish. Then you go home. If you need a bus ticket, I'll give you that too."

"Why?" he asked, suspicious.

"Because I don't want you to be selling gevreks when you grow up. I've told you this before." He was watching me without blinking. "Besides, no boy your age should be in the streets smoking cigarettes at this hour. You're inviting bad things to happen to you, don't you know?"

He looked down. "I'll pass by when I can."

I gave him a bus ticket as he was leaving and admonished him to go straight home. He said: "No need to repeat, teyze. I'm not stupid."

"Hmm!" I shook my head, "we'll see about that."

He put the empty wooden platter on his head and ran down the stairs, then was gone.

It got quiet in the house. I had to iron my pants for work the next morning. I hoped the boy would come often, keep me busy, and postpone this feeling of despair that squeezed my chest as twilight fell. I opened the ironing board slowly thinking of my chance encounter with Nuray, remembering what I'd told Aydın in Düsseldorf. "I run into all sorts of people, why not her?"

Perhaps I had conjured her with my wish. Or she had pulled me to her, the way the moon pulls our blood every month. Perhaps, I thought, she needed me, and crawled unseen through my dreams to plant this thought of a stroll in Karşıyaka. She cannot stand being far from me any longer. I almost burnt a hole in the trousers thinking about Nuray's mysterious existence and the ever-growing hope that at the edge of her married life was a narrow bench with my name on it, a place from which I could live vicariously those warm family moments, like a shy relative who comes laden with presents in return for some inclusion, a sense of belonging in those festive weekend rituals. I was beginning to feel happy. Running into them was a hopeful thing and all I needed to do was find the courage to make that phone call, hold it all together as I crossed the threshold into their house, then, keep it together until the end. Smile. Bring the child some treats. Auntie Mehtap. That's it.

When I called, weeks later, the conversation kept sputtering at the brink of premature conclusion, like those motorized dinghies whose pulled string fails to rev the engine, yet lasted too long. I was not myself in it. I couldn't find the doorway. There were too many "So, how are you and what have you been up to?"—a ludicrous effort to make everything seem unruffled as if we truly were some distant friends from work who had run into each other on the street and made an un-meant promise to call sometime, until my jaw, locked up in a fake smile, made my face hurt and I decided to say goodbye, feeling exposed for having mistaken her obviously fake invitation for an earnest one.

She said, "Mehtap, I meant it…"

"You meant what?"

"That I want you to come over and be part of our lives."

"It will be awkward. Thank you, but I don't think I can."

"If I can invite you, surely you can come too," she replied with irritation.

"There is no comparison between your invitation and my

acceptance, Nuray. You slammed the door on me, and left me without news for years; erased me from your life entirely. Got married, had a child, for goodness sake and not even a call.... You knew where to find me. Why didn't you? Then, we run into each other and you give me that 'come see us sometime' bullshit. You compare that silly invitation to my picking up the phone, swallowing my pride and fear, and speaking nonsense for almost an hour now, in the hope of ... so you can tell me that my acceptance equals your invitation? How dare you?"

I slammed the phone down so hard the table shook. Finally, I was slamming something. I was out of breath, my chest heaving up and down. The phone rang. I let it. I counted twelve rings. The ringing of a phone you purposely fail to pick up is shriller, more accusatory, and the silences in between are louder and angrier than the ring itself. Five minutes or so later, it started ringing again. I picked up and listened. She was weeping. I decided to visit the following weekend.

The doorbell. *Ding dong.* The threshold. Smiles. The little girl in a pink summer dress and white sandals. The gaunt man who bent his head not to hit the doorway. Nuray, all black curls and red lipstick and hips and voluptuousness in a brown summer dress, like some chocolate cake, like some soft, sweet edible thing that feels moist and spongy to the palate. How I missed her beauty. We hugged and it lasted too long perhaps. I was not going to worry about the gaunt man. His name was Ekrem. He helped his wife bring the cookies and tea cups to the coffee table while we chatted about this and that. The daughter was following him around the whole time, holding on to his leg. "So how did you two meet?" I asked once she had poured the tea into the delicate cups and they both sat down. My voice was sweet like sticky candy in my mouth. I wasn't good at faking admiration. When he smiled, I caught a glimmer of irony, something mysteriously clever in his eyes and thought I understood her attraction to him.

"I'll let Nuray tell you. She's so much better at it."

Ekrem finished his tea in one gulp to be done with it. It was clear the afternoon tea ritual had been imposed on him and he had been told to behave for the sake of the spinster friend. He rose from the sofa saying he was taking Mehtap for her afternoon walk. As soon as they left, we sat down and Nuray reached over to hold my hand from her armchair. We sat holding hands quietly as the apartment took on a strange aspect and the surrounding objects became unfamiliar. I shuddered. This was the space she lived in day after day while I sat in the sunlit extension of my house in Karataş. That was the buffet in which she kept her dishes, and the corridor leading to the bedrooms that echoed with her footsteps. There was the picture of her and her brother that used to decorate my bookcase, on the coffee table. A rhododendron in a copper pot. Hand-woven Bergama carpets. I looked at her hand as if some explanation would be released from it into my aching chest. I tried to occupy my mind with the ferry schedule for my return, so I wouldn't weep, not there.

"I'm sorry," she said caressing my arm gently. "I'm very sorry."

"Yes.... Me too. All this time, I went over everything, in detail, trying to find out what it was that I had done to make you leave."

"I got restless."

"I thought you were punishing me for saying I would leave you if Aydın loved me back. After that you went and had an affair with him. It was to spite me, wasn't it? To show me you could seduce him. To show me he would never love me back. It was ruthless, what you did. I don't even know why I'm here now. I should have just walked on. If I didn't call out your name, would you have walked on, pretending not to recognize me?"

"I don't know. I've missed you, Mehtap. You'll never know how much."

"Do you love him?"

"He is a good man."

"Is the child his?"

"Why are you asking me this?"

"I don't know. It seems you married Ekrem months after you broke it off with Aydın ... and me. And had the child soon after."

"Ekrem and I liked each other as soon as we met. He may not look like much, but he is very smart and gentle. There was no point in waiting. It isn't like we were young. We both wanted a family. Aydın never mattered." She seemed to want to continue, from the rhythm of her last sentence, but stopped abruptly and looked at me.

"I don't want to talk about this. I want to be happy to have you here, in flesh and blood, right here in front of me. I imagined this for such a long time. Could we not...?"

"Do you still splash around the bathtub, like you used to?"

She corked her head around and emitted her familiar neigh, somewhat tentatively. "Yes. I'm teaching my daughter to do the same."

I imagined Nuray and Mehtap in the bathtub singing marches and splashing.

"So where did you meet him?"

"Remember my cousin who used to pick us up when we went dancing?"

"The one with the Impala."

"That one. He and Ekrem are friends. One day the three of us went out. And..." she shrugged.

I was curious about so many things. I wanted to ask how it was for her to be with him, why this man in particular and what about me? I hoped that eventually I would figure these things out, if I visited once in a while and became more involved in her life.

"Let me show you the place!" She stood up and smiled, pretending to be the consummate housewife.

We walked from room to room. Little Mehtap's room had a small balcony with flowers hanging from the railing. Purple pansies. She had a flowery bedspread too. Curtains in the same fabric. "I made them all myself." She said. "New sewing machine. If you need anything, I'll make it for you..."

"I see you have become very tidy." I shook my head in disbelief.
"You haven't seen my closets." The curls moved about and the red lips parted letting out unrestricted melodies,, her enormous laughter making me want to float in the air. The coils of hair bounced around her face momentarily, her neck swayed and she giggled; it was done within seconds, and I was once again love-struck, despairing.

"Nuray, your laughter is life to me."

Tears were running down my cheeks, my hands rushing to stop the flow. She hugged me close, then gently led me to the living room and sat me down. I felt it was time for me to leave. I gathered my composure and said goodbye. As I walked down her street toward the quay, I looked up once and saw her silhouette at the window, watching me.

HEART-WRENCHING GOODBYES are the price one pays for a long life. They are all gone now, my loved ones: my grandmother Inez, my father, my mother, magnificent Nuray, and beloved Aydın. I have survived all of that grief, that immense liquid wave of aching that nearly drowns life out, then withdraws, leaving the whimpering body intact, relieved, guilty to be alive, hungering for three square meals during wakes and funerals, wolfing down the mourners' helva, easy prey to laughter, levity and the intoxicating scent of a neighbouring jasmine that comes to taunt nostrils here in the small rectangular space of this glass-covered cumba, as I write and write senselessly at a table which is even older than I, its wood borne with perfectly circular holes, side by side in telegraphic precision, by tiny worms who can trace their ancestry before the great fire of Izmir, maybe even from the time the tree was cut down a century ago, gnawing while Inez changed her daughter's diapers on it, leaving minuscule piles of dust beside their tunnels; those nests which entombed them. It is so. I am no different than the worm still struggling in the wood of this table. We both want to leave something of ourselves behind, to leave something that will continue or perhaps to simply be in action when death finally pounces on us.

I dreamt of my old teacher Gülbahar Hanım the other night. She was still skinny, tall and sour-faced, towering over me with her metal rod, ready to hit my hands. She didn't know that I had x-ray vision and could see her skeleton underneath her strict high-collared dress that smelled of naphthalene. I could see all her bones, one by one, and her wrist was broken. I exclaimed, "My teacher, your wrist is broken. Is that why you want to break mine?" And I awoke, feeling my nightgown wet around my abdomen, and the wetness was on my bed too. Did I pee from fear? Did my decrepit bladder find a cause in my agitated mind? They tell me I should go to a hospice; that I'm too ill to live here alone. They'll have to carry me out, I say. They'll have to come and scoop me from the floor and even then, perhaps I will still have enough rage to kick away their compassionate arms.

I have lived a life of secrecy, called it a modest life and it has been, in outward appearance, a most unremarkable one. Those few who knew me well have died and those who surround me now see a solitary old maid, a stubborn lady who will not give up her small corner of independence, her familiar objects. I still wear the same navy blue pants and black blouses, although more and more I wander around the house in my nightgown and hardly go out. I've given up dyeing my hair. I can't lift my arms up to apply the colour. The vegetable man does not come around with his cart anymore. Vegetables are in the supermarket. Emin, the gevrek boy has grown up and left. After that first night, he came back regularly and I taught him what little I know. I bought him the book My Sweet Orange Tree from a store on Mithat Paşa and every time he came over after that, we read it together. I would ask him to read to me, mostly, while I sewed buttons or washed dishes. I pretended to be busy at something, to encourage him to read out loud. I didn't know what the book was about when I bought it, but upon reading the story of Zeze, the young boy from the slums of Rio, I realized I could not have chosen a better one for Emin who would occasionally stop reading and pretend to have to go to the bathroom to hide his budding tears from me. He eventually graduated as an electrician from a trade school which he attended at night after he was finished selling his gevreks. One day he came to my door, dressed in clean pants and a white shirt, shaven and cologned, carrying a box of lokums.[25] He had gotten a job. He kissed the top of my hand and pressed it to his forehead. Dear Emin. Every Sugar Holiday, without fail, he came to visit with a box of fruit jellies and only stopped coming after he got married and had children. Perhaps he moved elsewhere.

---

[25]lokums: Turkish delight

Notebook II. The Cretans

MARIA LAY IN THE HOSPITAL BED in Konak, her face ashen, her fingers curled around softened palms on top of the thin grey hospital blanket. She had been hospitalized a few days before and her condition was deteriorating. Mehmet sat on the chair next to her bedside, his calloused hands clasped together on the blanket within touching distance of his wife's curled fist. There were large sweat stains underneath his armpits, hot July breezes blowing into the room from the open hospital window, bringing in the sounds of digging, shouting and honking from the busy street. Outside the room, in the hallway he could see the black-and-white photograph of a pretty nurse in a white cap, one finger pressed over her mouth to instruct silence. Mehtap walked to the open window, wanting to be doing something, to be engaged in actions that would help her mother regain her health, and found herself staring blankly at a pigeon perched on the sill, his head turning sideways to look back at her. They had been waiting for hours, obsessively watching the IV drip, ready to rush for the nurse the moment a bubble should form in the transparent tube between Maria's arm and the pouch hung on the pole. It hadn't happened. Father and daughter sat watching the pouch empty drop by drop, caressing her hands and arms, placing cold compresses on her burning forehead. Maria slept mostly, with the effect of the drugs entering her bloodstream, occasionally opening her eyes and moaning. She motioned for Mehmet to come nearer and he immediately complied, bending his head close to her mouth as she whispered something into his ear. He nodded and said, "Don't worry, my dove. It will be as you say. You just get better, please," in Greek and turned to Mehtap nodding his head for her to approach her mother. She got closer and held her mother's hand. Maria almost smiled, "Your hands are so cool, hrisomou. It feels nice." Mehtap swallowed the sob that was rising in her chest and smiled back. "Do you want another compress?"

Maria shook her head no. "I have to tell you.... Something you need to know. I may not have another chance to speak of it." Mehtap was about to protest and tell her mother that she was to get better and not speak this way, but Maria gestured for her to keep quiet.

"Something your father and I thought we could take to our graves.... But I will not rest easy. Come closer." Mehtap got close to her mother's lips to hear, "Tell your father to go get some fresh air now. He needs it." Mehtap nodded and went to tell him. He looked much older than his forty years with his sunken cheeks and hollowed eyes.

Mehtap approached the bed again. "Mama, you will get better. Please don't tell me you won't. I can't bear it, you hear?"

"We are all going there, my gold, sooner or later, and we will meet on the other side one day in the very distant future, God willing.... I'm grateful I have seen you grow up.... Don't be sad for me. Take care of your father. He doesn't talk much, but his despair goes deeper than even he realizes. I can see it in his eyes.... I told your father already, I want to be buried in the Catholic cemetery and please ask the priest to have a mass in my name. Can you do this for me?" She took a deep breath and looked as though she wanted to close her eyes and sleep.

"Shh, Mama, don't strain yourself now."

"The bracelets," she continued after another deep breath, "have been my greatest source of anguish. Your father and I had the same father. Yes. Mehmet the Great was my mother's secret lover. I wrote to her and she confirmed it. She raised me, all alone, and Mehmet the Great took care of her in secret. They couldn't have anticipated that your father and I would fall in love one day. My mother should have left the village, I suppose, but she didn't. Couldn't. I don't know.... I never told my mother about Mehmet's parents. She didn't know who he really was. We weren't close, we didn't talk much. All she wanted was for me to get as far away from the island as I could. She hated everything there. I'm not sure we could have stopped loving each other even if we had known.... I'm sorry darling. Please forgive me so I can die in peace."

Mehtap realized she had forgotten certain details of her mother's face many years later, when she became an old woman herself; the shape of her chin or whether she had freckles, but she could never erase from her memory the depth of suffering in her mother's eyes in that moment. It seemed as though her life had been a struggle that dragged her toward this instant. She could see the traces of nightmares that made her scream in the night, the sudden bursts of melancholia, her irritation, her sad relationship with the kitchen, all of those mysteriously sealed moments of unease she had witnessed as a child. She felt the petrified weight of powerlessness deep in her chest, holding her mother's soft and still very warm palm between her fingertips. Her own shock sprang less from the realization that she was the product of an incestuous love between brother and sister, than the poignancy and desolation in her mother's eyes in those final moments.

She leaned over and kissed her burning forehead, "Mama ... you couldn't have raised me better or given me more of your love. Do not fret about this. Leave the sorrows of the old country where they belong. Please do not be so sad." Tears streamed down her face as she whispered these words, wishing to erase her mother's sorrow.

Her mother nodded, and closed her eyes. Mehtap was grateful for this respite from seeing those eyes suffused with pain. Mehmet returned from his walk around the block still carrying the smell of chain-smoked cigarettes on his jacket and sat in the chair beside his wife. The death rattle soon followed.

She ran out of the room into the hot sunny afternoon, crossing streets and arriving, breathless, at the Konak peer just in time to see people disembark from the ferry.

Notebook III. Autobiography

I WENT TO SEE NURAY A FEW TIMES a year, once every couple of months after that initial visit. Every time I went, I brought a little something to my namesake Mehtap, a chocolate bar, or coloured pencils, a wind-up toy, whatever I could find. She was fascinated by the latter and had an entire shelf dedicated to them; teeth that clacked, a clown on a bicycle, a hopping bunny, a walking robot...

Nuray and I were never alone again after that first tearful visit. Not in her house. Ekrem would be sitting within earshot, reading his paper in his leather slippers. Mehtap would be either playing or doing homework at the kitchen table. Nuray and I would sit together and talk or knit. I've always hated knitting but I suppose she saw this as something to keep our hands occupied during those long silences when we gazed at each other with longing, like lovers at a train station except that neither of us was leaving. We sat, inhabiting islands of excruciating silence, our eyes playing hide and seek, my heart rising within my chest like bread dough, threatening to choke me. I still felt anger that she chose this life over ours; this life in which I was made to sit gingerly and behave like someone else. I understood her choices, but it did not help me better accept them. One such Sunday, as I was leaving, I said just loud enough for everyone to hear, "Nuray, I was wondering if you could pass by my house one of these weekends, for a little while, to help me sew curtains for my living room? You're so good at sewing ... and I'm having such a hard time. The material is too heavy for me to carry all the way here...." I held my breath in case Ekrem could hear the loud thudding of my heart. She raised her eyebrows and the familiar irony appeared on her smiling lips, like the ephemeral warmth of sunshine in an overcast sky and said, "Sure, if Ekrem and Mehtap don't mind not having me around for an afternoon next Sunday. What do you say, dear?" She often had this saccharine tone with him in my presence as if to purposefully highlight the unenviable position of her unmarried friend who lived alone and needed the support of a happily married couple such as themselves. He shrugged and nodded politely before going back to his paper. Mehtap asked if she could come too. "You'll get very bored, sweetheart. There are no toys for you to play with...."

"I'll bring my doll," she replied and her mother nodded, "We'll see..."

I ran down the stairs and into the street unable to contain my joy. She was not going to bring her daughter, I could tell from the look she gave me. She was going to get off the Mithat Paşa streetcar, like she used to so long ago, giving the conductor a good view of her curvy haunches as she swayed them down the steps and I would be standing there on the sidewalk, waiting for her, imagining long passionate kisses in my darkened bedroom, fumbling with buttons, hooks and other hurdles. I imagined not making it to that moment from a faint heart, from the constant weakness perfusing my thighs for an entire week. How slowly it passed. How thrilling to suffer the wait....

She called me at work on Wednesday to remind me to buy the fabric for the curtains. Her husband and daughter were going to come and pick her up from my house in the evening. "We will have to sew some curtains after all," she laughed in her usual neighing way, and I imagined that mass of black curls corking around the neck as she giggled into the phone.

"But I don't want to sew!" I exclaimed in exasperation.

"What do you propose, then?"

"I'll have to sew them before you come. What else?" I said after a long silence.

That left me three days to buy heavy curtain fabric I did not need, figure out how to use my grandmother's sewing machine which I had not touched in decades and make a convincing effort at sewing drapes worthy of a living room. She found the plan very amusing.

"Don't sew the whole set. Leave some for another Sunday, so I can come back to finish them."

She was about to pee herself from laughing, she said, catching her breath between guffaws and a snort, and slammed down the phone presumably to run to the toilet.

The next day after work I rushed to Saim Bey's fabric store in Kemeraltı to buy curtains. He kept asking me about my furniture, the colour of my living room walls, what kind of effect I was looking for and all I wanted to say was "I don't care! Just give me something. Anything." The material was costly. I resigned myself to actually changing the drapes of my living room. I didn't have the money for all those metres of material with glossy boughs in the colour of pomegranates; I didn't even know if this fit with the room or the furniture. A sense of despair was quickly replacing my initial excitement. Saim Bey proposed I pay in instalments, and I walked away carrying an enormous and heavy package that would become my new curtains.

Sitting in my extra bedroom with the material unfolded, and my grandmother's old sewing machine uncovered, I wanted to hurt myself for coming up with such an asinine plan. After some time pacing up and down I measured the windows to at least cut the fabric, and make some sort of hem and I figured if the room looked busy enough, it would convince her husband that some work had gone on before his arrival.

Nuray was apparently finding all this very amusing. She called me at work on Friday to find out how the curtain project was going. "It's a mess. I'm losing my mind!" I shouted into the phone.

"Why are you getting so worked up about this?" she chuckled. "You're blowing this thing out of proportion! What does he care about a boring sewing date on a Sunday afternoon?"

"He's not stupid."

"Stop exaggerating."

"What would you like me to prepare for you?"

Fried eggs, lots of butter it was. The sunrays filtering through the rustling leaves of the plane tree outside my bedroom window were casting elongated shadows on the walls and bed sheets, occasionally reflecting the amorphous grey silhouette of a branch going this way and that in sloppy zigzags over her profile or my arm, lighting up the curve of her upper lip, darkening the side of her long pale neck momentarily and moving away as if to highlight the drunkenness of the moment, as if to reproach, to show how blind we had been, how forgetful. The early afternoon was cool on our bodies, aching goose bumps rising to meet warm palms and lips. My left hand found the twin dimples in the small of her back, and rested there, as we lay face to face, and I daydreamed of Bedouins in the desert, imagining the moment they reached an oasis, crouching to wet their dusty lips with a handful of precious water. That afternoon was my handful of water.

"Do you remember the fairy tale you told me a while ago, here, one Sunday morning? It was a day like this."

"What fairy tale?"

"The monster in the labyrinth in Crete. Your bracelets. Tell it to me again. It was such a horribly sad story."

"Why do you want to hear a sad story?" I moved the curls away from her eyes.

She shrugged slightly, offering a melancholy little smile. "I don't know…. Maybe because I'm so happy right now. And life can be so sad…. Do you still keep them in that drawer?" She pointed at my dresser.

I nodded. "I've been thinking of giving them to your daughter when she grows up. Or if you have another daughter someday, they can each get one."

"I still think about that story, you know. The part when they enter the cave, and all the children soon to be eaten alive are cowering behind the brave prince, and it stinks in there making them want to vomit. The Minotaur opens his eyes.... It's so terrifying. Sometimes I dream of it. I'm one of them and I know I should be silent but I can't help screaming in terror. The monster wakes up because of me. Then I realize it is my eye that has opened and I'm inside the monster, looking at the shiny sword that will sever my head. Ekrem wakes up from my screams. I cannot tell him. Whenever he asks, I make something up."

I wanted to tell her the other story. The secret one I avoided. Or tried to. There is no avoiding a thought like this one. The harder you try, the deeper it gets; like water harnessed by a dam. Life is everything else that happens downstream. But thought ... who can trace the process that moves stuff through all that tangle of nerves and grey matter? Anyway, I wanted and didn't want to tell her. Primarily because if I told her, it would no longer be a secret. And it had to be a secret, because I was ashamed of it. I had done nothing to earn this shame; still it was mine to carry, in silence—that dark murky vat where secrets pool unheard, where they transcend life spans, centuries, where my mother thought she could hide her own burden until it leaked through her lips, having moved through the chest cavity, up her oesophagus to be released in that final rusty chime of words that strained her dehydrated vocal chords. An otherworldly tinkle ... I could say rattle, but she doesn't deserve that. I remember her voice coming to my ears like the tintinnabulation of small bells, in the old days when she was young and so beautiful. Did she tell me this to unburden herself or to warn me; the way her own mother ought to have warned her about her own secrets and didn't?

I did not tell Nuray about the bracelets that afternoon. I came very close to it. Among these pages which I may yet decide to burn I bury my secrets. We got out of bed and I put the tea kettle on. She sat at my grandmother's sewing machine and started that infernal noise. We took a break to have tea with biscuits. She tossed her curls around laughing, "I can't believe you paid all that money for the curtains. I think I will have to come back a few Sundays to finish them. You know why? Because I want to make a valance. It will really enhance your living room. Off-white, I'm thinking. Pomegranate will be too loud. You don't want to make a statement, just add a touch of elegance. You know what I mean?" She kept talking about the shape of the valance she had in mind, wondering out loud how much more material it would require as she munched on her biscuits and made slurping sounds sipping her hot tea from the glass after putting four sugar cubes in it. Four! For an instant, half listening to her prattle, I was transported to an earlier time, when this used to happen, and we went to bed with the assurance we would wake up together. I didn't listen, then. I complained about her splashing, not to mention her awful dietary habits while she lamented my poor taste in clothes and lack of spontaneity. Were we happy then? Or does happiness come from remembering such banalities through the frame of absence. Sort of like her valance that was supposed to lift my living room décor from its staid existence to a higher plane of elegance. I said to her: "I have missed this so.... Your talking to me and chewing and sewing while I listen and watch your bouncing curls, the shape of your lovely nose in profile. Is it like this with Ekrem too?"

It was an innocuous question that sort of burst out of me, but she took offence. "Why do you have to drag him into every conversation? When I'm here, I'm here. Forget about him, okay?" A pout formed on her cushioned lips and she began the infernal noise once again, shutting me out. I was about to defend my innocence, but decided against it, letting her believe I was making covertly jealous allusions. Perhaps I was too. Jealousy is an aphrodisiac, whoever denies it is a fool.

Eventually, the doorbell rang. The sun was setting over the bay and I offered her husband and daughter some tea in the darkening living room. Ekrem declined politely and we made small talk standing in the living room. The child wanted to go pee. She ran up the few steps toward the bathroom, on her way peeking into the sewing room where the bundles of fabric were laid out on a table. The empty tea glasses and plates with crumbs sat among scissors and pins. All was in perfect disorder. We heard the toilet flush. Mehtap ran out. Her mother asked if she had washed her hands; she was made to run back in and turn on the tap. Soon, they left.

When she came back the following Sunday, I found a way of asking her some of the questions that had been obsessing me since I ran into her again. How did it feel to make love with her husband? I wanted to know this, since she was the one who always insisted she didn't enjoy sex with men, yet she was living with one. We were sewing together, and I mentioned in passing that I had had an affair with a man, without divulging his identity. She became inquisitive, wanting to know when, how and why. I told her it had happened when I went to Germany on a business trip; someone I met there; my friend's acquaintance.

"Was he handsome?" she asked with apparent disbelief.

I nodded, feeling smug.

"No way!" she smiled, her lips curved up on one side. That was the tell-tale sign that she found the situation ironic.

"I still hear from him. He wishes I could spend more time with him...."

"Then why don't you?"

"He's married. In Germany."

"And if he weren't?"

"Well, he is."

"What was his name?"

"Why do you care?"

"Just tell me!"

"Hans," I lied.

"Well," she pressed, looking impatient, "was he blond, grey, brown-eyed, blue-eyed, tall? Go on, describe him to me."

"You know, it really bugs me that you never ask the important questions when I tell you something. Who cares what he looked like? You'll never meet him!"

"I want to visualize. Why do you get mad? Okay, so tell me what my questions should be, then. God, you're so annoying!" She pouted, waving her arm as if to chase a fly.

"How was he in bed? Did I like it? Did I fall in love? Why did I do it?" "Fine, answer your own questions then," She pouted, looking pointedly bored.

"Not if you're not interested!"

"Pass me the pins. You'll have to hold the fabric while I use the sewing machine. It's too heavy."

I gathered up the fabric and sat beside her while she slipped part of the curtain under the needle. She had a few pins sticking out of her mouth.

"You'll swallow one, and we'll have to go to the hospital."

She was about to press the pedal and make noise. She removed the pins from her mouth, sticking them on the pin cushion I handed her and scowled. "Happy?"

Our eyes met and we smiled.

"Still waiting for your answers."

"It was steamy.... I don't know why I did it. Maybe the drink... I'm not used to it."

She hit the pedal. I sat there holding the fabric while she manoeuvred the cloth this way and that for a while.

"Were you wearing your usual uniform when you seduced him?" That sideways smile.

"Dress, high-heeled shoes, and makeup. You'd have been impressed. I had my hair done too. Also the infernal corset you made me buy years ago. Remember?"

"So who took that thing off? Did he struggle?" she giggled.

"No, I hid in the washroom. I was worried he'd fall asleep by the time I got rid of it. Then, I had to suck my tummy in the whole time so he wouldn't notice the difference. I stopped breathing, basically. Made him turn off all the lights." I lied about the corset, and everything else to amuse her.

She continued sewing for a while silently. Then she took her foot off the pedal and looked at me. "Would you have been happy with him, if things had turned out differently?"

"How could I know? It was one night."

"Do you pine for him at all?"

I shrugged. I told myself, the last time you said something about him, she left you. Now shut up.

"Not really. But I do miss You… From the moment I open my eyes until I fall asleep. Even, while you're still here. Soon you'll disappear into another life, and I'll go from room to room, remembering you in this chair, smelling your scent on the sheets, your profile as you glanced out the window, the tinkle of your pee, the shape of your toes. There so much of you to remember."

She did not ask if I enjoyed sex with Hans. Nor did she say anything about how awfully I missed her. My unreciprocated declaration was followed by the dull rhythm of the sewing machine. I continued to help her with the fabric, holding it up so she could manoeuvre. She wasn't going to volunteer any information about her life with Ekrem. We were going to spend the rest of the afternoon playing with the valance.

"What about you?" I blurted. "How is sex with Ekrem?"

She lifted her foot from the pedal, stopped moving, her eyes still on the fabric. "You know what? I'm tired. Let's take a break from working. I'll make tea."

And that was that. We had tea. She told me some funny stories about her daughter. I pretended to be amused, even though I was preoccupied by my unanswered question. She never even got close to answering it the entire afternoon. I felt my ears growing hot with unspoken resentment. Finally, as we sat back to finish the sewing project that continued to nauseate me, she looked into my eyes before hitting the pedal. It was a gaze that felt like cool spring water, clean and unalloyed. "I will never speak about him to you. Just like I never speak of you with him. If you want to hear him somehow diminished in my regard now that I am with you, I might as well leave now. I'm not saying this to hurt your feelings; I just want you to know my life with him matters and it has nothing to do with you. I'm sorry I left so abruptly years ago. It was in part a fit of jealousy, I admit. I'm ashamed I seduced Aydın. I can't say I was truly interested in him. I did it because I could. I didn't contact you all those years because of shame. But I also have to tell you I wanted all that I have now, the child.... And I loved you more, so much more than you loved me. I did. And so, now that I've said all this, tell me why it is so very important for you to know about sex with Ekrem. How is any possible answer going to make things better for you? If I say 'it's good!' will you be happy? Or if I say 'not' will you feel sorry for me?"

She looked at the sewing machine and waited a few seconds. Then she hit the pedal focusing on the curves of the valance.

Notebook I. The Journal

A NEW NOTEBOOK TODAY. Bought it on my way back from visiting Aydın. I finished the last one after my return from Germany. Twenty years. One moment the smell of jasmine from the neighbour's yard makes you dream of love. The next, you're a sixty-year-old pensioner visiting the dentist too often and having teeth drilled and pulled and replaced by partial dentures that pinch. It's a way to fill the days I suppose. My dentist can hardly walk. He is at least eighty. His pink, shrivelled fingertips smell like plaster. Whenever I visit him, I pass by Aydın's apartment where he lives with a full-time nurse. His wife left him a few years ago. I take the elevator to the third floor. It's a tiny, noisy elevator and the lights are always blinking. I've told the janitor on three occasions. He nods sideways and smiles, "sure, Abla,[26] I'll do it." I come back weeks later and it's still blinking. "Not my fault, Abla," he protests, his oblong head bent to one side and still smiling. "The bulbs don't last long. I keep changing them all the time. The apartment manager thinks I'm stealing them."

Visiting Aydın is a sad affair. He doesn't remember me most of the time. At every visit I inspect the apartment, to make sure all is in order and nothing is missing. The cleaning lady goes on Thursdays and I tend to go on a Friday, to make sure she's done

---

[26]Abla: big sister

a good job. I run my finger on the furniture and check inside the fridge to see if the live-in nurse is stacking the appropriate kind of food, and the amounts required. Once I found a large jar of Nutella. "What is this for?" I questioned ready to pounce on her competency. She replied it was a gift from his Hanım. She visits once a month or so, and brings him a jar. His wife says he likes it. "But he has diabetes," I protest. "You know this." She shrugs. His wife seems to think it doesn't matter at this point.

"Throw it out," I order. She seems reluctant to touch it, as if it were some relic. I grab the jar and chuck it in the trash can; we both hear it hit the plastic bottom and bounce a little. Her eye is still on the swinging cover. "Do you like it, too?" I ask her. She blushes and moves her head sideways. "Well, if you'll be eating it, I don't mind." I bend to fish it out of the can, and since the plastic bag in the can was completely empty, I tell her it is clean still, she can put it back in the fridge. She was keeping it there, she explained after we safely restored it to its rightful place, because it's less tempting when it's cold and hard. We talk about how difficult it is to keep things from entering our mouths; my tongue is a magnet she laughs, her massive belly going up and down, sweets practically fly straight into my mouth and then... She slaps her large thighs and sighs, her puppy eyes seeking complicity in mine. For me, it is baklava, I nod. If I buy a box, I'll finish the whole thing in one day. We continue to commiserate about our gargantuan appetites as we enter the room where Aydın is sitting on a burgundy armchair with faded armrests and an assortment of cushions and pillows sticking out from behind his bony frame. "Go for a walk," I tell the nurse, "get some fresh air. I'll be here a while."

Every time I visit him, I approach his armchair with a lump at the base of my throat knowing he will not recognize or remember me. Sitting across from his shrunken frame, the crinkly skin barely covering large blue veins snaking up and down his limbs, the ever growing liver spots on his balding head, the sagging earlobes with curly white hair flourishing outwards, I recognize all of this as an aged version of the man I once loved above all. I accept this ruined husk for the wealth of memories it is still able to evoke in me. The lump comes from the unrecognizing, blank stare that greets me as I sit on the wooden chair across from him. The yellowed eyes move up and down my face and limbs, thinking me a stranger. He may say, "Are you replacing the other fatty?" Or "Why can't I get a young nurse for a change?"

He once said, "Come near me!" I approached him, hopeful he may have remembered something. He grabbed my breast and squeezed it with a demented grin and exclaimed a profanity I had never heard him utter before. "Show them to me. I'm paying you. I want to see them." He kept clawing at my blouse. You'd think such desires would have been erased from his mind along with everything else.

"Stop it. This is not done. Stop right now!" I scolded, holding his wrists, and he relented. His bent arthritic fingers returned to his lap and curled like sleeping cats. He started whimpering. "I'll be good if you show them to me."

Today was an excellent day. I entered the room and sat on the chair expecting he would either ignore me and keep staring out the window or call me weird names. I forced a bright smile, "Good afternoon Patron! How are you doing today?" I don't know why I said Patron instead of Aydın this time. He looked up and I saw the glint of recognition.

"Giritli!" he exclaimed. After some hesitation, as if realizing something was off in the current circumstance he continued, "You still work for me?"

I wanted to clap my hands and hug him for joy. "No, Patron. We're both retired."

"We're old."

"Yes, we are."

"We had fun in Düsseldorf...."

"You remember it?" He had miraculously recovered, I imagined.

"First you told me you were a dyke. Then we made love. On the floor. Not easy to forget," he smiled, showing greyish yellow teeth with gaps. After a moment, "After that, you rejected me."

"You were married, Patron."

"Am I still?"

"She visits you."

He looked out the window. "She has all my money, doesn't she?" After a pause he looked back at me. "I should have divorced. Did you wish for it?"

"I didn't think about it."

"I did. I wished for it. A lot of years. Too many. She would have made my life hell. Already she was…. What happened to … the woman with the black hair."

"Nuray? May she rest in peace, she died a while back in Canada. Her daughter Mehtap lives there."

"Another Mehtap…."

"Yes."

"I slept with Nuray, too." He grinned, offering a glimpse of the old Aydın, the flirtatious cad.

"Patron, you used to sleep with anything in a skirt…."

"You wore pants," he quipped.

I couldn't believe we were having this conversation.

"This is a wonderful day." I leaned over and patted his hands.

"Do visit me often, won't you?" he smiled. "Do you remember the fig tree we secretly climbed in Hasan Bey's garden when we were children? You got horrible diarrhea from eating too many figs."

From there on, confusion set in. He thought I was his cousin. I listened to his childhood stories mixed up with other remembrances tumbling out in anachronistic jumbles.

"Do you want tea or a fruit?" I asked, tired of sitting on the wooden chair.

"Is there scotch? Fatty hides it somewhere. Maybe in her room…."

"Wait here. I'll look for it." I rose and walked to the dining room. All the buffet doors were locked. I found the keys in a small decorative vase. I returned with two glasses of scotch on the rocks, the way he liked it.

We clinked.

"Şerefe!" he said.

Here we drink to honour while elsewhere in the world they drink to health, cheers and so on. "To honour!" I repeated after him. "I wish you good health and memory." I added, to deflect the absurdity of the circumstance. What's honourable about any of this?

He gulped the whole thing down in one shot and started sucking on the ice cubes, absent-mindedly, filling his cheeks with them, like hard candy.

"When are you coming back?"

"Next week Friday, same time."

He asked me if I remembered his father. I told him I'd never met his parents. They had already passed when he hired me. "He used to take me fishing…" he said and his voice trailed off. He became thoughtful.

"So, when are you coming back, then?"

"Next week Friday, same time."

He nodded and turned his head to look out the window. I heard the key turn in the lock and the nurse walked in, holding plastic bags. "I did a little grocery shopping while I was out. Did he behave?"

I rose and put on my jacket.

"Are you coming back soon?"

"Next week Friday, same time. When I come next week, I'll give you a haircut and a good shave."

"Will you bring me chocolates?"

"Sure."

"Who'll take care of me now?" He sounded alarmed.

The nurse walked in, "I'm here Aydın Bey. I'll take care of you."

"My Fatty," he smiled and pointed at her. She shook her head and disappeared in the kitchen.

I used to have a good cry after every visit. Nowadays, I come back to my house dry-eyed, make some tea and sit in the *cumba* sipping it, feeling depleted. It isn't only the absence of the man as I knew him all those years that I grieve, but the erosion of our complicity, of my sense of self from his vantage point. So much of me was invested in him. I used to not give in to his entreaties after Düsseldorf so as not to feel reduced the moment his attention inevitably strayed. Now we're wrapped in shrouds of forgetting. He can't see me for who I am, and he is not there for me to recognize. I feel lonelier than when I used to wrap presents for his wife and mistress in the office next to his. Every day, we awaken to the future within us, impatient as children, reluctant as pensioners. Who wants to face illness and forgetting?

Have I lived as I should have? This question haunts me. Have I taken all my chances, have I given life its due? How would I know if I'd done that?

Those among my friends who are religious find solace in fasting and praying. I'm unable to envy them. Faith is not something that comes with dedicated practice. I've tried to look deep into my childhood to find that attachment to God and the absolute belief associated with innocence, thinking perhaps it unravelled with time and I could get it back. Being assured of his existence by trustworthy adults, I used to picture a fearsome and bulging eye in the sky that saw all you did- when you went peepee, it saw you, when you stuck your finger in your nose, it did too—from the most trivial to your most intimate actions and thoughts, it was your unblinking witness, covering your intentions with a sense of shame and invasion. You could never see it, but all it ever did, or wanted to do, was watch you and your nose-picking, and your little lies and your gluttony. All this was made worse by the knowledge that God was a He, and not a She. No other He would see your privates, but this He did, like the ultimate peeping Tom. I suffered his existence, a feeling slightly moderated by my grandmother's belief in the Virgin Mary, whom I imagined in her floating robes and sheets blocking His view, my chronic constipation somewhat relieved by this vision.

  I did pray to him, whenever I needed or wanted something, before tests and for illnesses to pass and for my grandmother not to die. I prayed fervently. It was all about helplessness, I suppose. Being kept under tight surveillance on the one hand, and at the mercy of wish-granting on the other. God had grander designs and couldn't bother with little old me every five minutes, I was told, whenever the prayers didn't work. What grander designs? Watching wars unfold? Inciting people to kill in his name? The crippled or disfigured children I saw in the street, why did they deserve to inhabit such uncomfortable bodies, why did I deserve mine? Why did the creator of the universe and perfection personified see it fit to give me health and shelter and love, and took all of that away from others? Those were the wrong questions, apparently. My mind never found its way to the right ones, and I gave up trying. This is my secret. Even if on Judgement Day God in his magnificence will not judge you for the limits of your faith—which He is also responsible for, having put them there—people will. They will send you to hell. They are all waiting around the corner with stones in their hands, and matches, and froth on the sides of their lips, watching closely who is doing what, taking note and waiting for a sign to prove themselves God's fervent and righteous goons.

ANOTHER MORNING BY THE LARGE WINDOW of the cumba. Sunny with birds. Invisible sea and tea. Too many apartment buildings blocking the view. Some developer is patiently waiting in his office for me to die so they can tear this last house down, then build some condo monstrosity that will obstruct everyone else's view. Someone, someday, in this very spot, twenty floors up in the air will see the Bay of Izmir, with its boats and creamy waves soldiering, indomitable, toward the shore to finally crash and disintegrate.

Nuray's ashes are afloat in the bay. I will ask mine to be scattered in the same spot. Not that her dust is waiting for me. Does it matter? I mean, asking that my ashes be scattered here there, or this or that to be done, all this symbolic preparation of our afterlife, who is it for really? Was Nuray's wish a metaphor for her hidden grief of displacement? Or a figurative return to me, for having left me twice. A last wish made of guilt and forgiveness. Who knows? All posthumous gestures are absurd. They're meant for others to decode. Her dust, meanwhile, may have landed in someone's gourmet plate, derivatively, having fed a grilled sea bass in its better days.

Ekrem asked me if I wanted to partake in the ceremony, in a letter he sent me before returning to Izmir with Mehtap and Nuray's ashes. I never responded. I pretended not to have received it, arranging to be away in Bodrum visiting cousins when they arrived. I was out of reach. I couldn't face watching all that grey flesh-and-bone dust spreading into the water, sucked into liquid darkness like stars in a black hole, sinking like ordinary dirt. My beloved with the curly black neigh, and the soft black lashes and the equestrian ankles. I did not want to shed tears and sobs for lost time, for missed years, for my heart's deepest longing, under false pretences. My beloved. In our separate houses on distant continents, we were each other's moonlight. I imagined her stepping out on her brick balcony in Montreal on a starry night to see the same ivory light shining upon her. And here, sitting in my cumba, gazing at the dark universe above, or strolling by the sea, she illuminated my utter solitude. We always had that. I could not be around those who loved her and were loved by her, and had stood in the way of my life's happiness. In the end, we had all lost her. It was selfish of me. But I could not face it then.

Notebook III. Autobiography

THE DAY NURAY CAME TO BID ME goodbye we sat in the cumba, where the early afternoon sun filtered through the tulle curtains and fell on her black curls, the tip of her nose and the side of her jaw indiscriminately, illuminating a blemish on the side of her cheek and the dark circles under her eyes. She wore no makeup and her eyes were puffy. She grasped my hands across the table, squeezing my fingers together. There was an unopened package of Yeni Harman cigarettes and a green plastic lighter on top. She had quit smoking years ago, when she got pregnant and it seemed she intended to binge at some point during this long goodbye. From the way she had placed them on the table, one felt her determination to do herself harm by smoking the entire package. She and Ekrem had applied to immigrate to Canada, and their papers had recently come through. They were leaving soon. It was for Mehtap's future, she said. They wanted her to start school there in September. The timing was perfect.

"You don't look like you want to," I said and she burst into tears, her head bent into her chest, eyes shut, nodding as if to suppress violent hiccups.

"I do, I do…" she moaned and blew her nose with the handkerchief stuffed in her sleeve. "We're going to Montreal."

"How can you go to a place you've never even visited?"

"We did, we did … before Mehtap was born. Ekrem's older brother lives there and he's been wanting us to move for a long time. We went in February. Freezing. I figured if I saw the worst, I would be prepared for it," she sighed.

"You never told me...."

She waved her hand in front of her face as if to say it was of no great importance. "It's a new life...." She meant for it to be a hopeful utterance, but as it came out her face contorted and she resumed her hiccupped weeping.

"They have squirrels." She wiped her cheeks with her sleeve. "And so many parks! We saw the Olympic village." She folded her soaked handkerchief. "It looks like a gigantic erection." She blew her nose and sighed. "I will take you there when you visit. Ekrem wants to open some kind of shop...."

She was going on and on and it seemed to have a calming effect on both of us. I was too worried about her state to think about my own, and the definitive separation that awaited us. "Once you settle there and Ekrem opens his shop, maybe I can move and work with you two. I can do the bookkeeping..." I said encouragingly.

And she picked up from there, "That way Mehtap will at least have some family, an aunt...."

Tears sprang once more. "How am I going to do it? I have to decide what to take and what to leave. Mehtap, what am I going to do? How am I going to live without you?"

To this day, I haven't quite figured out why I felt compelled to put on a brave face. Perhaps it was helping me go through the moment without losing my mind. "Listen," I was firm. "I will help you pack. I'm good at that sort of thing. I will arrange for the shipping. Don't worry. And I'll come. I'll take the plane and come."

It was 1979. I was fifty. After she left with eyes puffier than when she had arrived, I sat down with a tall rakı glass filled with the banana liquor that had gathered dust behind my record collection, determined to numb my mind. As I gulped it down, I put on my favourite 45, the slow soft tango, "*To love you from afar, is the most beautiful of loves,*" that used to make me weep over Aydın in younger days, and wandered around the living room looking at the curtains and valance she had sewn over so many Sundays, with the pomegranate coloured boughs on the fabric positioned just so, and the red sofa she had made me buy as an accent in the room, and the ivory-coloured cushions to enhance the sofa and so on, wanting to feel melancholic enough to have a good cry and be done with it. It occurred to me that my living room had the panache of a classy whorehouse, not that I had ever seen one, but somehow I thought of that, and how she was so proud of her good taste, and how very far it was from my own and how I would have to live with it until I died, having sunk so much money to satisfy her decorative zeal and my need to be with her every Sunday. I burst into laughter, looking around. I laughed and laughed, hard enough to feel my belly shaking and then I had to run to the bathroom to pee. Hearing it tinkle into the water, still holding the glass, I began to sob. My voice echoed within the walls of the small bathroom with unrestricted force, just like the time when a kid had snatched my doll and I cried shamelessly loud in the schoolyard. I rose, managed to pull up my panties made my way back to the living room unsteadily and filled my glass once more, put the record on again. My sorrow smelled of ripe bananas. I was swallowing thick gulps that threatened to block my throat while I staggered into my bedroom in search of the bottle of sleeping pills I thought I had placed in the drawer of my bedside table. Five chalky white pills were scattered in there and I gulped them down with the remaining liquid which I was now chugging from the bottle directly, having done away with the bother of refilling my glass. I lay in bed, waiting for a forgetful sleep or death, preferably, my hands crossed on my belly and soon enough I passed out.

There were two cannibals, chests crisscrossed with white lines and masks covering their faces, talking about how they would eat me. One said they had to boil me first because my flesh was so tough. He showed me the large pot boiling a little farther away expecting the other to help him throw me into it. My wrists and ankles were bound with thick ropes and my head was stuck in a vise. His friend was not listening. He ripped open my belly with his bare hands and started removing my guts. I screamed in agony and found myself wrapped in sheets like a mummy. The hazy memory of sleeping pills flashed through my hungover mind. I rolled over unable to get out of my sheets momentarily and tried to open the drawer. The pain was pressing downwards; I knew I had to rush to the bathroom. In my efforts to rise, I fell to the floor and finally managed to disentangle myself and made it just in time.

From dawn to dusk I stumbled to and fro between bedroom and toilet. During one of my breaks, having sobered up from the exercise, I rummaged through my drawer in search of the bottle of pills. An unscrewed cap was sitting next to the rolling bottle of laxatives and the contents had scattered into the drawer. The box of sleeping pills was intact, tucked under a pile of handkerchiefs.

I took two aspirins for the hangover and slowly made it to the kitchen, holding on to furniture so as not to collapse. My mouth felt chalky and dry. The phone rang, drilling holes into my bruised brain. Cupping both ears, I rushed toward the living room to pick up the receiver.

"Mehtap?"

"Nuray, why are you whispering?"

"I don't want to wake Ekrem up. I had a nightmare. Couldn't go back to sleep.... I dreamt you couldn't make it and I died a horrible death. There was ... you were ... on this huge sailboat in the middle of the Atlantic. The wind wasn't blowing. I could see you somehow, standing on the deck. But the ship just sat there, never getting closer. I was jumping up and down, waving a white flag so you could at least see me waiting for you and not lose hope. But I tripped and fell down the cliff and broke all my bones on a sharp rock. I died waiting for you Mehtap.... Promise

me you'll come. If you don't, I will die, I just know it...."
"I promise you, Nuray. I promise. What an awful dream...."
"Did I wake you?"
"No. Been up for a while."
"What happened?" She sounded alarmed.
"I'll tell you later. It's not serious. Go to bed."

WHEN I CALLED HER BACK LATER that day, I told her about my sorrow-induced purge to cheer her up. I said something flippant to the effect that in good movies or novels, heroines always managed to take the perfect dose of sleeping pills or poison, even when they were drunk while the best I could do was try to end it all on laxatives. It was droll and pathetic, I thought I didn't have to embellish much to make her laugh, but it didn't work. She pressed on to know if I meant to sleep or die. Which one? "Tell me the truth or I won't forgive you," she insisted.

"I wasn't trying very hard. I'm glad I didn't succeed. I just wanted to sleep for a long time. What exactly is there to look forward to once you're gone? Not much.... I want to die of such sadness, but I don't want to be dead."

"Good," she said, "good. Promise me you won't do something stupid like this again."

Then, finally, she neighed. The laughter poured out of her and into me until I started rocking with it.

She was flattered by the depth of my sorrow, and reassured, I could tell. She whispered sweet names that she used when we made love, and told me she was in a state of panic every time she thought about leaving. We had three months left. I assured her I would help her pack after work in the evenings or on weekends, at her house if she thought Ekrem wouldn't mind it. I could also take my yearly vacation, that way we would be alone during the day, in her house, while packing. They had planned for Ekrem to take Mehtap to his mother's house, so Nuray could have the time to pack, undisturbed.

"He will be happy you're helping me. He can't take time off work; it's a busy time for him and he worries that I won't manage by myself, so he will be delighted to know this."

"Well then," I said, "let's start tomorrow."

I took a taxi to her house after work with a pile of cardboard boxes that were in good order and we started on the project.

It all sounds a bit tedious in the retelling, after so many years. The closer I get to the finish line, and I think I'm almost there now, the less significant my struggles seem under that vast expanse of stars, and as many ants scurrying in their tunnels below, in this ever-growing city with its millions of faces I can't commit to memory, each one containing a story of magnificent futility. And here I am, telling my own because Nuray once suggested I should. I never wear my wristwatch anymore; the gold rimmed one Aydın gave me as a retirement gift many years ago. Why keep his time when his own mind no longer comprehends it?

I've finally decided to take my Cretan bracelets with their fine engravings out of the drawer, out of so many years of hiding, and place one on each wrist, to affirm, unapologetic at last, that I am the child of a brother and sister expulsed from an island I have never visited. I want to show the world, the neighbourhood and especially those women whose beady gazes hiding behind lace curtains I have suffered and evaded all my life, that I no longer care to submit to their petty views. Not that I ever go out anymore, but if I were to.... And I daydream, mostly. I'm old. And I'm free. I have learned almost nothing. In youth we imagine it will all come together in old age, but it simply disintegrates and turns to dust in our souls before our flesh imitates.

The Letters

November 12, 1980

Dear Nuray,

I hope you're all settled in Montreal now. I want to hear all about it. Your neighbourhood, where you shop, Mehtap's school, Ekrem's work, your days, your thoughts ... everything. I hope you have time to write me a long letter.

Here, things are bleak. You left at the right time. We have to rush home because of the curfew. Military trucks are a frequent sight. Newspaper pages are littered with arrests. Soldiers with their machine guns seem to be stationed everywhere. I heard they just stormed into the dorms at Boğaziçi University and arrested some of the students in the middle of the night. The neighbour's daughter who was studying computer science there couldn't take the stress. She is home now and swears she won't return. It's all for our safety, they say.

Anyway, work is same old story. I find that I'm not able to sleep well, lately. I lie awake wondering about my future, yours.... This is inevitably linked to thoughts of death and dying; my mind wanders in that desert for a while, without a compass or an oasis in sight. Perhaps this happens to those like me who have been visited by love but spared its comforting domesticity. What do you think about this? I'm not looking for sympathy. I just have these observations and I couldn't tell anyone if not you, my sister moon, my shining half on the other side of the world....

I awoke to rain this morning. I love it so, the patter on the windows and streets, the perfume of earth rising, wet stones, wet trees and flowers and the sea scents wafting over the wintry smell of burning coal, and puddles gleaming here and there like soft dark mirrors into which burly grey clouds frown... Do you remember awakening to rain together long ago? I hold on to so much, I realize ... I hold on to all my memories of you. And memories of memories. Yes, I'm hopeless. I remember remembering things we did, and how it felt to remember them. I don't know what use it is or why it even happens. I suspect memories are parasites of sorts, mindless creatures that feed off our thoughts and senses until they are fat and bloated with all that stolen life. What use is it?

Dearest, I'm sorry for passing my blues onto this letter. I realize it's unfair to fill these pages with a sadness that will probably dissipate soon, but will still be there for you to open up and absorb after the fact. It takes ten to twelve days for your letters to arrive. And you always manage to sound cheerful in them, and to make me smile. I wish I had a bit of your light-heartedness. Please forgive me.

I've decided to take pottery classes a couple of nights after work. They have some evening classes. There is a lady who teaches art in the American Girls' School. She lives around there too, so I take the streetcar back and forth. It's very convenient. And I'm learning to make vases and jugs. It's soothing to have my hands in mud like that, and to spin the wheel. Mind you, I have sent gobs of wet clay flying across the room on a few occasions. Thank God her atelier is already messy and she doesn't pay much attention to the additional messes I make.

Anyway, I have to go to work soon and I'll mail this letter from there. Please take good care of yourself. I kiss your eyes. Please give a hug to Mehtap and my regards to Ekrem. Be well.

Yours,
Mehtap

December 21, 1980

Dear Mehtap,

Forgive me for taking this long to write you back. It's been difficult and I have no excuses; being busy is never a good excuse for someone like me. In this case, it isn't that I didn't want to write, but that I didn't want to speak of all those efforts I'm making every day. I'm exhausted. I want to stay in bed and make everything go away, most of the time.

Soon Mehtap will have her Christmas break, and I won't be able to write with her around, so I've decided that today I will devote all my time to writing this letter and mailing it. Maybe you'll receive it in the new year, in which case, I wish you the best: good health, joy, happiness. And above all I wish for you to visit. Will you?

You want to know where I live, where I shop, etc. One of these days I will take pictures and send them to you. Not yet. I live in an area of Montreal called Notre Dame de Grace, NDG everyone calls it. It's very nice—brick houses with tall maple trees in their front yards. We live on the top floor of a three-storey apartment building. Brick, also. And there is a fireplace in the living room but it doesn't work. I insisted on this place because of the fireplace, even though Ekrem kept saying the kitchen was small and shabby. Well, we're stuck with a small and shabby kitchen plus a fireplace that doesn't work, now. I've seen a few cockroaches too, lately, but anyway.... On the mantel, I have the pictures of my mother and brother and you. I talk to you when no one's around. Sometimes I weep, looking at your picture. I wish you were here to hug me. Mehtap, you haven't said anything about coming to live here. I'm waiting for you, you know. If you're so lonely over there, and me here, this only makes sense. Doesn't it?

Ekrem has found a job after four months. It's a factory job; it pays the bills. Meanwhile, he's looking into opening a shop of some sort. I don't know, maybe carpets and copper things, something specifically Turkish. He doesn't want to invest everything we have into something that may not work, understandably. If he opens a shop and it fails, then we will have lost all our money. He tells me I have to look for work also, if we are to make ends meet, until we figure out what to do. My English is barely sufficient, and here, you have to speak French as well. They were very helpful at the immigration office. There are courses I can take for free. In fact, I will also get some money to do this. So, as of next week, I'll be going to school full-time, to learn French and English. It'll be good for me, and most importantly, it will keep me away from the grocery store. My God, you should see the size of it! Think of a museum filled with food, shelf after shelf, row after interminable row. You cannot even begin to imagine such a sight, Mehtap. Shelves packed with cheeses and yoghurts (well, what they call yoghurt here, it's like a diluted version, all liquid and mixed with fruits) and meat packed in cellophane. There are no carcasses hanging from brass hooks, or the smell of blood and meat. Spotless rows of spotless food. I couldn't resist bringing home vegetables and fruits I have never seen before. One is called avocado. It's green and soft inside, and very bland. I wonder how you eat this. Another is called broccoli. Imagine a minuscule tree, with a green stem. That's how it looks. I boiled it and put some lemon and oil. It wasn't bad. Then they have tropical fruits called mangos. Anyway, I can spend my entire day wandering among the isles of this immense grocery store. I get hungry, and I keep buying food. I come home, and I want to taste all these things I buy. I've gained so much weight I can't fit into my clothes. I've bought jeans a couple of sizes larger and very loose fitting sweaters. I look awful, my dear. It's a pathetic life, when food becomes your main source of entertainment.

 Mehtap is doing very well at school. She has already made a few friends and I think she will learn the languages in no time. Maybe she will help me learn as well. Already she is pushing me to read and watch TV so that I don't embarrass her when I go to parent-teacher nights. She didn't say it like that, but she made me understand she feels embarrassed that her parents speak broken English. She rolls her eyes and says "Mom, stop saying 'v' when you see a 'w'. Repeat after me! Vase ... Wine. Not ... Wase ... Vine. Annecim, come on, try harder!" It is so hard on my nerves to feel utterly stupid and helpless at this age.

Sometimes, in the middle of the night I get out of bed and stand in the living room looking out the window. I see the street covered in darkness, the silhouettes of maple and birch trees, sleeping cars, nothing moving anywhere and I think of you. I think you must be getting ready to go to work on the other side of the world, having your gevrek with tulum cheese and your small glass of tea. I imagine you raising your arms to brush your hair, turning your face this way and that after putting your cream, and being ever so quiet while you move about your house in your slippers, all alone. You don't even turn on the radio. How can you stand such quietude? I can't even stand it in the middle of the night, when I'm awake and everyone else is sleeping. I think you would have handled this move I made so much better. I need to feel connected at all times. I need to be seen, noticed, acknowledged. Here no one pays attention. Bus drivers won't stop anywhere for you because you flirt with them or beg them. They see you running madly to catch the bus and still don't stop. Speaking of buses not stopping—I was walking to the bus stop and saw it coming. I didn't bother rushing, but a balding, chubby man in his navy suit and tie, holding a briefcase in one hand and a coffee in the other decided to run for it. He turned red and sweaty, with his coffee cup lifted up in the air for the driver to see him and stop. And as he was nearing the stop, his pants just fell off and he was in his white boxers, with the trousers around his ankles and his briefcase and coffee in his hands! Poor man, he didn't know what to do first; pull the trousers up or get on the bus. And everyone on the bus was laughing, so was I. I felt bad for him, but it was so hilarious, like a Chaplin movie. I wish I had a camera to send you this picture.

So this is my life these days, my dear Mehtap. I look forward to your letter. Please write soon.

Love,
Nuray

P.S. I had to hide your letter because you made a reference to waking up together. You know how it is, being married I don't want Ekrem to get the wrong sort of idea. I feel bad telling you this, because I want you to write these things to me and I don't ever want you to stop. But if you do talk about the past in ways that can be misconstrued, just want to tell you I will have to destroy it. Hope you won't be mad at me for this. I love you, always.

May 12, 1981

Dearest Nuray,
I apologize for taking so many months to write you back. I had to renovate my cumba, water started leaking from the roof after the rains, and there was plenty of that this spring. And you know, the only place where I sit down to write is in my cumba. My mind gets blocked in my bedroom or at the kitchen table. I'm a creature of habit, as you already know too well.

Work has been keeping me busy, as well. We're doing very well, exporting zippers all around the world. Patron hardly ever comes to the office, nowadays. Not that he spent much time there before either, but much less now. I'm still sending flowers to his wife, his mistress Gönül, and all the others on their birthdays. At his age, how he finds energy for all that activity is beyond my comprehension.

I was saddened to read about the difficulties you have in your apartment. The small and shabby kitchen, the cockroaches, etc. I hope you can move to a better place soon.

How is Mehtap doing? She is such a smart girl. I'm sure she will do very well and impress all her teachers very soon.

You're asking me when I will visit. My dear friend, you can't imagine how much I want to be there and see you all, but plane tickets to Canada are expensive, and with the renovations I had to do, I think I will have to wait till next year to come see you.

Do you remember in the old days when we lived together, you used to blow dry my hair with a funny plastic cap after putting rollers on my head? Guess what? I found it. You must have forgotten to take it with you when you moved out, and I found it in a box with all sorts of unrelated things, photo albums, etc. I didn't know whether I should laugh or cry, looking at it. So many memories came back just looking at that old thing. Our vacation in Istanbul, for example. How I wish I could rewind my life and be there again. Have champagne in Moda.... We couldn't stop laughing, we were so drunk, remember?

My pottery classes are going very well and if I could be sure that it would arrive safely to you and in one piece I would send you a vase I have named after you. It is asymmetrical, as if it were about to collapse to one side. I did it on purpose so it would be a bit shapeless. I have glazed it with pastels, and handpainted tulips on it—they're kind of leaky and imprecise with blues, lilacs, pinks, and yellows interlaced with fine green stems and brownish curly leaves, you know, the way leaves look when they are about to dry and curl inwards and get crunchy at the edges? Like that. The effect of those dying leaves I think is what makes the vase so special, for me. I wish you could see it. My teacher seems to think I'm talented. She's pushing me to take the classes more seriously. I have been thinking about changing your old bedroom into a studio. I can put vinyl covers on the floor. It is spacious enough. And I can take my pottery to my teacher so she can bake them for me in her kiln. This way, I can work in the middle of the night when I can't sleep and it gives me something to do on weekends. I will send you a picture of your vase as soon as I get a camera. I think I should start saving to buy one.

Well, this is it for me. Take good care my dearest friend.

Love,

Mehtap

P.S. Your story about the man running for the bus was very funny. I read that part a couple of times and it made me laugh out loud.

August 18, 1981

My dear Mehtap,

I have not been ignoring you. I have written you at least two dozen letters since I got yours, and they all ended up crumpled at the bottom of the bin. I couldn't bring myself to send them to you. But I feel better these days, so I'm hoping this one will make its way to you.

I have completed my English program and just started the French. Ekrem says he's proud of me for learning so fast. I can get by in stores and on the street. I watch a lot of TV. I think here everyone does. Then they talk about it. Back home we had a small black and white TV but the antenna never worked. So, we hardly ever watched anything. Here we have a colour TV and there are about a dozen stations. You can watch TV for 24 hours at a time if you wanted to. So I watch all the "sitcoms"—this means comedy shows. When the actors make jokes, you hear people laughing but you don't see them. It's the weirdest thing. Maybe they're not sure it's funny enough and encourage you to laugh, this way. Or they think people are too stupid to recognize a funny thing. I find I never laugh when I'm supposed to, and when I do, there is no background laughter. Also, you can't watch anything in peace, because when you least expect it commercials cut in and they are loud and go on forever. Ekrem says I should go out more, stop watching TV. You're not really living if you're watching other people pretend to be living interesting and funny lives. You're being a zombie. He scolds me a little; he never used to.... I made a new friend. Her name is Yelena. She told me she works as a stripper at night. Her husband owns the strip joint, apparently. She told me she jogs every day to stay in shape. Maybe I will join her. She lives in my neighbourhood.

I bought a jar of tahan at the grocery store, came back home and wept looking at it. How absurd it sounds! But that jar for a moment contained all I cannot have, can never have again, you know, the morning smell of the sea from my balcony, seaweeds and salty wetness, the sounds of the street down below with the tahan-pekmez vendor passing by singing, the small cup of Turkish coffee, that aroma, your *house with the stairs, the Churchill-faced woman who lowered her basket down for the vegetable vendor. Remember, we would stare in awe at the cigarette glued to her lips and how she could have an entire conversation with it stuck there, smoking away, and us sitting in our nightgowns in that cumba of your house having toast and tahan some lazy morning.... Oh God, everything familiar, everything I have ever known until now and will never ever experience again. Who would have thought a jar of tahan could do this to a person? I kissed the cold jar and pressed it to my stomach and sobbed and sobbed and called your name.*

I understand about your expenses, and you're right about how expensive it is to travel all the way here. If I could, I would have returned for the summer, a couple of months, and spent it with you. I would have taken Mehtap with me too and the three of us would have had a lovely time. Perhaps next year.

If you want to call me sometime, remember we have a seven-hour difference. When you wake up at six a.m., it's one p.m. for me. I'm done with school by that time and I should be home. Call me. I will try to call you as well. I know you have to get ready for work, so I won't keep you on the phone long. To hear your voice would do me a world of good.

I have changed so much. I think you may like me better nowadays. I'm done with singing and splashing in the bathtub, and I don't wear those high heels that hurt my feet. I also can't fit into my clothes so I wear loose sweaters so as not to attract attention to my widening hips. It's funny you found the hair dryer and the bag attached to it after all those years. Does it still work? I've lost a lot of hair and what is left hangs in large limp curls; even they seem depressed. I wonder if it is due to my age—you know, I mean my inability to find happiness here. Maybe we're too old to make such a change in our lives. But then I look at Mehtap and I see how easily she has made friends and how she talks incessantly with them on the phone. It's remarkable how happy she seems. As for Ekrem, he's always been the stoic type. He won't complain about anything.

He goes to work everyday and recently decided to take some night courses at a college nearby, to learn how to be an electrician. He's got it into his head that he has to reinvent himself because no one cares that he was some big shot in a Turkish company. It is all too far away and I suppose to them it could all be lies. When I ask him if he regrets leaving home he says, "I'm doing everything I can not to live with regrets and I wish you'd do the same." It must be hard for his pride to be working in an assembly line at his age after running a successful business most of his life. I asked him why he wasn't going to university to become an electrical engineer. He said it would take too long taking one course at a time at night. Then he turned around and asked me if I have considered looking for a part-time job as a sales person, in a grocery store, wherever. I don't know where to begin. He says, just go downtown and look for Help Wanted signs and walk in.

I guess I'll be doing that tomorrow. Pray that I find something. If I do, it may help everything else.

I wish you could send me the crooked vase you made for me, or at least a picture of it. I remember the doll you dressed up as a school girl for Mehtap. It was unbelievably beautiful. If you change my room to a studio, it means you'll be spending a lot of time there, where I used to sleep. The thought of it makes me happy.

I've got to prepare supper soon, so I have to stop writing.

I miss you and send you a big hug.

Nuray

September 9, 1981

Dearest,

The holiday of liberation, today. I'm home and I can hear distant sounds of the military drums of the great parade. It's a sunny day here and warm. I'm glad to have some rest. Aydın invited me to his summer house in Çeşme again, second time this season, but spending time with his glacial wife once a year is more than enough for me.

I know he invites me so he can have company. His daughters are overseas, and nowadays it's just him and his wife, and I suppose he can't stand her operatic moments. I love him dearly, but lately I find it very difficult to do things that don't please me for his sake. I have become selfish and unsociable I suppose. I'd rather sit here in my studio and play with clay. The happiness I derive from it is a strange one and not without frustration. If someone had told me that I would want to spend time doing something that leaves my fingernails, hair, and every crevice of my face filled with mud, I would have found it unbelievable. I never would have thought I would love the feel of mud under my fingers, the delight of shaping something soft and viscous with my hands, the spinning wheel, the pleasure of finding new forms and making objects that are not really very useful. I have changed Nuray. I have let go ... I can't find the right words to describe this transformation to you.

I miss you more than I can ever say. Tear this letter up after you read it, if you wish. I cannot be chained to pleasantries when my feelings surge and sear me the way they do. A volcano wants to erupt within me when I think about you. Perhaps this pottery business has something to do with all that wants to pour out of my heart. All the love I couldn't give you, all the sorrow I cannot shed in tears, the heights my soul yearns to soar toward and cannot, it is all stored here in my crooked and sad-looking vases. Hearing your voice the other day, so faint and filled with echoes, yet so real and so you, broke me entirely. I wanted to touch your face and neck and kiss your lips. I am tired of hiding everything all the time. I'm tired of calling you dear friend when I want to shout that you're the love of my life and your departure has turned my existence into a desert.

When am I going to see you again? You know our currency is so devalued now that a loaf of bread costs a hundred times more than it used to. Salaries are the same, but prices are a hundred fold. I barely make ends meet, and wonder how the poor survive nowadays. It is a very sad state of affairs. I think I could retire if I wanted to, but it's financially impossible. I would be destitute if I did. All this to say, whatever I have managed to put aside in the hopes of coming to visit you is not going to be enough now. There are banks that give very high interest rates and I am of two minds: putting my money there, or exchanging it to American dollars so that it will not devaluate further.

How are things with you nowadays? Have you found a job? Perhaps it will be easier for you to come here for a visit now. I hope you're all in good health. Please be patient and courageous. Remember that you will inspire your daughter to live a courageous life if you do so yourself. And that is the most important thing, isn't it? You've made this move for her sake, and you must continue this mission as well as you can. You are not alone. Ekrem is there to support you and your daughter is there to inspire you through the sadder days.

Be well darling, and remember that I love you deeply, and always shall.

Yours,
Mehtap

June 5, 1983

Dear Mehtap,

We will finally see each other. I keep looking at my ticket over and over. In four weeks, my plane will leave from Montreal, stop in Amsterdam and then Istanbul, and then Izmir. How lovely it will be, after so many years.

Do you need anything from here? I plan to bring jars of instant coffee. Is it still hard to find nowadays? What else do you need, want? Please send me your list quickly so I have enough time to shop for it. What size do you wear nowadays? I can get you Levis jeans. Anyway, Mehtap and Ekrem will stay here. Mehtap prefers to go to a summer camp while I'm away. Her classmates are going too and she thinks it will be more fun for her. Ekrem is staying in case Mehtap needs something, so he can be there for her. I feel a little guilty taking this trip by myself, but it will be wonderful, won't it?

I will keep this letter short. Don't forget to write me your list as soon as possible.

See you soon.

Love,

Nuray

September 3, 1983

Dear Nuray,

I still can't believe you couldn't come. Who breaks their legs crossing the street? I'm so sorry darling. Hope you're on the mend, now. Both legs! Are you in a lot of pain? Are you able to ambulate with crutches at all? When Ekrem called to say you'd had an accident, I panicked. We always imagine the worst. If it is any consolation, it could have been worse, you could have been hit by a bus and died. God forbid. Now you take good care of yourself and listen to what the doctor says and do it exactly.

Were you able to get your ticket reimbursed? Can you use it at a later date? I hope it wasn't a complete loss; I can imagine how expensive it was. Do you want me to tell your cousin, or anyone else who may have been waiting for you as well?

The weather is still warm here. I'm taking some time off work in a couple of days to go to Marmaris, for a week's vacation. It is not so busy anymore and warm enough for swimming. I desperately need to get away from the city and my work routine. I'm tired of it all.

I'll give you a call soon. We've been writing each other less these days, I suppose because we call each other more. It's extremely expensive, I know; but I need to hear your voice and be reassured that you're all right, especially nowadays.

I love you.

Mehtap

January 21, 1984

My dearest friend,

    In one of your letters you said that to call me your dear friend was to hide the true nature of your feelings. I have thought long and deep about that recently and I disagree. The word friend contains precisely the depth you assign to love in your life. It is surely a word of great relativity; if you have no one to love deeply, then the limit's right there. Doesn't Mevlana call the beloved Friend? When I call you my dearest friend, it means you're the closest being to my soul, the one whose presence in the world gives my senses joy and inspiration. The love of my child is in another category completely. If I have to choose between you and my child, I will always choose my child because she needs me, because my instincts lead me to protect her, because she has sprung from my body where I have carried her and fed her with my blood. Then there is you. Perhaps I'm not letting myself imagine the possibility that I could ever leave her to come to your side. Perhaps that is an unmentionable-unimaginable. You see, I have thought about all this at length and may write a long letter (to bore you to sleep, get ready!) today because I'm in bed and have nowhere to go.

    I have something to tell you, and I don't know how to do it from far away without the help of my arms to enlace you, and my lips to touch you. It is a difficult thing to share. Please bear with me if I take too many detours, and write senselessly for a while; I need it to find the way. What is difficult to say in words comes from those speechless places we have discovered for having lost our dear ones forever—you your parents and grandmother, me my mother and brother.

    When I tripped and fell and broke my two legs while crossing the street, I attributed it to simple clumsiness in high heels. When they took x-rays and prodded and poked me at the hospital, they discovered that I have some type of bone cancer and this is why both my legs broke when I fell. It is not normal for both legs to break thusly from a simple fall, they said. I didn't have the heart to tell you when you called the other day and asked me if I could still use my plane ticket later. You sounded so hopeful I just couldn't bear to cause you such distress over the phone. I have some treatments that will begin soon. They used the word "palliative" and I had to run home and check the dictionary to figure out what that meant exactly. It means that the treatment is not for a cure, but to help with the pain and prolong my life. The origin of the cancer is not in my bones but elsewhere, they suspect in the breast. It has spread now. I never felt a thing. I'm so sorry to share this awful news with you Mehtap. One has too many words or not enough words to talk about one's own impending finality. It is everyone's fate and mine's coming a little sooner than I expected.

Still, I am not hopeless. I hold on to the belief in a miracle. Why would such a word exist in the world, otherwise? A nun who was at the hospital told me of a place not too far from here where miracles have happened. It is a site of pilgrimage. She told me to pray. Pray for a miracle and for acceptance as well, she said, the ways of the universe are mysterious.

It would certainly help me feel better if you could come to see me now. Do you think it is possible for you to take some time off and come? I'm sure Patron would understand.

I kiss your eyes, my dearest.
Nuray

Remembering Mehtap

She drew me into her story unexpectedly that cold February morning, when I found her oversized package stuffed in my mailbox. There were two thick spiral notebooks within, pages filled with tight, studied calligraphy, in blue ink. The last pages of one book had apparently been written with great difficulty, by someone who could hardly hold a pen. The writing was shaky; it bled below and above the lines, and the spaces between words were uneven.

I have hazy memories of her house in Karataş, the red couch in her living room, a narrow street made of too many stairs one had to climb, the scent of jasmine through her open windows, bright orange pumpkin compotes I was given to eat from a crystal bowl. I must have been four or five, then. The next time I saw her I was already a teenager. She had come to visit us in Montreal during my mother's illness. The two of them would sit on the balcony of our apartment in Notre-Dame-de-Grâce having tea in small glasses, Mom wrapped in a blanket and Mehtap watching her every move. They would laugh to tears holding their sides, and sometimes they would gaze quietly at the park across the street holding hands. Often, my mother would lean her head on Mehtap's shoulder on that balcony and fall asleep to her friend's tender caresses. Mom seemed transformed when Mehtap was around. I can't quite describe the change except that it was palpable, as if this friendship created a universe around them complete with comets and constellations that shone brighter than the one my father and I inhabited.

If I felt somewhat envious, I was also grateful for her presence because it meant Mom had company while I went to school and Father to work, and we didn't need to worry about her being alone if she took a turn for the worse. Mehtap cooked for us, did the laundry and stepped in to mother us all in those few weeks of her stay. We all knew my mother was not going to recover, there was no remedy; we were sobered beyond the point of praying for miracles. Every coming day was going to be worse than the last. At night, no longer required to put on a brave face, I would lay in bed with my eyes open, my heart racing to escape the sharp claws of grief. I'd stare at the ceiling unable to stop imagining the precise moment when my mother, my beautiful mother, still breathing, laughing and living among us would be erased from existence. Would become an image in an album. A barely recollected memory receding in the haze of passing time. The curve of her brow, the precise location of the freckled constellations on the bridge of her nose, the soft pale valley between her left clavicle and neck where I loved to bury my face ever since I'd known myself, and even before, her scent of milk and lavender and cinnamon, the softness of her cheek resting on my forehead. All that. Gone. I knew Mehtap was awake, weeping quietly on the other side of the commode separating our beds, every night. I heard her sniffles. The night before her departure, I couldn't supress my sobs. She rose from her bed and came to mine. We wept holding each other tight. The next day she left, promising my mother she would return in a few months. We never saw each other again.

Before that time, I remember Mom's frequent phone calls to Turkey; father frowning over exorbitant bills, Mom on the defensive. There was also the doll. When I was about to start elementary school, I got a wrapped package. In it was my own doll, wearing a black plaited uniform with a white collar, and a tiny brown school bag complete with a miniature notebook, pencil and eraser inside it. She had sewn her a Turkish school uniform. I remember being overcome with admiration observing the intricate and painstaking work this woman had undertaken to make her look like a pupil so I would take heart on my first day of school.

These memories swept over the days that followed the arrival of the notebooks and the news of her death. I dreamt of my mother, of Mehtap and my father frequently, the words in the journals taking me back to the half-forgotten days of early childhood.

The summer following Mehtap's death, I travelled back to Izmir, took walks in her neighbourhood around Asansör, going up and down the steep stairs of the old narrow streets. I stood in front of her house with my pocket camera looking at the ornate corners of the cumba surrounded by glass windows, where I imagined she may have had her morning tea in a fine porcelain teacup, alone, staring into space. It was an old Smyrnian Greek house the likes of which have rapidly disappeared in favour of boxy apartment buildings all over the city. The house had already been sold by the estate. I took a picture knowing that next time I travelled back to Izmir I would find no trace of it. I could already visualize a concrete building with multiple flats whose wide open windows would spew loud commercials and soap operas, à la Turca music, and the sputtering of water faucets, mothers calling children to the table for lunch or having loud conversations on their cell phones. I put my camera away to protect the ghostly stillness it had just captured and climbed down the stairs to take a cab.

After returning to my life in Toronto, Mehtap and her journals receded in my mind for some time until I got a call: a few more journals and notebooks had been found stashed among some clothes, while emptying the house.

They arrived in a box about eight weeks after the call. These notebooks were smaller, thicker. Some of the pages contained multiple succinct entries, almost telegraphic, with dates. She had captured more than a decade, between 1958 and 1972 in the yellowed pages of these notebooks. Many of the entries were too hermetic to understand. One said, "Streetcar to Alsancak. Accident on the road. 45 minutes waiting in the heat. Her smile." One looked like a shopping list. I shuffled a few pages forward. "The mere sight of him…. Yet he is much too vain. Endlessly talks about beautiful women as if to remind me I'm not one of them." Then, "Nuray said today: '*I'm stuck. You take me for granted while you pine for him. Whenever he asks for you, you run. But he doesn't love you. I do!*'"

    I felt nauseous with unease as I turned the pages in which glimpses of private desires and deep secrets coexisted with the banalities of life. She was twenty-nine years old at the start of all these books and an old woman by the end. They contained things about my mother's life I could not have imagined. Things I wasn't prepared to consider. It would take a few readings.

    I never got her bracelets. Someone, somewhere in Turkey is probably wearing them in the naïve way people flaunt stolen jewellery, ignorant of their origins and carefully kept secrets.

    No matter. Mehtap's journals and the oblique light they cast on my mother's life are what I was meant to keep. If the lost bracelets from Crete were Mehtap's unwanted treasure, hidden among lavender-scented underwear and rarely worn, her words, like adumbrated foliage on a moonlit night glimmered here and there to reveal disquieting shadows, tremulous patterns unseen in the glare of daylight, and the occasional opalescent bloom of a jasmine so delicate and humble and ephemeral.

Toronto, June 15, 2014

ACKNOWLEDGEMENTS

Many wonderful people have believed in this book, starting with my family. Alfredo, Nikola, Maura and Jacques, you've all read a draft or two, encouraged me, given me space. I am so grateful for your love. Gerar, my dear brother, no one could have imagined that street, that house, the way you did. Thank you for making it come alive for the book cover. Hanna Edizel, for working on ideas for pictures and visual concepts with me. Morris Berman, when you said you loved the book, I felt I could, too. Hale Tenger and Kristin Micaleff-Botros, you took the time to give it a close and loving read, with invaluable feedback. Cecilia Ekbäck, Carole Giangrande, Dan Perry, Melinda Vandenbeld Giles, writer friends and peers, so generous with your time and words. I'm indebted to your kindness.

Luciana Ricciutelli, my dear editor, thank you for being the passionate feminist voice that you are, and for bringing diversity and change to Canadian publishing with your choices of books and authors. I am grateful for your encouragement.

Photo: Edwin Gailits

Loren Edizel was born in Izmir, Turkey, and has lived in Canada most of her life. She is the author of three novels, *Adrift* (2011) (long-listed for the ReLit Awards), *The Ghosts of Smyrna* (2013), and a collection of short stories, *Confessions: A Book of Tales* (2014). *The Ghosts of Smyrna* was also published in Turkish, in Turkey, in 2017. Her short fiction has appeared in journals in both Canada and in Turkey. She lives in Toronto with her family.